Julieta
and the DISCARDED
ROMEOS

MARIA E. ANDREU

BALZER + BRAY

An Imprint of HarperCollinsPublishers

To la Mami, who taught me to write in the dim basement light, sewed into the wee hours, scrubbed, drove, and lifted what needed lifting. When I think I'm trying hard, I remember you. Then I try harder. Thank you for getting us here.

Julieta
and the
ROMEOS

Love is a smoke raised with the fume of sighs;
Being purged, a fire sparkling in lovers' eyes;
Being vexed, a sea nourished with lovers' tears.
What is it else? a madness most discreet,
A choking gall, and a preserving sweet.

<u>Romeo and Juliet</u>, Act I, Scene I

Maybe? tbd. Not enough data to agree or
disagree.

one

If I could write this story, we would not be at the town pool. I would not be trying to make my flimsy beach towel stretch enough to keep my thighs from sticking to the plastic lounge. Ivy's island-sized hat would not be poking the side of my head while I blink to get the hastily applied sunscreen out of my watering, stinging eyes.

But I'm not writing this story, so here I am.

As a reflex, I reach down to pat the side of my mom's old pink beach bag to feel the outline of my writer's notebook through it. I won't take it out and risk slathering it in Coppertone just yet, but the feel of it through the bag reassures me. I will my brain to soak everything in so I can write it all down later, even how the sunscreen is causing a greasy film to obscure half the world. And by "world," I just mean the Alderton Town Pool, its concrete deck around the ice-blue water, the lap lanes cordoned off so that the oldsters can do laps undisturbed while the loud seventh graders try to jump on each other's heads. It's a whole microcosm of our town contained inside a chain-link fence: the kiddie splash pool with the anxious-looking young moms no more than a foot away from big-cheeked babies; the main pool where the middle schoolers' moms eat carrot sticks and ignore their kids entirely; the highly regulated diving boards you have to pass a test to even touch; the grass we're on littered with lounge chairs that have seen better days.

I am here for one reason and one reason only: Ivy Madigan, best friend extraordinaire and ride-or-die since grammar school. Ivy has impeccable taste in all things, like any girl who has grown up in a princess house. She has just one giant hole in her judgment: she loves it here.

I can't for the life of me understand why.

She looks absolutely thrilled. I mean . . . all of us Alderton lifers have loved this place at some point. The only difference is that, for most of us, the love affair ended sometime around first kisses and the onset of BO. But her love glows just as brightly today as it did since she passed her diving test.

She's talking beside me, animated, conspiratorial. "And then she said that if he was going to be like that about it, he was uninvited to her family vacation. Which, you know, it had been a bear for her to convince her parents to even let her ask him to go. This could make things really awkward at the epic party I plan to throw when my parents are away."

"Mm-hmm," I say absently.

Ivy cocks her head at me in disappointment, sunglasses like two giant saucers on her face. "Jules, that is the third bit of major scoop I have laid on you since we sat down, all fresh post-school, and we've only been out for two days."

"Makenna, Joshua, fight, check."

"You know I collect all this juicy gossip for you in the hopes of seeing it in a major blockbuster novel someday."

I laugh. "No, you don't."

"Okay, not *only* for that reason. But *also* for that reason."

Ivy and I may seem like unlikely friends to some.

With her flawless, salon-highlighted blond hair and baby pink acrylics, she fills out her pastel yellow bikini in a way that gets her free snow cones at the concession stand and adoring looks from the guy who checks passes at the door. I'm firmly under the umbrella so I don't get burned, am in a very sensible one-piece, and have a selection of three novels, plus my notebook, in my bag for when she inevitably decides she needs to swim laps. But we work, somehow. She listens to all my mad story ideas, encourages me, cheers me on. I come to the pool when she insists and let her drag me to more parties than I'd naturally go to on my own. It's been a winning formula for a decade. Well, it was more dolls and floaties at the start, plus long, lazy summer afternoons filled with scavenger hunts we used to concoct for one another. But we've grown through our various stages together.

"Speaking of novels, are you working on anything for your summer school thing yet?"

"A, it's not summer school. B, it hasn't even started yet."

"It's summer, and you're going to school, so . . ."

"Please stop calling it summer school. This thing is the most prestigious high school writing intensive in New York. Maybe the country. Led by one of my absolutely favorite writers."

"I didn't realize old Will was teaching at Fairchild."

"*Live* writer."

She seems to have taken it personally that I actually liked *Macbeth* when we were in English class together. She blamed it on my name. Which, *thanks, Parents, for inadvertently saddling me with that association*. But also I just thought the witches were pretty awesome, and I had a grudging respect for Lady Macbeth's steely determination. Ivy has not let me live it down since.

She settles back into her lounge. "Ryan won't show me what he's writing, either."

I let the comment go. Ryan is Ivy's twin brother. For as much as I adore Ivy, I'm . . . we'll say *challenged* by her brother, the overachieving twin without any of her winning disposition. I've been desperate to go to the Fairchild Summer Writing Intensive ever since I was a freshman; the application process is super competitive, and graduates go on to do amazing things. Their most famous alum and teacher, Paige Bingham, is my favorite author. She got a two-book deal while she was still a senior in college, and three of her books have been made into Netflix series or movies, including the absolutely swoon-worthy *Forged*, which introduced me to the sexy blacksmith I didn't even know I needed in my life. She's kind of this mix between Emily Henry and Rebecca Serle but you can also tell she's read some Flannery O'Connor, who I absolutely love. Finding out Ivy's brother had also gotten in put a bit of a damper on my triumph.

I say, "Writers are funny that way. But on this summer program thing, I'm serious. This is a big deal for me."

She puts a perfectly manicured hand on my forearm. "You know how proud I am of you."

"Do I?"

"Jules! *Yes*." Ivy scoots our chairs closer together, the meager grass trampled underfoot. "I'm sorry. I'm being a dick. Of course this summer is going to be amazing for you, because *you* are amazing. They're going to hand you a million-dollar book deal in your first week and tell everyone else to go home and stop wasting their time. I'm just going to miss you, that's all."

"It's a day program, Ivy." I laugh. "I'm not going anywhere. Also, I've heard million-dollar book deals aren't all they're cracked up to be."

She ignores this last part. "It's our last real summer, you know? Next year we'll be all distracted the summer before starting college. And you're already so busy with the restaurant and everything." She breaks off, is quiet for a second, then adds, "Forget it. I'm being a jerk. I'm probably just jealous, honestly."

"Jealous?" I make my best *You're not serious* face.

Ivy is effortlessly gorgeous, the kind of person everyone likes without her having to try. She's been dating the star pitcher of the baseball team since the start of junior year. And, not like money is everything, but it sure must not stink that her family takes fancy vacations as if her parents secretly want to be Instagram influencers. She also does not, nor has she ever, had any interest whatsoever in writing, and her life is pretty charmed, so I'm not sure why Fairchild would spark anything but benign indifference for her.

"*Why?*" I ask.

"You know what you want to do with your life," Ivy says. "Not only that, you've *always* known what you want to do with your life. You, like, popped out with a manual typewriter tucked under one tiny arm and a notebook full of ideas you'd been scribbling in there."

I laugh. "I don't know. I have plenty of doubts," I say. I know what she means about my focus, and she's not wrong. I've wanted to be a writer for as long as I can remember. When my brother and sister were tiny,

I wrote them little plays that made them laugh and kept them entertained for hours, asking for new scenes. Even before they were born, my mom taught me to write when I was four, and I'd fill up marble composition books with ideas I thought were totally original, but which upon later reflection read not-so-mysteriously like whatever my favorite Disney movie was at the time. I've written poems in math notebooks and character sketches on the backs of paper place mats during the off-hours at my family's restaurant. I survived middle school writing notebook-length stories in which every member of whatever my favorite boy band was at the time was madly, tragically, epically in love with me.

Whenever I picture my life as a grown-up, I'm writing in cafés and sumptuous libraries and on luxurious overnight trains in exotic locales. I'm giving readings in elegant lecture halls and signing copies of my best-selling novels to a line of readers that is so long I can't see the end of it.

Then I imagine my mother wondering aloud exactly how I plan to feed myself, and I suddenly remember I've never actually finished anything I've written.

It's not that my family isn't supportive. They are.

They're totally on board with this class, even though it's going to mean fewer hours I can help out at the restaurant. But my parents are immigrants and business owners, buffeted by the winds of up and down years. We just put an especially hard season at our restaurant, Las Heras, behind us. Dreams are fine with them, as long as I have the grit and talent to turn them into reality. And maybe *just a teensy bit* they wish my dream involved something more dependable, like a medical degree.

I wish I felt more confident that I've got what it takes.

"Your writing is epic, and you know it," Ivy says, reaching in her pool bag for the pistachios she always keeps in there. "Your *hair*, on the other hand . . ." She blows me a kiss, no hands, all pucker. "Maybe later you can come over and I can work on your tips? You need a refresh."

I twist the ends of my hair around my fingers. The blue ombré was Ivy's idea, right before finals: I wanted a change but didn't want to go blond, like her, so she bleached out the ends of my unremarkable brown hair and added a pale blue and lavender that sparkled in the sun and which I loved instantly. It has been one of my favorite things of this year, feeling like the kind of girl who can have hair that stands out.

I'm about to agree when I'm startled by a voice right next to me saying, "Jules? I didn't know you still came to the pool."

I spot the feet attached to the voice first: worn leather sandals I could pick out of a lineup.

I turn to face the voice. I didn't know Lucas came to the pool, either.

"Yeah, same, what are you doing?"

"I'm on little-cousin duty. He insisted."

I follow his line of sight. His little cousin, who was a baby like fifteen minutes ago but now looks maybe seven or eight, is doing a serviceable doggy paddle at the pool's edge, safe in floaties.

"What's your excuse?" he adds.

I point a thumb at Ivy. "Best friend duty."

She play-slaps my arm, and Lucas smiles in his crooked, familiar way. We've known each other since we were babies. His parents were the only other Argentinians in our neighborhood when my parents moved in, which was enough to make them immediate family. In the sixteen years since then, the two of us have buried a half dozen goldfish in our yards together, played four million games of Uno, and have survived a cringey YouTube-video-production phase. He's shared his potato-battery kit Christmas present. In the eighth grade, I insisted he teach me to tie a man's tie because I'd written a list of things cool girls know how to do, and I couldn't very well get him to teach me to drink whiskey at thirteen.

It's strange to see him here, though. He looks different, somehow. His unruly curls look a little sun-kissed, his squinty light brown eyes lit up somehow. He's in a Messi soccer shirt, but that's on brand.

"Anyway," he says now, "you working later?"

I shake my head. "Not till tomorrow."

"Well," he says, "see you tomorrow, then."

We wave goodbye, and he heads across the concrete pool deck, pulling off his shirt as he goes. The muscles in his arms and back shift underneath his skin.

"Um," Ivy begins, not even trying to act like she isn't staring.

"Don't say it."

"I'm definitely going to say it, Julieta Talavera Toledo," Ivy says, delighting in dropping my full, unwieldy name whenever she is making a particularly emphatic point. "When did Lucas get *hot*?"

"I said don't say it!" I wave my hand as if I can bat

away her words. "He's basically like my cousin."

"He's not *my* cousin," Ivy points out, pulling down her sunglasses to stare. "And he's clearly been doing his push-ups."

"What about M.J.?" M.J. is the boyfriend a photographer would pair Ivy with: ripped from his constant baseball practice, floppy haired, smart but not obnoxious about it. The fact that he's been her actual boyfriend for like a year feels like it has a certain cosmic rightness to it.

She pushes her glasses back up. "What *about* M.J.?" she zings back. "I'm dating, not dead. I can appreciate a fine specimen of humanity when I see one. And I'll add that from the look on your face right now it doesn't seem like your feelings about *this* particular member of the species are exactly chaste, either."

"Stop," I mutter plaintively, reaching for my bag and trying to ignore the sudden heat in my chest. Lucas was shorter than me for our entire childhoods. But he's grown like six inches since last summer. His hands and feet are suddenly enormous, the jut of his Adam's apple pronounced. Before I can stop myself I'm imagining how I'd describe him if he was a character in a story I was writing: his liquidy, big, yellow-brown eyes; the curls that look less messy and more consciously tousled now; the distinctly grown-up cliff off his jawline; that line between boy and . . . not so much anymore.

I wipe my sunblock-smeared hands on the edges of my pool towel, then reach for my notebook. I have to. I yank it open to a fresh page and grab a pen. Ivy laughs and heads for the pool, presumably to get a closer look at the muscly stranger in the spot where dependable childhood friend Lucas used to be.

~~If a familiar old shoe turned into a real boy and grew pecs.~~ omg that's terrible.

There are people you stop looking at because they're as familiar as you are to yourself. That's who L has always been to me. But life and muscle development have a way of surprising you.

Ugh.

~~He made his way to the pool with a distinct ripple to his muscles.~~

There is no easy way to do this.

Eyes: ~~brown. Light brown.~~ Golden brown. Hair: curly. ~~Lips~~ . . . No, let's stay away from lips for now. Smile open, like he's never hidden a single thing in his life. When dependable meets unexpected.

two

My sister, Lucesita, is practicing her violin when I get downstairs the following morning, the barely recognizable screech of "Cielito Lindo" that scratches at my eardrums as I wait for the kettle to boil.

"Luz," I growl, "could you possibly take that outside?"

Lucesita ignores me and keeps playing, her frizzy hair parted down the middle and held back near her temples with unicorn clips. My annoyance at the high-decibel violin fades at the sight of how, at eleven years old, she can so unselfconsciously still wear the trappings of the little girl she is fast on the way to not being anymore.

"It's hot outside," she mutters.

"It's hot in here, too," I point out, gesturing around at our small, cramped kitchen. "Also, do they really want you to play it so slowly? We'll all be several years older before you finish. And why 'Cielito Lindo,' anyway?"

"I wonder if they know that song is Mexican, not Argentinian," Jaime grumbles, looking younger than his twelve years. He's on the arm of the living room couch, where he's playing his Switch with the concentration of a royal jeweler cutting the world's most important diamond.

My mom bustles into the kitchen before I can answer, already dressed in one of the businesslike polos she wears for her shifts at Las Heras, her salt-and-pepper hair bobbed short. "Morning," she says.

"Morning," I reply, handing her a glass of water as my tea steeps on the counter. "Do you want some?" I point my magdalena in her direction. If there's one thing there's plenty of in this house, it's Argentinian pastries.

"Breakfast is for Americans," she says, plucking the bow from Luz's hand and setting it on top of the refrigerator; blessed quiet fills the humid air. "Drink your tea."

I smile and spike my Earl Grey with enough lemon to make my entire mouth pucker, then plop in two packets of stevia. My mom and I have some variation of this conversation every morning. The list of things my mother believes are "for Americans" could fill a freight train. Air-conditioning, unfortunately, is among them, except under the direst of circumstances. On the list are also shirts without sleeves (forget tank tops), food that's been frozen, opening the refrigerator at a house you don't live in, baseball, the phrase "it's just business," bug spray, and returning things to stores. I've spent most of my conscious life begging for Froot Loops or Pop-Tarts. Any and all breakfast foods, really. My big rebellion is sneaking a McDonald's Sausage McMuffin with Ivy.

"You know that you've been here just as long as you lived in Argentina," I remind her, math that's only recently occurred to me. "Plus we've all got that blue passport. So, ya know. American. Through and through."

"Passports are a piece of paper. The heart . . . that's different. It gets minted in place." Her English is impeccable, but her intonation singsongs like she's running every phrase through an Argentina filter, her tone lilting. She adds, "Jaime, querido, decime what you want for lunch."

Although she's decidedly anti-breakfast, no one should make the mistake of thinking that my mom doesn't care about feeding us. Every morning she spends at least half an hour apportioning and re-purposing whatever leftovers she brought home from the restaurant the night before, based on the complex and shifting set of wants of us all so that we can all have a sensational midday meal. She always remembers who likes what each week—lobster rolls for Jaime after a family trip to Maine, and broccoli with a special sauce when Lucesita briefly dabbled in vegetarianism. I was the only kid in third grade who routinely brought a lunch box full of empanadas and papas rellenas that everyone wanted to trade for.

Jaime's placing his order for today when my dad shuffles into the kitchen still wearing his pajamas, an espresso in one hand and a Red Bull in the other. He can officially be considered a part of the Not a Morning Person club.

"Who turned off the music?" he jokes, setting down the Red Bull to put a hand on Luz's shoulder.

My mom frowns, studies his bedclothes. "You didn't leave for Restaurant Depot yet?"

"Ya voy, mi amor. I'm headed that way."

"Nicolas, Route Eighteen is going to be a parking lot." She used to sound like a human checklist, full of useful reminders for him. But now her instructions have taken on a new tone and she seems more like a cattle prod trying to stir flesh to life.

"We need the backup vegetables," she reminds him. "And don't forget cups. I swear they put them in the oven to melt them. Oh, and pastry bags, and the little ramekins . . . Those are running low again, somehow."

"And carafes," I add gently. I don't want to pile more on him, but two metal water carafes suffered catastrophic handle loss over the weekend, one dumping ice water all down the front of my black waitressing pants. And before that we were already running short.

"Carafes!" my mom agrees. "Thank you, Jules. Anything else?"

I rack my brain, not wanting to forget anything. I'd hate to be responsible for putting any extra stress on them when we don't have some vital ingredient or tool in the middle of a dinner rush. "I think that's it," I say. "Unless you guys wanted to do any specials this week?"

The two of them exchange a look I don't quite understand. Although I suspect it has something to do with how empty the restaurant has been lately. We've been recovering from the pandemic in fits and starts. They've been trying everything: new menu items! Takeout cocktails! An impromptu patio we built in two feverish days out of marked-up Home Depot plywood. It's been a lot, and the jury is still out on how much longer it's going to be before the restaurant has fully recovered.

"No specials," says my dad, weary and spent like it's the end of the day and not the beginning. "Not this week."

My mom's lips tighten. "Nicolas—"

"We don't need to run any specials," he repeats, doing the espresso like a shot and then chasing it with the rest of his Red Bull as if he's headed into battle, but reluctantly. "I'm going to get dressed."

My mom watches him leave, bites the right side of her lower lip. Lucesita gets on tiptoes, stretches her fingers, trying to retrieve her bow from the top of the refrigerator; Jaime has drifted back to his game, oblivious to whatever is going on.

I don't know what to say to my mom, who is now all a crackle of tension I can't name. So I do what I always do when the world around me feels too uncertain, too intense.

I go up to my room, open my notebook, and begin to write.

Ivy always calls my writing "making up a world when you don't want to be friends with the real one." She's pretty spot-on. I mean, I like the real one just fine, but there's something extra-dimensional about the ones I imagine. As far as coping mechanisms go, it's probably better than some of the alternatives. Anyway, who *wouldn't* jump at the chance to escape into a world where they get to decide the weather, where everyone says and does what they say? When I'm writing, I can fiddle and fix until everything is perfect, no false starts or awkward silences.

"Julietita, querida!" My mom's voice echoes up the stairs.

I glance at my phone. Somehow, an hour has blazed by. "Can you drop Luz at her lesson on your way into the restaurant?"

I sigh and close my notebook, finding my way back to this world, the one with its stubborn rules I don't control. "Be right down!"

Story ideas

~~Two people go to the same faraway town to trace their roots and~~
~~Snowed in, two rival ski team members begin to . . . (Although.... I can't even ski)~~
~~Like To All the Boys, but on Mars~~
~~The Good Place meets Squid Games, but with a love story~~
~~What if, say, a shark, or a pebble, or a policeman?~~
~~Okay, not this, but this:~~
~~Not that. I'm babbling now.~~
~~What if two people meet and fall in love and everything goes great.~~
Okay, obviously not that

three

Lucas is already at the restaurant by the time I get there, and we move into our seamless dance of setting up the dining room: he smooths out white tablecloths on the tables we cleaned off the night before and left to air-dry, and I put two place settings on two-tops, four on the fours.

I nod my chin at him. "You got a little red," I say.

"Pesky pale parents." He smiles, putting on his clean black apron with long, nimble fingers. "It's the old Northern Italian heritage." He winks. Although his family is from Argentina for generations, his last name is Belmondo, a clue to some long-lost relative who started his journey in some picturesque Tuscan town, no doubt. For a second I'm distracted by the image my brain conjures of him buying fresh lemons in some hillside village in Italy wearing old work pants and a linen shirt, the sun making gold in his mass of curls, which once looked messy and unkempt but now is more along the lines of what I'd call "effortless." If I was writing him, of course.

I shake my head to clear it and hope he didn't catch me looking at his hair. It's good to have him around. He started working here during quarantine, when most of our business was delivery and my parents needed extra bodies to run food all over town. But even before that he was in here almost as much as I was: birthdays and holidays and eighth-grade graduation dinners, the two of us holed up in a booth working on our diorama of a hunter-gatherer village, or playing table soccer with the balled-up wrapper of a drinking straw, gorging ourselves on chorizo.

After the tables, we start our side work: me refilling sugar holders and pouring water into the tiny bud vases on all the tables, Lucas topping up bottles of ketchup—a job he took on specifically because I cannot do it without gagging—and rolling silverware into starchy black napkins fresh out of bags from the linen supplier. We don't talk, the silence comfortable and lived-in as an old pair of jeans. Filling sugar trays is repetitive: *Half sugar packets, four brown sugars, four stevias, four Equals, drop the tray on the table so that everything settles evenly, rinse and repeat.* This was one of the first jobs my parents ever gave me here—back before Jaime and Lucesita were born, back before I could even read. For as long as I've been alive, Las Heras has been another member of the family: relentless, constant, moody, with its own personality and unceasing demands.

But as it can be with things that are like family, my feelings about the restaurant are . . . complicated. I'm fiercely proud of it, with a deep vein of protectiveness and eldest-daughter responsibility: I can't stand to see empty water glasses or spotty silverware. Lucas still teases me about how hard I went off on one of our busboys when I caught him texting in the kitchen last spring during an insanely busy take-out lunch rush. I can't imagine life without the restaurant's distinctive smell of bread and searing meat and the lemon cleaner my mother prefers, without takeout containers full of great food for dinner, without the smiles of customers who have been coming here since I was little.

And, also, I cannot wait to pack up and move on.

I want so badly to escape, to write and travel and create a splashy, big life that doesn't hinge on the price of beef or the whims of the Saturday night dinner crowd. I want to put air and distance and book signings and writing accolades between us. But this restaurant is more than a place, too. It's like a character trait, a gene, a thing I carry inside and never, ever want to change. Or lose.

Lucas and I are back in the spotless kitchen listening to El Maestro, our chef, run through today's menu—ingredients, substitutions, what menu items can be made vegan if any of our customers insist and don't know that classic Argentinian cuisine is basically meat with a side of meat—when our hostess Zoe pops her head in through the door. "Just sat a two-top at table fourteen," she tells me. "You're up." Then she turns to Joaquin. "We've got someone asking for Adam and Eve on a raft on five. Can we do that at this hour?" Zoe tosses her bright red curls. She's an aspiring actress who somehow didn't get the memo that she should be working in a restaurant *in* New York City, not ten miles west. If wanting to be seen is the main require-ment for a successful acting career, Zoe is destined for an Oscar. She's got on a flawless black-and-white geo-metric pattern dress and stilettos that make my ankles hurt just looking at them.

All of a sudden my mother is there. "We can do anything at any hour," she says in an admonishing tone as I make my way out to handle fourteen.

I get them their drinks and take their lunch order, then find Lucas back at the wait station, where he's using an old box to practice toe taps for soccer ball control. "You could look at your phone or something, you know," I tell him quietly. "I won't yell at you like I yelled at Oliver."

"Yeah, right." Lucas raises one eyebrow and scrunches his lips into a half smile that is the facial equivalent of calling bullshit. "What do you think, I'm new here? No way I'm going to risk it. I can't believe I even let you catch me practicing."

"Shut up," I say with a laugh. "I wasn't *that* mean to him."

"Says you," he shoots back. "The poor guy is still in therapy."

I elbow him. His bicep is surprisingly solid, a realization that puts me slightly off-kilter, a sharp zing of contact going straight up my arm. *It's just Lucas*, I remind myself. Twenty pounds of new muscle does not a sudden love connection make. Still, I can't help but imagine how I'd write the scene in my notebook—suddenly I'm in the Tuscan village with him, we're on a class trip, maybe? A genealogical expedition to find his roots? I'm in a flowy light blue dress. I look up and . . . two old friends suddenly see each other in a new light and the sun is setting and . . .

Ugh. I have to stay on task.

We're quiet for a minute, looking out at the mostly empty dining room. Mrs. Richards is here with one of her friends from her book club, which meets here every first Wednesday. She's built in with the foundation. She's one of my favorite customers.

I stop by her table.

"How's your writing class going?" she asks.

I'm delighted and not surprised. She's thoughtful that way. Her white hair is chic in its Meryl-Streep-as-Miranda-Priestly cut and she's wearing a pale blue shawl that looks hand-knit. She runs the area's biggest art school, where Lucesita has taken sculpture classes and Jaime has taken cartooning.

"That's so nice of you to ask," I say. "So far so good."

"Well, with parents like yours, how can you do anything but succeed at whatever you try? Keep me posted. Maybe we can do a reading at the school or something."

"That's so nice, Mrs. Richards. How's everything

at the school? And your husband?"

Something clouds her lined face for a moment, but then she brightens back up. "Oh, you know, the ups and downs of running a business." She waves an elegant hand, and I notice her amethyst drusy ring, electroplated at the base in what looks like rose gold, which covers her middle finger from the base to the knuckle. "Please do tell El Maestro that he's outdone himself on this churrasco."

I nod. "I will." I head to the kitchen to do just that, then make my way back to Lucas.

The only other people in the dining room are the couple at fourteen. They're in their thirties, maybe. The woman in jeans and a ruffly tank top and the guy in a slightly square-looking polo shirt. They're sitting against the wall with the large painting of El Acon-cagua on it—hand-painted years and years ago by my dad, back when he still painted. The guy is deep in the weeds of some exaggerated story, waving his arms while the woman smiles gamely.

"He is . . . really going for it," Lucas observes.

"I think they're on a first date," I respond, low, so my voice won't carry.

"Yeah?" He turns to face me. "How can you tell?"

"Well, look at her. She's leaning in. Clearly putting

out the *I think you're cute* vibe. But he's too wrapped up in impressing her to pick up on it, so he's all in on his story. Notice they haven't touched hands or kissed once."

Lucas tilts his shaggy head to the side like, *Point taken.* "I thought they were just awkward."

I roll my eyes. "No. They're trying to figure each other out. She recommended this place and hopes he likes it. He ordered scrambled eggs, which suggests to me he's never been in an Argentinian restaurant before and doesn't know what's good to order. He's trying to act like he's funnier than he is."

"All this from standing twenty feet away from them?"

I smile. Their story is written all over them. Most people's are, if you know how to read it. I try to look busy but notice the woman reaches out and puts her fingertips on the guy's arm, just for a second. He lights up in response as if he just hit some secret jackpot.

Something about them makes me think of my parents then, their *Don't forget to go to Restaurant Depot,* all-business relationship. I feel a tiny stone of dread plunk to the very bottom of my stomach. *They're fine,* I tell myself. *The restaurant is fine. Everything is—*

"You want to know something kind of pathetic?" Lucas asks me. "I'm seventeen years old, and I've never actually been on a date. Like an official one."

"Really?" Just like that, I am not thinking about my parents anymore. "Nah. What about Meredith?"

Lucas spent the better part of last year hanging out with Meredith Epstein, an alto in the glee club with extremely straight teeth and a penchant for wearing capes and cape-like coats.

Lucas shakes his head. "You're going to laugh."

Now I'm intrigued. "I'm not."

"So . . . I did ask her to go to Applebee's a couple of times. One time after soccer practice, I remember, specifically. She was there, and I asked her."

"Classy," I quip.

"You said you were going to be nice," he says, giving me a mock shove. More contact. "I figured it was a low-risk, not-trying-too-hard type of suggestion."

"So that's a date," I say.

"No. We never went. She always just wanted to go to her house and hook up. Which, like, don't get me wrong, I was not . . . mad about that." He looks down, his sun-reddened cheeks getting a deeper color. "But I don't know. It would have been nice to do something else once in a while. Plus her room had an inordinate number of plants in it, and it always smelled vaguely mossy in there."

The idea of Lucas hooking up with someone—even quirky Meredith Epstein—makes me feel about a hundred things at once, most of them Not Good. My fingers itch for my notebook. It's like I can never name my emotions until I write them down.

"Oh yeah?" I manage finally. "What, you want to be romanced?"

I'm kidding. At least, I'm trying to. But Lucas doesn't laugh. He looks straight in my eyes, his big, brown, black-lash-ringed peepers looking solemn and open and a thousand miles deep.

"What if I do?"

"I—" I open my mouth, close it again, heat creeping in my ears, down my neck. My entire body feels like it's on fire. "I mean—"

I'm saved from myself when my mom pops her head out of the kitchen.

"Jules?" she calls, holding up a bundle wrapped in a brown paper bag. "Can you run out and take this to Abuela?"

I don't fling myself into her arms in gratitude, but

almost. "Of course!" I snatch the bag from her hands as if it contains lifesaving medication. I call to Lucas over my shoulder. "Can you cover my tables?"

I don't wait for him to answer before I dash out the front door.

Abuela Bubbles, or Abuela Nélida, my father's mother, lives a few blocks from the restaurant. Lucas named her Abuela Bubbles when we were little, because she was never without a container of bubbles in her purse back then. I'd have jumped at the chance to go spend a few minutes with her even if I hadn't just forgotten how to make sentences in front of my oldest childhood friend. I push back the nagging feeling that my mom would never have let me leave if she thought there was even a chance the restaurant was going to get busy. I focus on the fact that Abuela is basically my favorite person on the planet, and I'm always happy to do a lunch run for her benefit. She moved to Alderton a couple of years ago, after Abuelo died. She flat-out refused to move in with us—"I need my space!" she insisted. Still, I hate to think of her sitting in her apartment all alone.

I park in the lot outside her building, then let myself in with the key my parents keep for food-delivery emergencies. I run up to her apartment, 3L. The steak sandwich is warm through the paper bag, the familiar weight of it comforting. There's also a well-wrapped cañoncito on top, I'm sure, since that's what my mom almost always sends. Abuela loves her steak and her dulce de leche.

The door is open a crack. I rap my knuckles on it backhanded, then take a tentative step in. "Abuela?" I call out. "It's me."

"Jules!" She appears like a whirling dervish, springing down the hallway. She's a kaleidoscope of color, as always, a patterned sweater that looks like a Miró painting, loose black pants with tiny yellow flowers, and hot red puffy slippers to complete the look. Her hair is battleship gray, her face lined and alive with electricity, like all those lines are conduits. Her lips are a goopy maroon.

She barrels toward me, throws surprisingly wiry arms around my neck. "¡Que hermosa!" she says, then holds me back.

I hardly look *hermosa* in the restaurant apron I'm just realizing I forgot to take off and my nondescript black polo under it, or the black jeans that are the uniform. But I warm at the Abuela goggles she's looking at me through. It is nice to just be loved madly. I hand her the food.

"Ay, m'hijita, only one?" she says.

I laugh. "Did we get your order wrong?" I ask, following her down the narrow hallway into the tiny kitchen in the back.

"No, no." Abuela waves a hand. "I just don't want to be, como se dice, rooood."

"Rude?"

She puts the bundle on her table, then swings her arm game-show-hostess style. I follow the motion. A guy in skinny jeans is wriggling out from underneath her sink, his soft-looking white T-shirt riding up to reveal a strip of pale, smooth stomach; he yanks it back down as soon as he notices, a faintly sheepish expression on his face. He's about my age, with a mop of dark red hair and a nose sprinkled in freckles. He looks vaguely familiar, though I'm not sure from where.

"¿Conoces al calvo?" Abuela asks me. I suppress a laugh. Calvo means "bald" in Spanish. This guy is the direct opposite of bald.

"Calvin," he says, sensing my confusion.

"That's what I said, Calvo," says my grandmother,

unwrapping the food. "There, wash your hands. Calvo, this is my granddaughter. She brought you lunch."

"Jules," I mumble by way of introduction. I am certainly not in the mood to explain the pronunciation of Spanish J's right now, so I skip it.

"Oh!" Calvin shakes his head. "No, no, that's okay. You didn't have to do that. I'm fine."

My grandmother tsks at him, and whether he's a regular handyman or a new guy, he obviously hasn't learned that you can never escape a feeding from my abuela. She fusses at him until he washes his hands in her stamp-sized sink. Then she leads him over to the table and puts the sandwich on a plate for him. I try with minimal success not to stare—one, because there is a strange boy alone with my grandmother in her tiny apartment and I want to make sure he's not a pervert or an ax murderer, and two, because he is awfully cute.

"Acá, dale, you sit, too," she says to me.

"I have to get back to work, Abuela." I shake my head, then turn to Calvin. "It was nice to meet you."

She dismisses that notion with another wave of the hand and pulls out the chair to block my escape. I sit down obediently. She goes to the fridge and produces two cups of homemade rice pudding—my favorite—plunking one in front of me and the other in front of herself. Her kitchen is tiny, and three is about as many as you can sit at her café-style table. I feel the heat from Calvin's knee next to mine.

"Calvo is my new neighbor," she says by way of introduction. "He fixed my sink."

"So I see," I say, smiling at him over my rice pudding. "Thanks for the assist."

"Anytime," Calvin says. His voice is pleasantly gravelly, with an accent that's more New York borough than North Jersey. "You go to Alderton, right?"

"I do," I admit, still trying to place him. "Do you?"

"I did," Calvin explains. "We just moved here in February, so I kind of snuck in for the very end of senior year. Unpacked just in time to graduate, basically."

"Yeesh," I say, before I can stop myself. "That sounds miserable."

"I mean, it wasn't great," he admits, looking a little uncomfortable. "But it's done now. And I still see my friends from Brooklyn pretty often."

"Calvo is very good with the sinks," Abuela pipes up. "And he also likes my arroz con leche."

He smiles at her. "And your telenovelas."

Something about the way he says the word—his accent, maybe—makes me chuckle. "I'm sorry," I manage. "What now?"

Abuela fixes me with a look like, *manners*. "I made Calvo and his mother some of my rice pudding the other day," she explains patiently, "and when I mentioned how these lazies from the apartment building hadn't come to fix my bathroom sink yet, he said he knew how."

Calvin nods. "This was last Thursday," he clarifies. "Which was, I discovered when I got here, the very same day that *La Periodista* was starting." His pronunciation of that is fairly hilarious.

"He came right in the middle of it," Abuela continues, "So he had to watch."

"No other choice, clearly," he adds. They sound like an old married couple telling the story of their meet-cute; already I'm imagining the true-crime book I'm going to have to pen when he absconds with all her money and her collection of rhinestone brooches shaped like bugs.

"Big fan of the novelas, are you?"

"I mean, I wasn't." Calvin's smile, when it comes, does not *seem* like the smile of a con artist, though probably that's exactly what a con artist would want me to think. "But I have to admit, I'm kind of into the whole thing now. Plus I've been trying to teach myself Spanish for like a full year and getting a fat lot of nowhere, and Mabel and Rodrigo are way more interesting than Duolingo."

"Mabel and Rodrigo are . . . ?"

"¡*La Periodista!*" my grandmother chirps, like I should keep up.

"Okay," I point out, still looking for the snag in the story, "but you were working on the *kitchen* sink when I got here."

Abuela shrugs. "They all stink," she says.

"Evidently." I finish the last of my rice pudding. "I missed the plumbing class at Alderton, I guess."

"My dad used to . . . I used to help my dad when he fixed things," Calvin says, his voice a little quieter than it was a moment ago as he runs his thumb around the fussy filigreed edge of Abuela's sandwich plate.

His hands are all dinged up, his knuckles thick, a raised white scar near the edge of his hand, plus assorted scratches. For one completely deranged second I imagine reaching for his hand across the table, tracing the lines of his scars with my thumb.

"I like fixing things. I like figuring out how things work, if that makes sense."

"He's going to do my closet light next," Abuela reports happily. "And then some bookshelves."

That makes me laugh. "Did you agree to all this?" I ask, turning back to Calvin. "Because I gotta tell you, you better make sure you finish my grandmother's honey-do list before you go off to college in the fall, or she's liable to show up at your dorm with a box of alfajores and an even longer list."

But Calvin shakes his head. "Oh, I'm not, actually," he admits. "Going to college, I mean."

I blink. *Gah*, how many dopey things am I planning on saying today? "Oh, no, of course not," I blurt too quickly. "I mean, not *of course not*, I'm sure you *could* go, but I was just saying to a friend of mine the other day that it's . . . Honestly, the idea that as a society we're encouraging teenagers to take on hundreds of thousands of dollars in debt with no guarantee that they'll ever be able to pay it back is just crippling entire generations of . . ." I stop, take a breath before I go into full-on-manifesto mode just to cover up that I feel awkward about my assumption that college was the only way.

"Jules," Calvin interjects gently, holding a hand up to stop me mid-prattle. "It's okay. It's, like, a reasonable assumption for someone our age to make, especially in a town like Alderton, where it seems they make you pick your safety school in kindergarten. And who knows, I might go eventually. But I'm going to work for a while. Maybe travel. I haven't decided."

I nod, busying myself, gathering up the empty pudding cups. There's something so different about his vibe, what little I know about his worldview. He's right that you don't meet many kids who go to Alderton High who don't plan on going to college, and suddenly it feels like my world needs expanding. My brain goes to how I'm going to write about him later, just me and my notebook. He is a blank page of a person, a thrill so complete it's almost a buzz. Is he a self-taught polymath with a talent for taking things apart and putting them back together? Might he end up busking in Edinburgh and get discovered by a record producer? Will he give out water to migrants at the border? Maybe he could restore a vintage school bus in Spokane, then make an art gallery out of it that becomes all the rage. He might be great at bargaining at a souk in Marrakesh, or start a dance school in Vienna. He could be anything. Everything.

I think what's heady about all these thoughts is that he makes me imagine myself there right with him. In some magical, instant way, he makes me want to be a bigger version of myself. And all I've ever seen him do is fix a sink and smile at me, revealing adorably crooked incisors at my abuela's tiny kitchen table. Not for the first time this summer, I wonder: *What is going on with me?*

four

On the morning of my first day at Fairchild, I spend a ridiculous and uncharacteristic amount of time picking my outfit. *It's a writing program, not a fashion show,* I can imagine my mother saying, so I don't let her see how much attention I'm putting into it. As someone who cares about details, I know that we're sometimes defined by a small one. I once listened to a writer panel on YouTube in which one of my favorite authors said that her agent automatically deleted any query email with a mistake in the first sentence. I don't want to roll into Paige Bingham's class in the typo of outfits. But I also don't want her thinking I'm a try-hard.

Finally, I settle on a pair of gray jeans, comfortable New York–appropriate flats, and a top with a bit of ruffle in the capped sleeves. The whimsical pattern says *I don't take myself too seriously*, while the cut says *I could throw a jacket on over this and make it work in a boardroom*. Not that I've ever been in a boardroom. But I've read my share of books with them in it, and I know jackets are required.

I leave myself half an hour to get to the bus stop, even though it's only, like, three blocks away from my house. I turn the corner onto long, tree-lined Elmwood Road, the dappled morning sun turning everything golden as if lit by pixies. The front gardens are the best on this road: riots of lilacs and hydrangeas and dahlias and zinnias, everything lush and start-of-summer hopeful.

I step into the road to look down it to watch for the bus. It's a straight shot, and I can see for several blocks. Nothing yet.

Slouching on the bus stop bench, I buckle and unbuckle the front of the special messenger bag I bought just for this program. Then I scroll my phone for a while, clicking from Lucas's Instagram profile over to Calvin's. Lucas has stopped posting soccer game shots, which used to be the bulk of his posts.

Calvin has three posts, all travel stuff, and nothing in his Stories. I found him because he gave me his number at my abuela's the other day.

"Calvo," she instructed firmly, "give my granddaughter your number. Emergencies," she added cryptically and with classic Abuela flair.

But it's not like I've done anything loony, like text him. What would I even say? *Seen any good Spanish-language programming lately with anyone literally old enough to be your grandmother? Just FYI, I recently wrote several hundred overwrought words in my secret notebook about you? Please don't scam my abuela?*

I get up, step back into the street, and let out a sigh of relief: there, several blocks away, is the profoundly unsexy New Jersey Transit commuter bus that will cough its way to me, pick me up, then lumber along this main street, through several towns. It will then get on the turnpike, go through the Lincoln Tunnel, and deposit me in the Port Authority. From there, I'll take the A train uptown. I have a screenshot of the route in my phone and, in case of battery emergency, also printed out and tucked inside the blue notebook.

Overkill, maybe. But I want to get this right.

It's summer, and a little past rush hour, so until now I've been the only person out here. But just before the bus pulls up to the curb, someone comes dashing around the corner onto Elmwood and careening down the block, edging in front of me and hopping up onto the bus just as the doors belch open. I'm about to snap at him for cutting the line, or, at least, I'm about to give him major huffy attitude, when I recognize the precise haircut and the slouchy Abercrombie T-shirt I've seen before.

"Ryan?" I sputter.

Ivy's twin brother turns around, fixing me with his most future-corner-office lawyer smile. "Come on, Jules," he says. Even though he just ran the last block and a half like he was trying to qualify for the Olympics, he's not out of breath. "Don't want to miss the bus."

"What are you doing here?" I demand, bracing myself against the headrests as I follow him down the aisle. The bus is jam-packed with manspreaders and offensive-perfume wearers, and there's not a seat to be found. The bus lurches into the road with deep weariness.

"I'm going to Fairchild," he reminds me with an inscrutable smile.

He has a messenger bag, too, except his is probably made from camel's tears and trust fund wrappers

(*Write later: Do trust funds come in wrappers? An exploration*). Anyway, it's expensive, buttery leather that looks beat-up and neglected, which I'm sure means it's brand-new and he paid extra for the pleasure of having it look like Thomas Jefferson left it to him in his will. He's got it slung across his tall, slim body. My parents could probably pay the restaurant's rent for a month with what I bet that thing cost.

"Just like you," he says.

"No, I know that." When I found out Ryan had gotten in to Fairchild as well, it temporarily took the shine off the whole thing, like maybe it wasn't as special as I'd thought if they accepted any rich, fratty, know-it-all who could buy his way in. "I mean, why are you *here*?" I repeat, waving my hand around to denote "bus."

Ryan and Ivy drive matching BMW convertibles, hers in white, his in a color I'm sure must be called Ample 401(k) Gray. In fact, she suggested I text him for a ride to the program, and I worked hard to fight off the look of *you can't be serious* before making some noncommittal comment to deflect. I mean, she says sibling-level awful things about her brother, but I'm sure she wouldn't love it if I did. So I didn't. But I wasn't about to ask for a ride from the guy who beat me out for sophomore-year class president while barely launching a campaign beyond "But I'm Ryan."

"How come you're not driving in?" I ask.

Ryan mock shudders. "You must know what parking is like on the Upper West Side," he says with the casual authority of a person who goes into the city way more than I do.

"I guess," I mumble, just as the bus hits a bump and I almost go tumbling to the sticky, rubber-coated floor. Ryan grabs my arm and steadies me.

"Get your sea legs, there, Jules," he says with a smile.

He didn't even budge, although I was nearly airborne. I consider hissing at him to get him to unhand me. Ugh, I can't believe I'm going to have to stand all the way into the city. *With Ryan Madigan.* What the actual hell?

I take a breath. I don't know why Ryan ruffles me so much. I think, not for the first time, that it's so weird that humans who grew in the same belly and were made and raised by the same parents could be so different. First, they look very little alike. Ivy is blond, although I know that's helped along by the pricey salon she goes to to get her highlights done with her mom. Ryan's hair is dark and clipped short and precise. Ivy has light, swimming-pool-blue eyes, while his are a darker blue. Ivy is California tan, but Ryan looks like he could easily be cast in a vampire movie. Ivy's privilege has made her warm and generous, quick with a hug or a compliment or a social media rallying cry to help a GoFundMe reach its funding goal. Ryan's privilege just makes him . . . Ryan. Kind of snooty and impossible to read. We always had a certain distance between us, but he's been harder to take since the sophomore-year class-president thing. True, it may be time to get over that. But I guess I'm not.

The bus slows for the next stop, its brakes screeching like dying demons. Right in front of Ryan, two passengers get up to exit. He makes eye contact with me.

"Window or aisle?" he asks.

I consider telling him neither, but I've ridden through the Lincoln Tunnel standing up before, and it makes me want to barf.

"Window," I decide, and slide in without further comment.

Ryan sits down next to me. We settle into a deeply unsatisfying silence, with me staring out at the highway and Ryan popping his earbuds into his ears, presumably to listen to some podcast about the stock market or how to buy your way out of a white-collar felony conviction. I like to know things, guess at motivations, surmise intent, imagine everyone around me is a character awaiting their inciting incident. But he is one I can't figure out.

"Can I ask you something?" I say finally, turning to face him. "What are *you* doing going to Fairchild?"

Once it's out of my mouth I realize it's way ruder out loud than it was in my head. He pops a headphone out of the ear nearest me, but answers the question. "It was either this or intern in the mailroom at my dad's office. And because, you know." His full lips twist. "I like to write."

My eyes narrow. "Since when?"

"Since . . . always?" Ryan looks amused.

"You've never mentioned it before."

"In any of those long, intimate heart-to-hearts you and I have had over the years? Also, I write for the paper?"

"I . . . Fine," I have to admit.

Ryan and I have never spent that much time together, partly because I find him and his *I know everything* air tough to take and partly because he's hardly ever around: he's always out with friends or at some party or hanging out in the school newspaper office, where he's deputy editor. Which is, I guess, tangentially writing-related.

Ryan adds, "Anyway, I applied without even telling my parents and got in. No one had to be bribed." He lifts one elegant eyebrow, like he knew exactly what I was thinking. "My parents, as you can imagine, have never been prouder or more thrilled."

It almost—*almost*—makes me feel bad for him. Ivy and Ryan's parents are what you might call "high-powered." Their dad does corporate law. Their mom runs a real estate office where she barks orders at a small army of agents and sells million-dollar houses. They have one of the biggest, oldest Victorian houses in our town, on an elegant lot bordered by an elaborate wrought iron fence. The house looks like if you let it get a little bit more beat up it might work as the set of an old ghost drama. Except, no, because there's always an army of landscapers and handymen around. There's usually little-to-no parental supervision there because their parents work these intense hours, more intense than my parents, even, and that's saying something. I can see how they might not be super supportive of Ryan spending a whole summer in a writing workshop. Not exactly the cutthroat corporate-raider skills they'd want him developing, I imagine.

Which is not a reason to feel sorry for him, I remind

myself firmly. There is literally *no* reason to feel sorry for Ryan Madigan, who spent spring break in an over-water bungalow in the Maldives. I know Ivy lives that life, too, but she wears it differently, somehow. I can't help but reflexively draft his villain origin story in my head: a dad who doesn't understand him, a mom who's never around. I reach for my notebook without quite knowing I'm going to do it, opening to a fresh blank page.

"What are you writing?" Ryan asks, craning his neck and trying to look over my shoulder, close enough that I can smell the faint, sandalwood-y scent of . . . is that cologne? Shampoo handcrafted in small batches by cloistered nuns and hand-carried by devoted follow-ers down from the mountain on holy goats?

"Nothing," I tell him, slamming the notebook shut and jamming it back into my messenger bag.

Neither one of us says anything for the rest of the ride into the city.

Arriving at Fairchild requires a train ride to the Upper West Side and a walk from the subway station. Ryan and I navigate this in that hinterland between "I'm not with you" and "together," walking near each other without quite acknowledging that's what we're doing.

He walks faster than I do, long legs in a pair of slim-fit flat-front pants, but he doesn't try to outpace me, either.

The check-in separates us naturally. Long tables are set up with a range of letters—A–G, H–M, N–S, T–Z. He goes to the second, I go to the last, since my last name starts with a T. It's a painful transaction to spell *Talavera* for the person behind the table, who insists on making the joke that it sounds like *television*, like I've never heard that one before. Finally, she hands me a packet and directs me to the auditorium for the welcome. There is a big group of us, more than can fit in one classroom. This lifts my hopes a little. Maybe Ryan is in a different section of the course and I won't have to see him at all.

No such luck. He's already taken a seat up near the front of the classroom when I arrive, his smooth, serious face turned toward the podium at the front. I sit in one of the only available seats, at the back. The high-ceilinged room looks like it might have been intended for the visual arts kids and not the writers. There are splotched easels crammed together in one far corner, and floor-to-ceiling windows with sunlight streaming in. There are about fifteen of us here, not a huge number. But the relief at that is outweighed by the "serious writer" vibes a lot of the other students are giving off. One girl with an under-cut has an ancient, dog-eared five-subject notebook crammed with tiny writing that she flips back and forth through as she scribbles furiously. A guy in the seat next to me types soundlessly into his Mac at a surprising speed for a two-finger typist. He intro-duced himself to me with some formality right before class began, telling me his name was Wyatt in an in-scrutable, half-British-but-not-totally accent. There's one "I Read Banned Books" T-shirt and at least two book-cover totes in class. Everyone is brow-furrowed and serious. Writers. Intense. Probably more expe-rienced than me. Maybe even veterans of this class from other sessions.

Paige Bingham strides in at four minutes after the hour, an author photo come to life. I have read so much about her meteoric literary rise that I forgot to pay attention to the fact that this was fifteen years ago and she looks closer to my parents' age. She's in a black dress over black tights so dark they look like yoga pants. She's got beaded bracelets from her wrist to halfway to her elbow, and a set of marbled green beads with a tassel around her neck. Her eyebrow is pierced and, beneath the bracelets, I glimpse the edge of an elaborate tattoo twining its way up her forearm.

My brain starts doing flips. There is so much to remember to write down later.

Paige clears her throat, leaning against the podium in front of her. "Who here is a hard-core writer?"

Tentative glances around the room. A smattering of hands go up.

"Come on. No wrong answers. I wouldn't have raised my hand at your age."

One more hand goes up. I keep mine down. Am I? I'm not sure.

"For those of you who know you want to be writers, congratulations. For those of you who don't, you are still in the right place. This is a course on writing, yes, but it's not about the technical stuff, and it's not so much about the business, either. It's about storytelling. And storytelling is going to serve you no matter what you ultimately do in life."

"So we won't have to write?" a kid quips from the back. He's got a wide, friendly face that looks like he's stressing this class less than the rest of us.

"Spoken like someone coerced into being here. Nice try. No, you'll definitely be writing. A lot. But I'm going to encourage you to play, to find different vehicles to express yourself. Talk to me about what you like to write. Or even what you like to read."

A guy in front of me whose desk is all but taken up with a giant binder calls out, "Fantasy!"

The wearer of the "Banned Books" T-shirt calls out, "Werewolves!"

A bunch of snickers. I glance at Ryan. He doesn't jump in. I'm curious what his answer would be. Then I'm annoyed at my curiosity.

"Okay. Take out your notebook. Or let me know if you need loose-leaf. Now write it down."

I pull out my notebook, flipping past the blank front page. When I was little, my mom used to tell me that in Argentina they always made caratulas on the front page of their notebooks, drawings to illustrate them. I always skip the first page of my notebooks intending to do the same, although I usually end up just scribbling quotes on there.

Paige clears her throat, and the room falls to silence. It's so different from high school. It thrills me, like a peek into what college might be like.

"I'm sure at least some of you have that image of the solitary genius typing away at the old-timey typewriter. Show of hands, honest hands now, who imagines that that's what the writing life is like?"

The room ripples with soft guffaws and about half the hands in the room go up. I don't raise my hand because I'm not sure.

Paige raises her hand too. "Once upon a time, if you'd have asked me that same question, I would have said, yes, of course. It's a solitary genius creating something brilliant in a vacuum, that's what's created all the writing we've ever loved and held up as worthy. But the fact that you're here hopefully means that you're at least somewhat aware that's not the way it works at all. Writing takes a community. Publishing *definitely* takes a community. But we'll leave questions of commerce for later. For now look around and let it sink in that if you do decide to get serious about a writing life, many of the people in this room could be your community for a long time. The hive mind you go to when you're stuck on a plot point. The ones you call when you're sure everything you're saying is derivative or small. Writing flourishes in a supportive community, so that will be part of what we'll be building here.

"Okay, another show of hands, for those of you who feel okay sharing: who here has dipped a toe in putting your work out there? Could be StoriedZone or Wattpad. Or a publication. Anyone? Come on, I've read all your applications. I know your secrets," she teases.

A few hands go up, fewer than for the other questions.

"Good! A head start, then. So here's my assignment to you for this week: get your writing out there. Send a story to a small journal. Or a big one." She laughs. "If you don't want to jump on the rejection train yet—and, believe me, there will be a lot of rejection if you choose the writing life—then put something up on a site like StoriedZone. Stake your claim. You are a writer. It's not enough to think about it. Being a writer is an act. Do it. Out loud. Somewhere. Come prepared to talk about it next week.

"And read the syllabus. By the end of the summer you'll either have five completed stories or the start of a novel and a full outline. Polished, workshopped, ready for whatever is next for you. My goal is to give you a jump start on achieving your writing dreams, whatever they are."

She lets it hang there: sparkly and promising, a writing career made magic orb right in the center of the room, and all of us staring at it, aching, hoping, imagining, daring. "And don't forget the Best Work Prize. That's an incentive for you, a literary agent to give you feedback on your work, plus a few other cool perks. Details on the class website. So go forth and write your best," she says. "Or . . . write what you can. *Best* is a high bar. Aim for it but don't get hung up on it."

All afternoon I feel a heightened awareness of Ryan at the front of the classroom: the way he twirls his pen between his fingers, his long legs stretched out underneath his desk, his shoes even nicer from the back of the room. I'm fully expecting him to be one of those guys who loves the sound of his own insights so much he can't imagine everyone else won't, too, with an endless supply of questions that are "really more of a comment." But he's quiet and attentive, taking notes in a notebook that complements but doesn't match his bag.

I lose track of him once class lets out for the day, his tall head disappearing in the flood of people streaming outside into the muggy city afternoon. I stand around awkwardly for a moment, unsure if I should wait for him. Do I even want to? Finally, I give up and catch the train back to the Port Authority, hanging on to the terrible subway pole, and wishing for biohazard level 4–style decontamination showers at the stops. By the time I collapse into an aisle seat on the bus, I feel like I've fought a WWE fight above my weight class. I desperately need a shower and a week on a mountain-top meditation retreat. Then Ryan bounds in. He looks just as put together as he did this morning, clothes smooth, face unshiny and calm.

"Hey, Jules," he says as he passes. I open my mouth to say something but can think of nothing, which is fine, since he then heads for the back of the bus before anything occurs to me.

I shake my head in confusion before pulling my computer out of my messenger bag. If I'm going to put our first assignment up online somewhere, it makes sense to start it on my computer and not doodle in my notebook. I open a new document.

The empty page smirks at me.

I pull out my phone instead. I've got a WhatsApp from my tía Chiqui, my mom's sister and favorite aunt.

"¡Ya pronto!" she says. Soon. There's a picture of her with a new suitcase, presumably for her trip here.

I'm going to see her in a few weeks for the first time in years. "I'm excited!" I write back with a heart emoji.

I turn off my phone. Enough procrastinating on this writing thing. It's not usually this way for me. *Editing*, now that's a beast. But the blank page is usually my friend, an invitation, a play buddy, an adventure waiting to happen. But the cursor blinks, unforgiving. This feels different. Unsettling. When it's only for me, writing is a release valve—a joy. But I imagine the kids in class reading it, or, worse yet, Paige Bingham, and I can't start. I just can't.

This is ridiculous. Type words. *Type.*

I begin deliberately. Since the story won't come, I try a description of Paige's classroom.

The paint-splattered easels stood guard as the . . .

Ugh. Terrible. I smash the back button hard until it's all gone.

The smell might be described as higher education meets teenage ambition.

Even worse. Smash back button. *Smash smash smash.*

I might as well try one line that could somehow make it into a story.

Everyone called Gideon Giddy, a terrible description for her. Especially since Thomas had walked off with half her fortune and most of her dignity.

None of this is getting me any closer to the Best Work Prize. I'm about to punch the back button one more time when Ryan's voice blooms behind me, low and quiet.

"How's it going?"

I jump. At some point, he slipped into the seat directly behind me, but I didn't notice because I was too busy self-flagellating. He still smells like sandalwood, the faintest note of . . . *Is that basil?* underneath it. I am . . . pretty sure I smell like subway and frustration.

"Peachy."

"That's what I figured." Ryan smirks. "I could tell by the way you were punishing that poor keyboard." He waves his arms to demonstrate, earning a dirty look from the woman in a business suit sitting beside him. "I thought, *Wow, Jules must really be on a roll.*"

"Did you need something?" I ask impatiently.

"What are you working on that's got you so . . . animated?" Ryan asks in reply. "Are you doing Paige's assignment already?"

"That falls squarely in *none of your business* territory," I kind of hiss. "Like, deep, *deep* within the capital of None of Your Business."

"Okay, fine." Ryan gets up then, coming around my seat to stand in the aisle beside me. From this angle, he looks very, very tall. "Let's talk about the class. What did you think?"

I inhale deeply. This is Ivy's brother, I remind myself. Not just her brother, her *twin*. And as much as she loves to talk smack about him and his annoy-ingly symmetrical facial features, I assume she would not love to hear that I elbowed him on the knee cap on a bus on the way home from our first day of writing class.

"I thought she was amazing," I admit, leaning my head back to look up at him. "But, I mean, I already knew that."

Ryan makes a face like, *I guess*. "Okay," he allows, "that 'no adjectives' exercise was pretty good, but you've got to admit she was off base on Hemingway."

I laugh out loud at that, I can't help it, one loud, mean cackle. "Oh, Ryan," I say, as kindly as I can man-age. "Please don't."

Ryan frowns, like he's genuinely confused. "Don't what?" he asks.

"I just, I honestly cannot have this conversation with you right now. I'm tired. It's been a long day. Twelve trees were chopped down in the Amazon since we started talking. Let's just . . . not and say we did."

"I truly have no idea what you're talking about."

I heave a loud sigh. "Paige was not 'off base on Hemingway,'" I begin, barely managing not to mimic Ryan's bro voice. "Like, what was her fundamental premise, exactly? That literature is a living, breathing

thing and that we should evolve with it, not revere some stodgy old white guys because other long-dead stodgy old white guys said we should, and everyone's been following along ever since? I'm pretty sure that's like . . . directly on the base."

"No, of course." Ryan leans forward, bracing one arm on the seat in front of me and ducking his head closer to mine. "I'm not saying there isn't some quality stuff being produced today. Or that we shouldn't read all of that, too. Like, obviously we should. But when we, as a society, have identified genius, why should we no longer pay attention to it in the service of progress? Like, let me put it another way: Who's your favorite contemporary author? The one whose career you'd most like to have? Whose work speaks to you?"

"I mean, Paige's, to start with."

Ryan makes that dubious face again, his lip curling slightly. It makes me want to yank his hair, second-grade-style.

"Sure, if you like romance."

The bus emerges into the light then, but only for a second, before being plunged back into the yellow glow of the tunnel.

"What are you saying, exactly?" I demand. "That writing romance is a diminishment of something?

That it's not a worthy genre?"

Ryan holds his hands up. "Listen, I'm not trying to rehash some old, tired argument with you. I'm not saying that women's fiction is, like, less than."

"Because all romance is women's fiction."

"I mean, let's be honest with each other here. Historically, yes. I've never seen a men's romance section. Have you?"

"No," I retort, staccato, "because they put that stuff in 'Literature.' You don't think Hemingway wrote about love?"

"Of course he did," Ryan says, his words measured. "But that's not all his books were about."

"No. And it's not all Paige's are about, either." I'm vibrating with irritation and frustration and I truly hate when guys—and it is always, *always* guys—take this position. It's so annoying! So un-self-aware. But it's not exactly like I'm going to be the one to educate, or that it's even my job to do it. So I pivot. "What are you working on, even?"

Ryan hesitates. "It's like . . . a war story."

"It's *like* a war story?" All at once, I smell blood.

"I—yeah," he explains, a little haltingly, "except it takes place in this cursed land, with two warring factions that have been mortal enemies for centuries, but in each generation in order to appease the beasts that live on the fringes of their settlements, they have to kidnap the heir to each other's— You know what?" he says, breaking off as he studies my face. "Never mind."

"I'm sorry," I say, trying to keep my face straight and largely failing. "It's just . . . it's a *fantasy*?"

Ryan sets his jaw then, but I can tell he's embarrassed. "Yes," he grinds out, "I guess you'd call it a fantasy."

I nod slowly. I love fantasy, actually, and I read a ton of it, too. But for a guy to turn his nose up at romance knowing the crap fantasy gets from the "literary" crowd is pretty rich. "You know Hemingway didn't write fantasy, either," I can't help but say, smiling my most dazzling smile.

"I can see that you're enjoying yourself right now," Ryan says dryly. But he smiles.

I can't help but laugh. I feel goofy and not nearly as annoyed as I did a minute ago. Ryan Madigan, writing high fantasy. What a total geek. I wonder what his future law partners would think of that pastime.

"You know what I did think was interesting?" he asks. He's still leaning over my seat, the heat from his body radiating off him like a pizza oven. "What Paige was saying about the Best Work Prize at the end of the summer."

I nod. The prize is judged anonymously and based on our end-of-summer portfolios; the award is $500 and the chance for an actual literary agent to read the first ten pages of our work. I want to win it desperately, and from the look on his face, I can tell that Ryan does, too.

"Yep," I say, trying to keep my voice even, to not sound too eager. "That is interesting."

"Well," he says, "may the better man win, I guess."

"Yes," I reply crisply, then turn back to my laptop. "Except in this modern retelling, the best man is a woman."

And that's the end of the conversation for the rest of the bus ride.

Top Ten Reasons Romance Rocks

- Love makes the world go round
- Seriously, love is like the OG thing
- Sexy, brooding leading men
- But not a psycho like Heathcliff. But a little bit Heathcliff, except Heathcliff after counseling. Or Romeo without the death wish
- That fluttery feeling that literally nothing else can give you
- Because human connection is everything
- Abs
- Smoochy scenes with abs (side note: in the "be the mate you want to have" category, should I tell Ivy we should join a gym? But literally with what time?)
- Ryan can STFU with his Hemingway fanboying. Also: Hemingway totally wrote about love.
- What does Ryan know anyway? He writes about beasts. Maybe he said "beasts" because he was afraid to admit it's actually gnomes. Gnome wars.

five

Tuesday nights are usually quiet at Las Heras. Well, the last few years, every night is quiet at Las Heras. But Tuesdays are more than most. That's why it's always been when we have the asado. Asados are the Argentinian version of American barbecues, with a unique flair. My parents and Lucas's sit out on the restaurant patio. Music from the sound system piping through the tinny outdoor speaker while they talk and laugh and even dance, on occasion. Lucas and I sit with them sometimes, but we're mostly in the dining room to handle walk-ins. It's kind of fun, them as the patrons and us as the servers. It feels like being grown-up and in charge.

Even though the restaurant isn't what I want to be in charge of when I'm a grown-up, I like the feeling.

I bump the door to the patio with my hip, balancing a tray of small plates: empanadas, a selection of olives, churrasco sliders, a plate of thinly sliced chorizo sauteed just so. The conversation is in full swing, Lucas's dad telling some long, convoluted story about trying to get directions to the beach when he was first learning English and being epically, comically misunderstood. It's a story I've heard before, but that's part of the warm feeling of these nights: stories like familiar old blankets passed around lovingly and with care.

"So the wine is flowing freely. Are they . . . already hammered?" Lucas murmurs in my ear, coming out behind me with a tray of soda and handmade chips for Lucesita and Jaime.

"They're working diligently on it," I crack. My mother's eyes in particular are a little red, which is unusual: she's generally not one for relaxing or letting her guard down within half a mile of the restaurant. But things have been different with her for a while, a feeling I keep pushing back. *She's just letting loose*, I tell myself. *It's fine*.

"It's not for the faint of heart, a long marriage," my mom says, apropos of some exchange I've missed. She reaches for her wineglass, takes a swig. "Listen, chicos, do you hear? Take your time. See the world."

"No, Magda," Lucas's mom says, chiding. "Don't scare them off. It's nice to get married. Get a good, solid job—not this soccer player thing—and get married." She turns to Lucas and me, raising one eyebrow pointedly. "You'll see."

"Okay, Mom," Lucas says with an eye roll. He avoids looking in my direction. "I'll tuck that bit of wisdom away."

"Oh, dejenlos." My mom waves a hand. "It's not like marriage is everything. Take your time, m'hijos. See the world," she says again. I wonder if she's tipsy enough to not realize she's repeating herself.

I glance over at my dad, noticing for the first time my parents aren't sitting next to each other. Although my mom made what was considered by her family a radical decision in coming to the U.S. for college, then staying, she's not exactly a bra-burning "you don't need marriage" revolutionary. *What the hell is up with these two?*

As I push back into the hall to the kitchen, I think of a story my mother told me casually when I was thirteen. I was crying because nobody had asked me to the eighth-grade dinner cruise. At the time, the story was just one of those things I figured my mom was saying to cheer me up. But it comes back to me now, full and rich and imbued with a meaning I didn't give it then.

My mother grew up in town in Mendoza, the daughter of the owners of the local ferretería, a hardware store. They weren't wealthy by any stretch, but as owners of a bustling business, they were considered to be doing better than many. Part of being raised in a family with a business meant working in it, a habit that made it down the generations, apparently.

One day, as she was dusting an aisle, she found a note folded up beneath a small can of paint. It said her name on it. Curious, she opened it up. The writer of the note had long admired her intelligence and beauty, it read, but he was from a poor family and knew she would never accept him. Still, he thought she was too special a girl not to at least tell her that someone felt that way about her. A week or so later, there was another note.

The game went on for a while. She left him a few notes back, asking him to reveal himself. He never did. His notes captivated her. They were peppered with lists of songs and original poems, keen observations on life and love. They were obviously written by a sensitive, romantic soul, and she ached to know who he was. She wondered if maybe she was falling in love with this shy writer, but, of course, that was silly. She didn't even know him.

But my mother was a girl with a plan. She'd been accepted as a foreign student to a university in Michigan. When the time came to leave for college abroad, she did, leaving her secret admirer behind. College is where she ended up meeting my dad.

They were two of only a handful of foreign students from Argentina, so they spent more and more time together. My dad was majoring in business and came from a hardworking small-business-owning family, too. He worked tirelessly to pay for his schooling, putting in long hours at a restaurant off-campus. She liked that about him. My mom majored in computer programming, and it was the job she landed after college that put her on the road to American citizenship. When they married a year after that, it meant my dad would get his papers, too.

Sometimes I've wondered what it is that keeps my parents together, with their all-business demeanor with each other, their *Don't forget the scallops at Restaurant Depot* tones. I even know that they hurried their marriage along for immigration purposes: once my dad graduated, he would have had to go back to Argentina without that marriage certificate. Do I exist because two people chose convenience? Because she never found out who left her that love note? Because love lost out?

I don't know. My mother wouldn't talk about it after she first told me the story. My attempts to gently prod were rebuffed with a smile, or an "If you've got so much free time, how about you go fill the saltshakers, m'hija?" If I pressed some more, she'd say, "Sacá la cabeza de las nubes," a gentle rebuke. *Take your head out of the clouds.* But if taking my head out of the clouds means losing my chance at real, sweeping love, at holding out for the biggest dreams, not just the easy ones, I know for sure I don't want that.

I also know that I have the power to write a different ending to my mother's story. An ending I would have wanted. All at once, I know what I want to write on StoriedZone. I duck back into the kitchen, dig my laptop out of my bag, and open it up in the empty dining room to write:

It would take a covert operation to discover who'd been leaving Maggie the love notes incandescent with romance and hope. But she'd have to do it, and do it quick: in three days, she was set to leave her small town. She'd never forgive herself if she didn't find out who her secret admirer was. He could change the course of her whole life.

And, maybe, she wanted him to.

"Jules?" comes a tentative voice behind me.

I swing toward it to use my body to block the screen.

"What are you working on?"

The initial flare of panic dies down as fast as it roared up. "Hi," I let myself relax. After all, it's just Lucas, my lifelong co-conspirator. He knew about the little towers of Elmer's Glue I made on the windowsill behind the curtain in the dining room when we were six. He read my extensive canon of BTS fan fiction all through middle school. I'd let him in on my mad crush on Bobby Dennison in the seventh grade, which ended in disappointment when he failed to show up for our hastily planned rendezvous during softball practice and then pretended he didn't know what I was talking about when I asked him what happened.

Which is why I'm so surprised to realize I kinda don't want to talk about this idea with him.

Normally writing calms me down and helps me get my thoughts organized. If anyone asks me about it, I'll happily blabber on and on until I realize the well-meaning person who asked is slowly glazing over into a mound of moss. But something about committing the story of my mom and her love letters to paper makes me feel like a trapdoor has opened up inside me. I think of the way my mom's face clouds over when she thinks nobody is paying attention, as she absently folds laundry or sweeps the sidewalk out in front of the restaurant. Was my mother's true love somewhere else, in a boy too shy to reveal himself? Did she spend time wishing she had worked harder to find him? It feels vital, an ongoing emergency, suddenly, to focus on how not to miss love when it shows up.

I look from Lucas to the screen of my laptop, back again.

"It's nothing," I tell him, and close the computer. But even as I try to stuff it back, I can't wait to finish what I started writing. I can *see* the story unfolding. I want to catch it and get it down on paper. But that will have to wait until later. "Come on, let's go out there before they set up a net to capture us."

I turn him around by the elbow. At the door, he lets me through first.

Maggie was the child of some of the last sailmakers left in a sleepy downstate seaside town. Most sails were made in big factories now, but Maggie's family still made theirs in an old open barn of a room with ancient equipment her dad tinkered with endlessly.

Maggie liked the small fishing village where she'd grown up. She liked the smell of salt and sea near the docks as the fishermen brought in their daily catch. She liked scallops for dinner and sunrise over the water.

But Maggie wanted very much to get away.

She wasn't sure if she wanted to go forever, or just for a while. Seventeen years were a lot to spend in this tiny backwater town. She wanted to go places as opposite her small town as she could find. Instead of sea, she wanted to get lost in the desert. She wanted land so dry and vast that the water molecules in her felt like the last precious H_2O for miles. She'd applied, and gotten accepted, to a school in a big desert city. She was leaving in a few short weeks.

Maggie's job at her family's sail business was to add the final touches to the carefully packaged sails right before the weekly visit from the UPS delivery truck that came to take them to their destinations. She did some of the not-fun stuff, like print out shipping labels and put the final packing tape on. But her favorite part was writing the notes.

She had a neat box full of sea-themed stationery, and she'd pen a special note to each recipient. To Carmen in Key West she wrote, "May your seas always be sunny." To Joel in La Jolla she wrote, "Wishing you endless sunsets full of joy." Business was busiest in the spring, so she'd get up first thing to get her work done before school.

One morning in March, she made her way into the quiet front room of the factory. The sea threatened churn, steely and choppy, and low-slung clouds hovered out where the sea met the iron sky. She let herself in to the work room with the key under the mat and found the neat pile of boxes with instructions. She loved this room, with its three sides of floor-to-ceiling windows that give her a glimpse over the slumbering town, and its chippy old rafters made from reclaimed ship's wood back when her great-grandfather first built this place. It was usually unlocked during the day, open to the public in case any of the local fishermen came in with a special request for netting or a new mizzen sail. If no one was behind the desk, the fisherman would leave a note and Maggie's father or uncle would get to filling the order, left on a different pile than the ones that shipped out across the country.

She sat on her favorite padded stool to begin the day's work. It wasn't a surprise to find a note, as the spring was when the fishermen liked to get their own boats up to snuff too. She raised the volume on the radio when one of her favorite songs came on, Avril Lavigne's "Complicated," a song that really spoke to Maggie about honesty and being herself, and unwrapped the notes.

She only had to skim a line to understand this wasn't a request for new rigging. It wasn't a note for the business at all. It was a note *for her*.

She read it through, a smile spreading over her face. It wasn't just a note for her. It was a note that felt like it could change everything.

🎣 Posts 3   💟 Likes 12

six

I swing by Abuela Nélida's house to check on her a couple of afternoons later. There is something about her living alone in this apartment that feels so vulnerable to me, though I'd never say that to her face, for fear of being denied even a taste of her rice pudding for all eternity. Still, back when my grandfather was alive they owned a cottage near the water that was tiny like a dollhouse, with brightly painted rooms and cozy nooks for reading and a garden Abuela tended with obsessive care. It's hard not to compare that place to this one, with its dull engineered faux hardwood floors, and windows that only open six inches for safety.

I rap my knuckles softly on her door. She opens right away, in a tan-and-fuchsia dress that hugs her thick middle. Her lipstick matches the tiny hot pink flowers, her close-cropped curls perfectly coiffed. She looks like she's about to go on a garden tour.

"You look fantastic." I smile and go in for a tight hug.

"Ay, y vos tambien." She hugs me. "You smell like dulce de leche and maybe un poquitín the picadillo."

"Restaurant life," I say with a grin, thrusting a container of arroz con pollo at her.

"Veni, veni, you're just in time," she says. "You missed Mabel starting her job, but I think she's going to run into Reinaldo again soon. I can just feel it."

Ugh. The telenovela. "I thought *La Periodista* was on in the afternoon," I say.

"DVR," Abuela explains, like it's not bizarre that she knows what that is when she's still kind of figuring out how text messages work. "Decime, how was your class?"

"It was good," I reply, pleased that she remembered. "I posted the beginning of my first assignment on a website so people could read it. But I'm too nervous to go look and see if anyone has. There's this prize you can get, and I really want it. But I don't know if my writing is good enough for that."

"Of course it is," Abuela says. "People will love it if you put your heart into it. How could they not, when my nietecita is hermosa and brilliant?"

"We'll see," I say. I do appreciate her confidence. I sometimes wish I could see myself through Abuela goggles. "It's actually kind of based on—"

"Hey!" Calvin is sitting on her sofa in jeans and a navy-blue T-shirt, a pair of scuffed-up work boots splattered in paint. He's eating a powdered doughnut out of a bakery box. "You're just in time for Mabel and Reinaldo." Like that's not an extremely unusual thing to say.

"I—" I stop, cartoon-abrupt, looking from him to my grandmother and back again. "What are you doing here?"

"Watching *La Periodista*," Abuela answers for him. "I just told you. Mabel used to be a street urchin," she continues helpfully, gesturing at the television. "But now she's a crackerjack investigative reporter." She nods at the box on the coffee table. "Have an alfajor."

I reach down, take one, and squint at the screen.

A young woman dressed in what a third grader might imagine a journalist's outfit looks like: wool pants, billowy white blouse, a vest so tight it looks like a corset. She's having a heated exchange with a man in a gorgeous suit that looks like it was built especially for his big-chest body, and three-day stubble so neatly trimmed it almost looks painted on.

"So," Calvin tells me in a voice of authority, "Mabel is an assistant, but the main reporter who is supposed to go report on a court case for a mobster has been kidnapped—"

"Seriously?" I laugh.

"Seriously," Calvin promises with a grin. "Anyway, Mabel has to cover for him. But Reinaldo, whose family owns the newspaper, is arguing against sending her, under the pretext of her lack of experience, but secretly because he loves her and doesn't want her in danger. But she doesn't know how he feels and is angry that he's trying to thwart her career."

"He's got it bad for her," Abuela stage-whispers, winking at me across the room.

I perch on the arm of the sofa. I hate to admit it, but give me some drama and I am hooked. Mabel trots off on assignment. Her story on the trial is brilliant, of course, putting her on the path to having the career that she wants. But as the episode ends, we see one of the mobster's stooges watching her from behind a corner. Menacing music plays. The message is about as subtle as a fire truck siren: she's a target.

"Ay, la pobre," says my abuela, looking worried. "I hope she's going to be okay."

"Somehow I suspect it will all work out for her," I promise, getting to my feet and tucking my hands into the back pockets of my jeans. "In the meantime, I should probably go."

Abuela jumps up from the sofa with the speed and agility of a runner coming off the blocks. "¡Huevos!" she announces, bopping her forehead dramatically with the heel of her hand. "I just remembered, I'm out of eggs." She frowns. "M'hijita, would you run down to the store around the corner and pick some up for me before you go? You know I keto now."

I cock my head in her direction. She just scarfed down an all-carb pastry. She most certainly does not keto. I'm surprised she even knows what it means. But I can't say no to her.

"Sure thing. I'll be right back."

"Calvo," Abuela says, "Why don't you go with her? In case she needs help."

"Eggs, Abuela?" I say with a shake of my head. "I'm fine."

"No seas tonta; you never know," Abuela says in a voice that leaves no room for argument, ushering both of us down the hall. "And besides, you can talk about Mabel and Reinaldo, guess what happens next, no? You don't need an old woman getting in the way. Go, go."

The door clicks shut behind us before I can protest further. Calvin and I stand awkwardly in the beige-carpeted hallway with the sickly fluorescent light. It clicks that this whole thing, the pastries, the teleno-velas, the three dozen things she suddenly needs done around her house—might be a part of a grander plan on Abuela's part.

I look at Calvin, who seems to be coming to the same conclusion in real time.

"Uh," he says, tucking his rough hands into his pockets and smiling sheepishly, "I think this might be a setup."

I snort-laugh. "Oh, no way," I deadpan as we wait for the elevator. "The buddy system is key when pur-chasing groceries." I hit the elevator button a few more times, even though it's already lit up. "You don't have to come with me. I can make your excuses for you. I doubt she'll hunt you down. Not very fast, anyway." I wink.

"It's fine," Calvin says. "It's a nice afternoon. I'll walk with you."

It's perfect early-evening summer weather, the sky a silky blue showing hints of darkening, the leaves rustling gently overhead. I spot the first firefly of the season, and the cicadas sing in the park across from Abuela's apartment. Somewhere, someone is playing a jazz album, and its languid tones offer a soundtrack to the laid-back vibe of the block.

"So you moved here from Brooklyn?" I ask as we head down the sidewalk.

Calvin nods. "Bay Ridge, yeah. My folks split up last spring, and my mom has family here, so."

"I cannot believe they made you move two months before graduation," I say, shaking my head. "Like, seriously, they couldn't have waited a tiny bit longer?"

"No," Calvin says, no hesitation in his voice at all. "They couldn't."

"I . . ." That stops me; I glance over at him to see if he's going to say more, embarrassed that I pried, still curious what the story is.

Calvin relaxes a little. "I don't know," he says, pulling open the door of the small corner grocery and waving me through, "I probably could have finished out the year if I had been totally set on it. Crashed with a friend or something. But it's just the two of us now, my mom and me. I didn't want to leave her, you know? It wasn't so bad."

I think of my parents back at the restaurant, the strangely comforting weight of the responsibility I feel, equally too heavy and comfortingly inevitable. "Yeah," I say. "I know."

We keep up a steady conversation as I make my way to the back of the store and pluck the eggs from the cooler. It just flows. I tell him about the restaurant and what my job there is like. He mentions the plot of a Sequoia Nagamatsu book he's reading and how one of the chapters touches on the theme of what it feels like when you think you're disappointing parents. After I jot down its name in a note on my phone, I get into what my first week at Fairchild was like. Because the conversation is so smooth, I blurt out the plot of the piece I just posted to StoriedZone before I realize I'm talking to someone I barely know.

"Wait," Calvin says, "so I can just go read it if I want to?"

"I mean, sure, theoretically," I say, my ears getting hot. "I guess that's how the internet works."

He laughs, full-throated, like he's in the middle of some primordial forest and not in the cramped aisle of a neighborhood grocery store.

I take the eggs to the register. Calvin throws two bags of candy onto the counter at the last minute, saying, "I bet Abuela needs some Sour Patch Kids in her life, too." He pays for both items over my protests.

"That was chivalrous, if financially unsound," I tease, the bells over the door jingling behind us as we leave the store. "Abuela would approve."

"I gotta tell you," Calvin says, ripping open the bag of candy with his strong-looking hands and holding it out in my direction. "It is possible she's not the only one I'm trying to charm, here."

His directness feels like a pop to the sternum, but in the best possible way, which makes my breath catch and then sends my heart in a gallop. I take a piece of candy and put it into my mouth. Its sour sweetness gives me a sharp pang in my jaw, surprising, mixing in with all the other fun and confusing feelings of hearing Calvin tell me he is trying to charm me. And realizing he's doing a pretty good job of it.

"Good to know." I smile. Mostly because I don't know what else to say.

As we go through the front door of the apartment

building, our shoulders bump gently.

He tucks the rest of the bag of candy into the back pocket of my jeans, and I feel it there like a four-alarm fire all the way home.

It's nearly bedtime. I am staring at the screen of my computer. But I can't make my fingers log on to Storied-Zone.

It's been a full day since the story has been up. One of the features of StoriedZone is that new posts get highlighted on the front page, if only for a few minutes, so it may be that a few people have read my words. *Actually read my words.* The site has a view counter. The thought of it is exciting and vaguely nauseating. If someone has said anything mean, I may spontaneously combust.

I log in, breath held.

Twenty-seven views. No reviews. I'm relieved. Also disappointed. Wanting to be seen and not wanting to be seen are at war, and it's a dead heat.

In the corner, there's a red notification circle. Curious, I click. "Collab request," it says. I've never noticed this before. I click into it.

It says, "HappilyEverDrafter would like to collaborate on this project. Nothing they post will be visible publicly on 'Untitled Teen Love Story' until you approve it. Would you like to accept this message?"

Collaborate? What does that even mean? I've seen the StoriedZone tagline: *Publish. Collaborate. Read.* But I've never thought about what the "collaborate" thing meant. But then I think of Paige going on about the community of our class and how writers need to support one another. I hit Accept.

There's a note from HappilyEverDrafter.

"Hi, AldertonGirlAconcagua. Your story sparked some thoughts. I'm taking a chance and sharing them with you. Totally okay if you don't want to hit *publish* on them. I'll know you want to keep playing if you do, though. Your move."

Um, what? I scan ahead and a smile breaks across my face. I can't help but think of a new story idea right then and there: *The perfect boy finds main character through her writing.*

1:04 a.m.: HappilyEverDrafter posted to "Untitled Teen Love Story."

Maggie:

I hope you don't think it's strange that I write you. I've seen you through the windows, up so impossibly early, and there are so many times I've wanted to tell you all the things I think are awesome about you: how hard you work, the way you smile as you write notes to tuck into the packages, the picture of Arches National Park you've got tacked up on the bulletin board behind you.

But I'm shy, and I don't know how to say these things out loud. My heart is pounding even as I write this note. I'd so like it if we could talk so we could see if I'm someone you might want to know better. I might have left this all as a wish, letting the inertia of my shyness keep these things unsaid, except I heard today you are planning to leave. (Small towns and our gossip rumor mills!) I realized I wouldn't forgive myself if that happened without me at least writing this note. But hopefully more.

You'll be surprised to learn who I am. (Yes, you know me, because doesn't everyone know everyone here?) I hope it will be a pleasant surprise. Whether you are happy to learn who I am or not, I want you to know I think you're amazing, and I wish you smooth sailing wherever you decide to go.

seven

"Okay, all," Paige announces the following Tuesday, "I've got feedback on your most recent assignment."

The idea of finally hearing what Paige thinks about what I turned in shakes me loose from the question I spent the entire weekend obsessing over: *Who is HappilyEverDrafter?* I've pressed refresh on my StoriedZone dashboard roughly five hundred times in the last few days, waiting for my inbox to ping with a response. But nothing yet.

Paige passes back my work, her beaded bracelets making a clinking noise on her wrist. At the top of the paper are only two words: *Keep going.*

Ryan is sitting beside me, and I can't help but turn to look as she hands him his pages: an entire essay is scribbled at the top of his paper with an arrow pointing to more comments on the back. "Spectacular world-building, Mr. Madigan" is all I can make out before he stuffs it in his bag.

Spectacular? *Spectacular?* He gets *spectacular*, and I get *keep going?* What does that even mean? "Keep going" is what you say to someone who has run out of gas in the rain and is walking with a red container to the nearest gas station to get a gallon, soaked through like a drowned rat. *Almost there! Sorry, would stop to give you a ride, but I'm in a hurry! Keep going!* As they zoom away.

Of course, I'm going to keep going; we have five more weeks of class. That's hardly encouragement. It isn't exactly praise. With a tight feeling in my stomach, I think about how *keep going* isn't a glittering sign that I'm in the running for the Best Work Prize at the end of the summer. I thought I was special, getting into this program. But in a room full of kids who got in and want it as much as I do, I don't feel so special.

"Feedback is so nerve-racking," Ryan murmurs, leaning close enough that our shoulders touch. "How'd you do?"

"Great," I lie, shame and jealousy flooding through me, mixed in with a tiny bit of surprise that he'd say feedback is nerve-racking when he basically got the equivalent of a big gold star on his. I shove my paper into my messenger bag.

Keep going, I tell myself. It's not much, but it's what I've got.

Paige wraps up class for the day. I stumble out into the furnace-blast air of the midafternoon. I don't want to be this person, envious and insecure. I came to Fairchild to get better, didn't I? I came here to meet other people who want what I want. But I can't get over the idea that maybe I'm not good enough to be here after all. That Paige, this person I idolize, this writer whose words move me and stun me and make me want to go back to the page over and over until I get it right, sees something in Ryan that she doesn't see in me.

I'm reminded of an ancient movie my parents made me watch a few years ago. I think they intended it to be inspirational. But it put a thunderbolt of fear in me. It was about Mozart but told from the point of view of his biggest rival, who hated him. The man was jealous and spiteful and worked so much harder than Mozart ever did. I don't know if it's a true story or not, if Mozart really was the screwup that the movie made him out to be, but this other man, the court composer, knew enough about music to recognize Mozart's genius but not enough to replicate it. I wonder if that's what I am, too, someone who can see what good writing is but can't create it herself.

"You going home?" Ryan asks right next to me, where I hadn't even noticed him. Recently, I've looked for him at the bus stop in the morning. We've fallen into a predictable travel rhythm, not quite coordinating but finding each other most mornings. Last week, he was carrying a collection of Flannery O'Connor stories, which I'd recommended to him the week before that. A few days ago, he brought me a dog-eared copy of *The Chronology of Water* and said softly, "You're right, I need to read more women writers." Yesterday, after we slipped into our seats, he wordlessly handed me a muffin.

But after the shock of *keep going*, I kind of just want to sulk in silence all the way back to Alderton. Still, what am I going to say? *Leave me alone, I'm in a bad mood because our teacher thinks you're a better writer than I am? Some days I wonder if growing up without some of the advantages other kids have had, with parents who always struggle for money, means that I'm never going to be able to compete with the likes of private-tutor, Harvard-summer-program you?* I'd sooner admit to plagiarizing all my ideas from Jonathan Franzen.

"Yeah," I say, heaving my messenger bag over my shoulder. "Let's go."

Outside, the sky is low and slate gray, a moody summer storm forming. The subway is only a few blocks away, but it's iffy whether we're going to beat the rain. A moist gust of wind blows, swirling and hinting at drizzle. A drop splotches on my cheek.

Ryan reaches to put his phone away, I guess to get it out of the impending rain. A super-old Avril Lavigne song blasts from inside his bag.

I stop walking and gawk at him—that is the song that was playing in my story. I picked it because since my character is loosely based on the note thing that happened to my mom, I figured I'd pick a song that might have been popular around that time, and I didn't want to burn Google down figuring out what that would have been in Argentina, where she was at the time. So I relocated the story to Maine and picked an American song.

Ryan stops a few steps ahead, turning around to look at me. "You good?" he asks. "Did you forget something?"

I shake my head, still staring a little. "That song. It's just that my mom says Avril Lavigne is for Americans," I blurt.

"Ooookay," Ryan says, smiling at me a little while scrunching his eyebrows. "I mean, I'm American, so, I guess that tracks."

"I . . ." My face gets itchy-hot. "Right."

"Come on," he prods, nodding in the direction of the subway. "It's going to pour."

I speed up after him, mind racing. It doesn't mean anything, necessarily. It's not like I wrote about music no one has ever heard of. I mean, it's literally *popular* music. It doesn't mean he read my story and is trying to send me some kind of secret message.

It definitely doesn't mean he's HappilyEver-Drafter.

Right?

Another lush drop falls on my forehead, then another. All at once, the sky splits open with a strobe of light and, a moment later, a crack of thunder I feel in my elbows and shoulders.

"Run!" Ryan shouts over the sudden roar, but he's laughing; all around us people are ducking into doorways and trying frantically to flag down taxis, holding their bags and newspapers up over their heads.

"Here, let's wait for it to slow down a little," he says, signaling in the direction of a bicycle shop with a deep overhang and no one sheltering under it. I follow him under. The rain is so hard it's bouncing up onto our feet and ankles.

"These are the moments when being anti-umbrella becomes an issue." He smiles, water running down his face.

"Are you anti-umbrella? Me too." I smile. It's a small similarity, but something about finding such a quirky and specific one delights me.

"I figure until they perfect the technology so that it doesn't only keep the top half of you dry, I'll opt out, thanks." That is almost word for word my argument for refusing an umbrella even when Doña Faustina is apoplectic in her insistence I carry one.

I look at him. The small side street we're on has all but cleared out and we're all alone, everyone else in the vast city in their own little bubbles away from the rain.

He looks off down the block at the splashing cabs and one lone guy in a tank top walking at a leisurely pace like it's not pouring buckets on him. He adds, "I like what you said in class the other day. About how all narrators are unreliable in some way? I've been thinking about it a lot. Like it sort of makes me want to reread everything I've ever read through that lens."

It surprises me that I have the power to challenge Ryan Madigan's thinking, that he's willing to let it be challenged. I can't say I dislike it. He looks at me and I smile and the moment is long and lasting, set to the beat of the rain as it slows down.

Finally I say, "I think we should brave it now."

He nods. We head to the subway station. Right at the top step I skid on a wet patch and almost go flying down the steps. Ryan grabs my arm to keep me from falling. Am I imagining that he holds on just one second too long? Or am I wishing it?

We swipe our MetroCards and slide into a train that's about to leave the station. A small puddle starts to form around our feet. The subway floor is already damp in places, almost muddy in others, New York mixed with water. My hair is plastered to my forehead. Ryan's shirt is sticking to his chest. I'm suddenly freezing in the arctic air-conditioning. I shiver. I take a step closer before I realize what I'm doing. Ryan puts an arm around my shoulders and squeezes. Once.

"Always an adventure with you, Jules," he says,

low, in his throat. Then he lets go as the train plunges into the tunnel, the lights flickering out.

"Oh yeah?" My heart does something unexpected and electric, throbbing in my ribs. I look up at his profile, the line of his nose and his jaw. "Is that good?"

He's just a shadow, a magnetic one I want to get closer to.

Ryan laughs into my ear. The darkness feels like permission, an open door. "We'll see," he says softly.

Then the lights come back on.

When I get home that night, I can't wait to log into StoriedZone. A few more comments, ten more likes. I click into messages . . . nothing new. But! The icon next to HappilyEverDrafter is green. He is online *right now.*

I start a message, my heart beating wildly at the back of my mouth. *Hello, phantom writer friend.* Ugh, too cutesy. I delete it, try again: *Hey there!* No, that's not right, either; what do I think I'm writing here, a cheerful business email? Finally, I just type the first thought that popped into my head when I first saw his handle on the screen, that bone-deep sense of recognition: *It's you.*

The three dots that indicate he's writing back pop up right away. *It's me*, he types back.

Who is this? I write, giddy, my throat getting tight as I hit Send. It could be a stranger, obviously, or some rando in his mother's basement. But in my gut I just . . . don't think it is. I think of Calvin tucking those Sour Patch Kids into my pocket. I think of Ryan in the dark of the subway car. I think of Lucas that day in the restaurant, that loaded moment passing between us. I've been writing stories for so long without ever really experiencing one, but now all at once it feels like I might be on the edge of possible, with more than one amazing door to walk through. But which one?

Nope, he responds. *Too soon.*

Oh, come on. *Seriously?* I type, hitting Send before I can think better of it. *Why?*

The three dots pop up. I watch them dance. Then they stop.

How's the writing going? he asks instead.

I sigh, dropping my head back against my headboard; downstairs I can hear my mother washing dishes, the insistent screech of Lucesita's violin.

You're really not going to tell me?

I am . . . really not. Not yet, at least.

I feel like I know you.

Maybe you do.

I have two choices: I can dig my heels in and insist that he tell me, possibly leading to a stalemate—or worse, scaring him off altogether.

Or: we can just . . . talk.

The writing is . . . going, I type cautiously.

Going is good, he replies with a smiley face. *Although why do I feel like there's something you're not telling me?*

"Ugh," I murmur, feeling seen in the same way I did when I first read HappilyEverDrafter's pages: like he'd instinctively understood the things I didn't have the words for, like he's known what I was thinking without me having to say. I chew my bottom lip for a minute, then start typing, telling him about Paige's *keep going* and the Best Work Prize and how anxious I am that I have nothing of value to say. I spill everything I've been keeping bottled up inside me since I started at Fairchild or possibly even before that; by the time I'm finished I've filled the entire chat window, and I feel both exhausted and deeply relieved. If it's Ryan, I just majorly exposed myself. If it's Calvin or Lucas, it still feels like a lot to reveal. Still, it also feels good, being able to be so real. The distance the screen provides gives me courage.

I blurted a lot, pouring out of my fingers in that furious way when my brain is going faster than my hands.

His response, when it comes, is an exercise in literary restraint: *You're talented*, he tells me, his words calm and confident even through the screen. *You got this.*

And I can't wait to read whatever you write next.

**7:14 a.m.: HappilyEverDrafter posted to
"Untitled Teen Love Story."**

All Maggie was able to think about in her clapboard school was the note tucked neatly in the pocket of the army surplus bag she used to carry her books. It nearly vibrated with hope, with meaning, with mystery. Nothing interesting ever happened in her storm-soaked town, nothing beyond the occasional boat wreck or a disturbance in the price of lobster.

But here, in her very own beat-up brown bag that she'd dug out of a closet at the start of high school, was the most interesting thing that had happened to her in . . . ever.

Ms. O'Shea was droning on, poor thing, something about medieval bathing habits. Even if senioritis and her early-decision college acceptance letter hadn't made it nearly impossible to focus for weeks now, Ms. O'Shea would have still managed to achieve full zone-out.

Close to bursting, Maggie quietly reaches for a piece of loose-leaf and places it inside her notebook so she can do an approximation of paying attention.

She writes,

Dear You:

Your note made me happy, if a little surprised. Why not come into the office and strike up a chat? If we really do know each other, I'm sure that wouldn't be too hard.

Maggie stops a moment. If they really do know each other, it's more than likely from school. It's a small town with a small school. This is her third time having Ms. O'Shea. He could be in this room right at this moment. The thought makes her throat throb with her heartbeat. She scans, wondering who it could be. Every head is bent over the desk, although only about half of them seem to be engaged in any form of trying to capture what Ms. O'Shea is saying. The rest are doodling or looking off aimlessly. She goes back to her note.

Although I get why that might feel hard. If you're not ready, I understand. But maybe some hints? If you want to give me clues, I'm game for following where you'll lead, until you're ready for us to meet.

eight

"Whoa, whoa," Ivy says a couple of days later, holding her hands up to cut me off midsentence. Fairchild isn't in session this Friday, so I met her at the pool before my dinner shift at the restaurant. The afternoon sun sizzles on the back of my neck.

"Back up. What makes you think this HappilyEver-Drafter person is a guy you know, exactly?" She frowns from behind her pink mirrored aviators. "Actually, how do you even know it's a guy? It could be anyone. Don't you think?"

I cock my head at her. I suppose she could be

right. But it just all feels too familiar, too close to be a stranger.

She crosses her long legs in front of her. She's wearing a high-waisted bikini bottom and a cross-shoulder top with a polka-dot edge and a tiny keyhole; the guy manning the snack bar gave both of us free fountain drinks, and I suspect the two things are not unrelated. She clears her throat. She adds, "Just . . . be careful, okay?"

"What, like you're worried that the next chapter he writes is like, 'I can see what you're wearing through my binoculars'?" I shake my head. "It's not like that, Ivy."

"That's not what I'm saying," Ivy counters. "You don't have to wind up on *Dateline* for it to turn out . . . not how you think it's going to turn out, that's all."

I frown. "Meaning what, exactly?"

"Look," Ivy says, "you know I love that beautiful, creative brain of yours. But I just feel like sometimes you get so wrapped up in the story you're telling yourself— thinking about how you're going to describe it when you write it down later, or imagining what the perfect ending might be—that you miss out on experiencing what's happening right in front of you."

"Wow." I'm not imagining the connection I have with HappilyEverDrafter. I'm certainly not imagining the work he's done on "Untitled." "That's rough, Ivy."

"I don't mean it in a bad way," Ivy says, a furrow in her brow. "I'm your best friend, that's all. I just don't want you to get disappointed." She takes a deep breath. "Anyway, now that I'm done being a buzzkill, tell me about your suspects."

I brighten. "Well," I begin, "There's Calvin, my grandma's neighbor."

"The boy next door," she says with an enthusiastic nod, tapping her fingertips together. "I like it. Continue."

I fill her in on the way he's been helping Abuela and our little trip to the convenience store, the way he hinted about going on StoriedZone and reading what I'd written. "He would have had to have guessed my username, though," I point out, "so I don't know how realistic it is to think it's him."

"Well, that would be true for any of them, right?" she points out. "Is your username that hard to guess?"

I twist my mouth to one side. "It's AldertonGirl-Aconcagua."

"Ugh, Jules. For a word girl, that is a deeply uninspired username. Why didn't you just make it your street address and social security number?"

"I don't know!" I laugh. "I wasn't thinking about whether anyone would figure out who I was. I just literally made it the first three words that popped into my head." But now I realize that the website has a feature where all the latest people who signed up are in the "Say Hi to a Newbie!" column on the right of the site. It's how they encourage interaction with new members. I got like twenty followers the day I signed up because of it. Anyone going to the site the day I signed up who knew I was doing it would not have had a hard time figuring out my username.

"Okay," Ivy says. "Let's put a pin in Sink-fixing Calvin. Who else could it be?"

I tilt my head to the side. "Well, Lucas . . ."

"I knew it!" Ivy exclaims, jazz hands and all. "Finally. I mean, how could you *not* be thinking of him like that, with the new pecs and the big brown eyes and the whole 'destined from birth' thing? I mean sure, it might be a little odd to get with—what did you call him?—basically your cousin? But also, too perfect. *This summer . . . is he a friend or is he more?*" she adds, in her deepest movie-trailer voice.

"Ive, seriously!" My face is prickling. I give the pool a quick scan, sure that Lucas, or worse, his mom, is going to materialize and hear what I'm saying. "You seem overly invested in the Lucasness of it all."

"Yeah, yeah." Ivy waves a hand and laughs. "I'm Team Lucas, for what it's worth."

"Noted." Then, before I lose my courage, I blurt out: "There's actually one other person it could be."

Ivy lifts an eyebrow. "I'm sorry. Are you telling me that my little Julieta has three of her very own Romeos?"

I roll my eyes at her. "They're just . . . guys who I may or may not like."

"I'm so mad I already did my movie trailer voice!" Ivy is practically vibrating with excitement. I'm never the source of interesting gossip or boy speculation. She is eating it up. "Okay, so tell me about potential number three. Do I know him?"

Ugh. Now that I'm about to tell her, my nerve dissipates. It is *so* weird. "Kinda, yeah," I say. "Actually, yes, totally." I wrinkle my nose, throw a silent *Don't let her hate me* prayer out into the universe. "Ryan."

Ivy stares at me like I've fried her motherboard. "I'm sorry, what now?"

"You heard me."

"I did," she admits, "but you and Ryan have hated each other since time began. Especially since the

Great Class President Debacle of Sophomore Year. You wouldn't even take a ride from him to summer school, as if you thought I hadn't noticed your conspicuous dodging of that question."

"First of all, it isn't summer school! And second of all, I know it's *so* strange. Nothing has happened between us, and I'm not even saying I want anything to. But we've been talking a lot on the way to and from the class, and the other day . . ."

Ivy scrunches up her nose and holds up a hand in the *Stop* position. "God, please don't tell me anything gross about my brother."

"Let me finish, please?" I blow a breath out. "The other day, when we were coming home, he played this song I wrote about in my story. Accidentally. Like he was putting his phone in his bag and I guess he hit Play by accident and it blared out."

"What song?" Ivy asks immediately. "Cardi B? 'I Kissed a Girl'?"

"No," I say. "Avril Lavigne. 'Complicated.'"

"What? That's not evidence." Ivy sags back into the lounge, disappointed. "Literally everyone who has ever listened to the radio has heard that old song."

"I know," I admit, "it's thin. But still." I think of adding that I just have a feeling. That sometimes the way he looks at me while we're walking through New York, or the way he asks questions when I tell him a story or a plot idea make me feel like he listens more deeply than almost anyone else I've ever met. But that's even thinner evidence.

Ivy sighs. "I am going to take this opportunity to reiterate my original position," she says, pulling one leg up in front of her and resting her chin on her knee as she looks at me. "Does it occur to you that it's this sweeping, writerly imagination of yours that's making this Happily person into something bigger than they are? That's making you see signs where there are only coincidences? It sounds like you've got three great guys right here in front of you, Jules. Do you want to waste what could be an amazing, romantic summer trying to figure out which one of them is also your imaginary friend? Or do you maybe just want to go for it? Like what if your collaborator is just trying to get you to take action in real life?"

"I mean, when you put it that way . . ." I trail off. Suddenly I don't want to talk about it.

Ivy frowns, shifting her weight on her lounge chair. "Actually," she says, "we've sort of been . . ."

"Hey," I say as my phone buzzes with a notification

from StoriedZone, "hold that thought. I have a notification from the site."

My ears thrum with the hope that HappilyEver-Drafter has posted. But when I click on the notification, it's just a comment from another user: *Nice job, guys! This story is rad.* Likes are firmly in the double digits for every post now.

I turn back to Ivy. "Sorry." I try not to feel too disappointed as I slip my phone back into my bag; normally a comment like that from a total stranger would have me walking on air for at least the rest of the afternoon. But there's only one person I'm interested in hearing from.

"I posted another chapter last night and thought maybe HappilyEverDrafter had written back, but . . ." I tell her about the scene I wrote, about Maggie and what she wants to accomplish, about the mysterious notes.

"These clues she asked for. They remind me a little of the scavenger hunts we used to do," Ivy says.

There was a time in our lives when Ivy and I were inordinately obsessed with scavenger hunts. As kids, we would make hand-drawn maps and leave clues around each other's houses and backyards leading to whatever random thing we had hidden. Once, we did a Ring Pop. Another time it was a friendship bracelet, which I still have in my jewelry box. It was a fun way to pass the time, and it was the birth of my obsession with books with maps in them. Ryan always gave us crap for it, and even Lucas thought it was kind of silly. I realize now that's probably where I got the idea. "Yeah, I guess so. Why?"

Ivy shakes her head. "Nothing," she says with a smile, looking over the blue of the pool. "I'm going to go jump in the water for a minute." She hops up off the lounge chair and heads for the water, turns around at the very last second with a sly grin. "But also: Team Lucas. Although the handyman is a close second. You'll understand if I abstain from commenting on the brother theory."

The pool surface glitters in the sun as she dives into it with barely a ripple. I let out a long breath and let my mind circle the mystery of HappilyEverDrafter. Maybe Ivy's right and I'm making too much of it. But I can't not. It feels so good.

Alternate endings to **Romeo and Juliet**

Option 1: Romeo says, "Hey, I think you're super cute, but how about we both finish high school? And I'll take you to a dance."

Option 2: Romeo and Juliet, inspired by his balcony prowess, take up rock climbing.

Option 3: Romeo and Juliet date, drift apart, he goes to war (note, research: war in Verona at the time?), she has eight babies, they find each other when they're old, and they do die together, but on a great vacation after finally reuniting.

Option 4: Juliet didn't die, wakes up in present day after a long suspended sleep, finds out people are touching the boob of a statue of hers in Verona (true story) and launches a campaign to have the statue melted down, only to come into direct opposition with the mayor's son, who wants to "preserve" the town's heritage, even though Shakespeare totally made up the whole thing. Enemies to lovers with the super cute mayor's son.

nine

It's Saturday night, and the restaurant is busier than it's been in a while. Zoe is zipping around the floor as she seats table after table. My arms ache pleasantly from carrying heavy trays full of plates from the kitchen. We ran a two-for-one ad in the paper this week. It was my mom's doing, over my father's strenuous *no specials* objections, so I don't know how profitable the crowd will be. Still, it's nice to have bodies in here for a change, the buzz of conversation and the clink of glasses making a warm thrum.

It's been so busy I've hardly had a chance to wonder what is going on with my next chapter of "Untitled," which I posted a couple of days ago. As I think of it, I dig my phone out of my pocket to check. I push through the swinging doors to the kitchen, where our sous-chef, Joaquin, is bent over the line.

"Do you know where we source the salmon?" I ask him. "The couple at twelve wants to know."

But Joaquin shakes his head. "We're eighty-six on the salmon," he says, wiping his forehead with his forearm.

"Ugh. *That's* going to be a fun conversation. What are we doing instead?"

"The bass is real nice today. It's from Chile." He says *Chile* like you say it in Spanish: Chee-leh.

Then, as I'm turning to go: "You working the floor all by yourself out there?" he asks. "Where's Romeo?"

I frown and ignore the "Romeo" joke. It's an oldie. "That's a great question, actually."

Lucas texted earlier to say he was running late and would be here as soon as he could; it's almost six now, nearly halfway through the dinner shift.

"Listen, m'hija," Joaquin tells me, "you're a hard-working girl. You're smart. You don't need to settle for no guy who doesn't go to work on time."

I snort. "Noted, but I've told you a thousand times, that is not what's happening."

"I'm just saying be careful, mi niña."

"I'm going to tell Lucas you said that," I joke.

"And I'm going to tell him to come to work on time!" he says as I swing out of the kitchen again, stopping in the wait station to sneak a look at my emails and notifications. Ugh, not a peep from HappilyEver-Drafter. What if he's bored of the game? What if he hated what I posted in reply? What if he doesn't write back?

I take dessert orders for a two-top and deliver appetizers for a family of four. I refill waters and drop checks and run credit cards through the MICROS, receipts spitting out with a satisfying zip. It feels good to be moving, like I'm remembering the steps of a dance I haven't done in a while. It feels, more than anything, like coming home.

I'm brewing a new pot of coffee when my phone finally buzzes: HappilyEverDrafter has posted! I'm about to click the link, my heart pounding, when . . .

"You look like you just got a notification that you've won the lottery. Beware the emails asking you to put in your bank information so they can deposit your millions into it," says a deep voice behind me; I whirl around to find Lucas already wearing his apron, sleeves rolled up.

"Don't be jealous," I manage to quip, slipping my phone back into my pocket.

"Right," he says with a grin. "My mistake."

Neither of us says anything for a moment. Instead of our usual comfortable silence, something feels . . . off.

Lucas clears his throat. "Sorry I'm late," he says, offering exactly zero explanation. "Joaquin already let me have it. But it's awesome that we're this busy. What can I do to catch us up?"

I wait for another beat, expecting a story about his car getting a flat tire or a close encounter with an extraterrestrial, anything. But Lucas just looks at me innocently, waiting for instructions. *Where were you?* I almost ask. But I don't, the question suddenly sounding much too personal in my head. It's strange. He's never late.

Unless . . . unless it took him longer than he expected to write the response to my chapter and he lost track of time.

Unless he's HappilyEverDrafter.

"We need to restock the soda cans," I say finally, ignoring the flush I can feel creeping up the back of my neck at the idea of him being HED.

We descend the brightly lit wooden stairs down to

the basement of the restaurant. I've seen some dingy restaurant basements at my parents' friends' restaurants, but ours is spotless and well lit. I used to joke with my dad on busy nights that it was nice enough to put the diners who were waiting on tables down here. The ceiling is higher than the average basement, and whether it's El Maestro's influence or my parents being clean freaks, too, it is impeccable, everything organized with precision. I could find anything, from the stash of tablecloths to spare chairs to a random hoard of foot warmers someone thought was a good idea at some point, and I wouldn't have to ask anyone. Things are labeled and stacked on gleaming metal shelving.

We make our way to the neat stacks of soda cans lined up by the office door. My parents keep a tiny office down here, which I'm pretty sure started life as a closet. A voice comes through the thin door, muffled but unmistakable.

"We're going to have to decide soon. We can't keep robbing Peter to pay Paul." It's my father.

"I refuse to accept that, Nicolas. We made it through the whole pandemic and came out the other side. We're not going to start laying people off now." They always talk business in English, even when they're alone. The language of business is English, keeping it from cutting too close the way Spanish does. My mother's voice is trembly, near tears, not her usual, in-control voice.

"Mi amor, you've seen the receipts. It's everything, the pandemic, the price of everything, but let's be real. It's Tierra del Fuego. After all this being cooped up, people want what's new. We've always been dreamers, I know, but we can't ignore the numbers."

Tierra del Fuego. A few months ago, another Argentinian restaurant opened up on the other side of the strip. It caused a ripple, because how many Argentinian restaurants does one town need? They opened up with a slick sign, a visit from the mayor, and a feature in the local paper. I was worried, but my parents told me that long relationships mattered more than flash.

Now it seems they feel differently.

"We *can't* lay off Joaquin," says my mother, sounding more definitive.

"I can do what he does. For a while. He can collect unemployment until we get it together, mi amor. This is only temporary. We have to stop the bleeding somehow."

And then, the worst sound of all: my mother starts crying.

Lucas looks stricken. He grabs three shrink-wrapped trays of soda cans off the top of the stack and signals wordlessly that we should get back upstairs. Shell-shocked, I take one and follow behind him.

We get back upstairs to the small fridge where we keep the sodas and he begins cutting the plastic off, wiping each top individually and placing them inside in the pattern we've been taught: Sprites on the top shelf, Cokes on the one after, the combo of the slower sellers—Fanta, root beer—on the shelf beneath that. I feel like a boxer who's taken one too many shots to the head, woozy, unsteady.

He leans in close so the rest of the kitchen won't hear. "I'm so sorry."

I shake my head. Water is rushing somewhere. It takes me a moment to realize it's coming from inside my head.

"I had no idea," I confess, feeling like an utter child. "I mean . . . I've seen the slow nights, but I figured . . . start of summer? Plus who even knows what a successful restaurant looks like at this point? I figured it was the new normal."

"I know." Lucas's voice is quiet. "It's so . . . I don't even know what to say."

I get down in a squat, then let myself fall down on my butt onto the floor cross-legged, my weight suddenly too much to hold up. "Can I tell you the worst part?" I ask, looking up at him. "It's not just the restaurant. It's just . . . them. They're miserable. They never seem to have fun together anymore. Even at home, all they talk about is the restaurant. So all-business. It's like they don't even love each other anymore."

"Don't say that." Lucas gets down so we're eye level. "He was literally just calling her 'my love.'"

"That's a placeholder, and you know it. It doesn't mean anything. People stop meaning words they say all the time."

"I don't think that's true."

"It's true," I say, leaning my head back against the wall, a deep need to cry tightening my throat.

"I can tell you one thing," he says, his big brown eyes suddenly wide and serious. "If you ever hear me say it, you'll know I mean it."

I blink at him, not sure what to say to that. Our faces are very close. "I . . . ," I start. Before I can say anything more, Lucas stands up again, brushing his hands on the seat of his work pants.

"You know what we should do?" he asks, holding out his hand to help me up. His tone sounds like the same one he used when we were eight to convince me to sneak frogs from the local park into my family's aquarium because no one would ever notice. "We should take a field trip. Go check these douches out."

"Who?" I ask. "Tierra del Fuego?"

"Exactly," Lucas says cheerfully. "Get a sense of what all the buzz is about. Cut their gas line. Drop a Tupperware full of roaches into their dining area. Leave them some scathing Yelp reviews. Who can say?"

I snort-laugh. "Okay, maybe not that vermin thing, but going to stake them out is actually not a bad idea. Sometime next week, maybe?"

Lucas nods. "It's a date," he says; then, blanching a little: "I mean, not a *date*, but . . . You know what I mean."

Do I? I want to ask him. But he's headed out into the dining room before I can reply.

1:17 a.m.: HappilyEverDrafter posted to
"Untitled Teen Love Story"

Maggie:

I like this game. Okay, clue # 1: You'll find it where the seagulls gather, past Marchmeadow and the Little Free Library.

ten

Jaime taught Abuela to text a few Christmases ago, and I'm working on my latest assignment for Fairchild the following afternoon when my phone buzzes with a message from her number: *Tonight*, she tells me, and already I know it's not a question. *My place. 6:45.*

Then, a minute later: *Wear a dress!*

I know better than to ask any questions. Plus I'm squarely in the land of HappilyEverDrafter. It has been near impossible to concentrate on my Fairchild homework when all I can think about is his latest addition to our story. *Our* story. I swoon a little. I'm being ridiculous, I know, but I kind of love it.

I send Abuela a thumbs-up. I write a few more paragraphs of my assignment. But time is doing the thing it does of expanding and contracting while I write, and suddenly I've barely got time to get dressed if I want to make it to Abuela's place at her precisely allocated hour. I slip into a blue-checked Gap dress with spaghetti straps and a pair of espadrilles. I grab some leftover costillas from the fridge because I never show up at Abuela's house without a food offering, then head out the door.

I imagine the entire scene in my head on the way to Abuela's apartment, focusing on practicing some *spectacular world building* skills of my own: perhaps she's got an old friend visiting who is an aristocratic polo player, and she's planning a fancy dinner party with lots of courses, soft music, a hundred candles, and a gaggle of fascinating, sophisticated people to talk to.

And if I'm imagining Calvin there, too, in a button-down, offering me sparkling cider out of one of those little old-fashioned coupe glasses as the candlelight catches glints of his russet hair, well, that's between me and Paige Bingham.

When I get to the apartment, though, my abuela is the only one in it, the hallway behind her dark and empty, no light in the tiny kitchen. I'm not sure exactly where I thought the aristocratic polo player and his retinue would fit in this shoebox of an apartment, anyway. I can't help but be a tiny bit disappointed.

But her eyes are shining. "Come on," she says, nodding approvingly at me before linking her arm through mine and squeezing. "We're going out on the town."

She leads me across the street to the side entrance of a large stone church, pulling open the heavy wooden doors with surprising strength. She leads me down a short hallway, then through another set of doors and into a large, bustling multipurpose room. A handwritten sign on a piece of poster board reads *Senior Night* in cheery bubble letters.

The room is surprisingly full, brightly lit, and noisy with animated conversation. It's like walking into an invitation-only club you only hear about through a friend—like the Alderton version of a puerta cerrada, except the median age appears to be about eighty-two. Abuela steers me up the row of tables with purpose, like she's headed somewhere specific. I study the setup at the front of the room: there's a giant golden metal cage full of mini golf ball–type balls, a table, an older man with a potbelly standing behind it.

We are legit about to play bingo.

"Abuela," I say as she weaves me through the

maze of long tables, "don't get me wrong, I've always admired your commitment to a glamorous life, but I'm *pretty* sure we could have come to play bingo in our regular clothes."

Abuela shoos me toward a table near the front. "We could have," she says with a wink. "But we're more fabulous than that."

She lets me in first. I move to the open seat.

And there he is. Calvin.

"What's this?" I smile.

"Huge bingo aficionado. Considering turning pro."

I laugh. "You're a terrible liar." I turn to my abuela. "I'm on to you." I poke her playfully in the shoulder.

She opens her eyes wide in mock innocence. Suddenly I want to laugh and laugh, and it's almost not ridiculous that I'm in a bingo hall. Suddenly *wear a dress* makes a whole lot more sense.

But Calvin shakes his head. "She had nothing to do with it," he tells me, sliding a couple of game sheets across the table in my direction.

"Right." I'm still smiling. I can't help it; suddenly the canned music sounds like a brass band, and the church basement looks like a ballroom, and for the first time I notice the flowers on the bingo table are a bright, vibrant orange.

"I can see that you don't believe me, but just wait until you see my mad skills."

"Uh-huh." It's not exactly a suit, but he's more dressed up than I've seen him before. He's wearing dark jeans and a charcoal Henley pushed up to his elbows. I'm momentarily distracted by the pale jut of his collarbones. But the announcer up front has finished telling us the important news about the spaghetti dinner next Friday and tickets for the fifty-fifty raffle on sale at the back, and a studious hush falls over the crowd as he starts hollering out the numbers.

"B-fourteen! G-five! O-nine!"

It is as if he were announcing free trips to Maui or something, the whole crowd hums so excitedly. But when I scan my card, I've got nothing to mark. I look over at Calvin. He's got his little stamper at the ready, poised like he's sure he's about to win. To my left, my abuela, who I'm pretty sure has never played bingo before, is already deep in conversation with a little old guy in a bow tie and a sweater vest. I don't think she even has a game sheet.

It's only a couple of minutes before someone yells out, "Bingo!" and a sweet-faced but fiercely focused blue-haired lady runs up to the front of the room at a pace that makes me wonder if she used to be a sprinter.

"Tough break," I say to Calvin.

"It's early yet."

He doesn't win the next round, though, or the round after that; when I glance up at him a little while later he's abandoned his card entirely and is gazing back at me with an intent look on his face.

"You," he says, reaching out and running the feather-light tip of his finger over my knuckles, his voice so quiet that only I can hear him, "Look really pretty."

It sends a shiver through me. It's extremely chaste, as far as touches go. Also, my grandmother is *literally* sitting right next to us, but I can feel it all over my body. "I bet you say that to all the girls at senior night."

"You'd lose that bet," he says as I'm dimly aware of someone else calling bingo in the back of the room. "But if you're a betting person, let's make a bet. If I win this next one, we go out one day this week. Just you and me."

My gut does a full-on, circus-worthy tumble down like it's hurtling toward earth in a trapeze act, possibly without a net. "For a guy who's considering going pro, your bingo record is not stellar so far."

"Then bet me."

They call out the next number. He doesn't have it.

"Bet," I say, smiling, sure one of the rapaciously competitive bingo players up front is going to beat him.

He has the next two. He's got bingo. He's about to yell it out, but then leans forward and stage-whispers, "Abuela!"

She turns to him, distracted, face alight with whatever is going on with Sweater Vest.

Calvin slips the winning bingo sheet to her. "Yell 'Bingo!'" he says.

She scans the numbers for a microsecond, then yells "Bingo!" She shoots to standing, then runs up, Sweater Vest in pursuit.

Calvin smiles, full glow, putting the moon to shame. "Friday?" he asks.

On the nights when you're all moonglow
And you're floating on the glassy sea
And the earth's deep sigh blows through you
When you fear that love will never find you
Or that it will fool you
Like a secret note whose author you
        should have found
Ages ago
Before it was too late.
Be still a moment
There deep in your moon-self, your voice will
        meet you
Elegant like a dancer, brave like a bird.
And say now
The time is now.

eleven

"I gotta tell you, Jules," Calvin comments on Friday night, one hand hooked over the wheel of his ancient Ford Explorer, "when I said I'd take you anywhere you wanted to go tonight, I wasn't necessarily expecting you to say Hackensack."

"Excuse you," I chide, holding up one imperious finger. "Hackensack is the municipal seat of Bergen County. It has a brewery, a kick-ass performing arts center, an awesome library, and, like . . . sixty different limo companies. Not to mention a Barnes & Noble where I have spent many happy evenings eating chocolatey goodness and imagining owning every book in there. Or, maybe, seeing my own name on its shelves one day."

"That is quite the list of local attractions." Calvin nods with a grin.

The ice cream shop is Pepto Bismol pink and hospital green inside, with a handwritten menu behind a series of round hot plate–ish contraptions where they melt the ice cream, then freeze it and roll it into scrumptious little tubes. It's fascinating to watch how they do it, which is why I suggested this place when Calvin texted to collect on his bingo bet.

Calvin orders something called the Chocolate Tower, which is apparently the world's most massive ice cream concoction, with four rolls of ice cream, a waffle behind it, two graham crackers sticking out the top, a chocolate-covered cookie stick to the right, a marshmallow speared on to the left, and two Oreos stuck in the middle. Plus it's smothered in gummy bears.

"A light snack," he says when the girl behind the counter hands it over, beholding its already-melty heft with a satisfied nod.

We head back outside, sitting down at one of the tiny bistro tables lined up along the front window. It's a low-ceilinged, gray evening. The air has weight to it—still and heavy, laden like a fruit about to drop from a tree.

"Better get to work on that," I tell him, plucking the plastic spoon from my cup of strawberry and gesturing at the Chocolate Tower. "The only person I've ever seen finish it is my little sister, Luz, and if you get shown up by an eleven-year-old who still secretly plays with Barbies, I don't know that I'll be able to respect you in the morning."

"That's fair," Calvin admits, biting the end off a chocolate-covered pretzel. "How many siblings do you have?"

"Just two," I tell him. "Both younger."

"That tracks," he says with a nod. "You've got real big-sister energy."

My eyes narrow. "Is that a compliment?"

"Yeah, of course," he says easily, though it doesn't necessarily feel like one, coming from someone so laid-back and resolutely plan-free. "Reliable. Helpful. Goal- and family-oriented." He grins. "You just seem like the kind of girl who always has to go someplace after this, you know what I mean?"

"I do have to go someplace after this," I admit with a smile. "Party at my friend Ivy's house." I've been so busy with the restaurant and Fairchild—and, okay, with HappilyEverDrafter—that the two of us have barely talked this week.

Calvin tilts his head to the side like, *See what I mean?* "Well," he says with a lopsided smile. "Thanks for fitting me in."

"It's not like that," I say. "I'm not, like, some social butterfly. I just . . ."

"Have a lot of balls in the air?"

I feel my shoulders drop with the weight of recognition. "Yes," I allow. "A lot of balls in the air." The truth is it feels strange even to sit here in one place with him just talking, not to be multitasking or working or being on call: I've checked my phone like three times for a text from my mom saying Lucesita needs to be picked up at a friend's house, or somebody called in sick at the restaurant, or can I bring Abuela some dinner on my way home. I don't mind those texts; after all, that's what families do for each other. But I can't shake the constant urge to escape, either, even if it's just into the stories I make up in my own head.

"I want this writing thing to work so badly, you know? I want to live this big, creative, romantic, exciting life. But it feels irresponsible to be chasing some one-in-a-million dream when the restaurant is . . . When my parents are . . ." I break off.

"Your parents?" Calvin prompts.

"I don't know." I dig a crater in the center of my ice cream. "Stressed all the time, but that's not it. Not the only thing, anyway. It's like the pressure of the restaurant has cracked them apart in some way I can't fully understand. I guess I thought that if I picked up some of the slack, did as much as I could to pull the restaurant along, plus also built some brilliant, solid future for myself, the pressure would go away and they'd be back to how they used to be. The last couple of years have just felt like one long crisis, you know? So I've just been . . . living in crisis mode. For a long time. Maybe that's the energy you're picking up on."

"That's a long time to be in crisis mode," he says quietly. "And I get what you mean, but you realize your parents aren't your job, right? Making your own big, creative, romantic, exciting life is your job."

"Says the guy who skipped the end of senior year to move to a new place because his mom needed him."

"That's different, though." Calvin takes a bite of his chocolate tower. "I didn't care about where I graduated. And I'm not going to stay here forever. It was . . . well, I guess it was our own form of crisis mode."

I take in a long breath. "I'm sorry about your parents," I tell him.

"I'm not." Calvin shakes his head. "It was the right thing for them. For all of us, really. They'd been unhappy for a long time. If anything, it really underscored for me how we have to live in this moment, take in all the happiness we can, not worry so much about the future, you know?" He smiles and stuffs a full Oreo into his mouth, then hands me the other one.

I take the Oreo but make no move to eat it, my hand dangling in midair, static. I feel like an idiot. Here I am complaining about my parents because they work too hard and don't exhibit enough PDA to reassure me, while Calvin had an actual parental crisis that upended his whole life.

"Don't do that," he says.

I blink, still holding the Oreo. "What?"

"Whatever story you're telling yourself in your head about how I've got it harder than you do," he says, "Don't do that. It's not the tough-childhood Olympics. Everybody is dealing with their own stuff."

"Fair enough." I take a bite of the Oreo, fighting an urge to take his hand across the table. "I'm glad you're here, then."

"In beautiful, scenic Hackensack, New Jersey?" Calvin winks. "Anyway," he says, "Let's not talk about parents," he says.

"Okay," I agree. "What do you want to talk about?"

We sit there until it's dark out, fireflies lighting up even this urban block, this spot between the Lebanese restaurant and a botanica. The conversation flows the same way it did at the grocery store that night. He tells me about his favorite places to hang out in the city and what bands he likes. I tell him where I want to go to college.

"The city," I admit, though I've never actually said it out loud before. "I know a lot of my friends want to get far away to other states, not right in our backyard. But when I think about book readings and events and the library on Fifth, New York has always seemed to me where I want my writing career to be born. If it's *going* to be born," I say. "What about you? What are you going to do?"

Calvin swallows the mouthful of chocolate. "I don't know. I'm working for a landscaper part-time. He's my uncle, so I can kind of make my own hours. And I'm taking a carpentry class. I can make a mean end table. I really am not sure what's next, but I'm cool not knowing. Just sort of letting it unfold. I read a ton. I kayak on the creek a couple of mornings a week. I let myself talk to strangers. I watch telenovelas with your abuela to learn Spanish. I try not to make life, but to let it happen."

I nod, but I can't say I get it. In response to things getting hard, buckling down feels like the only option. I wonder what it would feel like to let go. Even the thought feels scary. But pure, somehow. Brave. I admire him, the peace he emanates.

I'm about to reply when my phone buzzes on the table: *Are you coming????* Ivy wants to know, followed by half a dozen beer emojis. *I need to talk to you.* Then, a second later: *Also, just as a heads up, I might have . . . underestimated the number of people I invited over.*

"Oh no," I mutter under my breath, then text back to let her know I'm on my way.

Calvin lifts an eyebrow. "Duty calls?" he asks.

"Something like that." I look at him across the table for a moment: his auburn hair and curious expression, his big marked-up hands.

Maybe it's okay to fly by the seat of my pants a little, I tell myself. *Maybe it's okay to change the plan.*

"Actually," I say, then blurt the rest out before I can think better of it: "Do you want to come to a party with me?"

twelve

Ivy and Ryan's house looks like it belongs in an old English romance movie or a novel with a brooding young protagonist who doesn't want to inherit his title, some manor house dutifully tended by a hundred stouthearted, animated townspeople. It's got three levels, an actual turret, an elaborate patio, and a lot bigger than just about any other in town. The arched front door, antique and imported by her mother's decorator from somewhere medieval and fabulous, is propped open with a box of hard lemonade when we arrive. Raucous laughter tears from the house's interior and onto the leafy quiet of the cul-de-sac.

"Your best friend *lives* in this house? Is she, like, a cursed princess or something?" Calvin asks as we make our way up the stone walkway, which is flanked on either side by tasteful lanterns and a perfectly manicured front lawn.

"She does," I admit sheepishly, "But I promise she's super chill."

"Okay." Calvin looks skeptical. "Is she, like, one of the Real Teen Housewives-to-Be of New Jersey?"

I smirk at him. I try to imagine seeing all this excess for the first time and not just as a place I've been coming to since I was little. I get his reaction. Ivy's parents can be pretty over-the-top with their shows of privilege.

Ivy wasn't kidding when she said there were a lot of people here: the house is packed. It looks like half our class is here, along with a bunch of graduated seniors, all the pool people, and a whole lot of people I don't even recognize. The bass from the sound system thumps up through the soles of my feet. The neighbors in Ivy's part of town aren't the cop-calling type. Plus the houses are spaced far enough apart that it's easy to ignore the occasional party or domestic disturbance. Last winter Mrs. Gardella across the street got so hopped up on painkillers than she forgot where she lived and went wandering door-to-door in a silk bathrobe, and nobody even batted an eyelash. Still, tonight's vibe is more *Pretty in Pink* obnoxious rich-people party than romantic adventure. I can tell by the set of Calvin's shoulders that he is not loving being here.

"Sorry," I say, shouting so he can hear me over the music as we weave our way through the crowds. "Ivy's parties aren't usually quite so . . . much."

Calvin nods, his jaw set. "It's cool," he says, jamming his hands in his pockets like he's afraid to touch anything. I've spent so much time at Ivy's place over the years that sometimes I forget what it looks like to the unaccustomed eye: a living room large enough to fit my entire house twice over, one of those staircases that leads to a catwalk overlooking the first level and a deep, rich oxblood-colored leather sectional the size of a yacht. In one of our many scavenger hunts, Ivy hid a tiny handmade doll I used to love behind it and told me I could keep it when I figured out the clue. There's an original oil painting hanging over their ornate fireplace with its marble mantelpiece. I suddenly worry for those vases perched precariously on it and hope they aren't some heirloom, because I don't see how they'll survive this night.

Through the archway that leads into the dining room I spy Ryan in a pair of khaki shorts and a T-shirt, presiding over a game with red Solo cups on his parents' antique dining room table. He's got one arm slung around Emily Thurnauer's narrow shoulders. Her cheek is tucked cozily against his chest, which— huh. I didn't realize they were hanging out. He looks up, his eyes far away, and I freeze. He lingers a second, but I can't tell if he sees me. Then he looks down at Emily.

I mean. Not that I care.

I take a deep breath, then reach down and take Calvin's hand gently from his pocket, weaving his fingers through mine. "Big house," I say, squeezing. "Don't want you to get lost."

Calvin smiles at that, seeming to relax a little: "Buddy system," he agrees. "Never fails."

We round the corner into the massive kitchen, which is outfitted with the kind of gleaming stainless steel appliances that would make even the restaurant's look puny by comparison. Ivy is standing at the marble-topped island, dumping a bag of Tostitos into an oversized Pyrex bowl.

"You're here!" she says, wrapping me in a hug. She's in a pale pink dress, and she's gathered her hair up in a bun. She spots Calvin over my shoulder. "And you brought company!"

"Calvin, this is my best friend, Ivy," I tell her. "Ivy, this is my . . . Calvin."

"Nice to meet you, my Calvin," Ivy says, offering him a dazzling smile before turning and dumping a jar of salsa into a bowl. I know from experience that nobody would care if she just tossed it all onto the patio table outside, but for better or worse, Ivy is her mother's daughter. She's not about to let people eat chips out of the bag like a bunch of heathens. Not on her watch.

"Jules," she says, handing me the bowl, "can I borrow you for a second?"

I smile apologetically at Calvin before following her down the hallway. "What's up?"

"I . . ." Ivy hesitates, looking back over her shoulder at Calvin.

A kid I don't recognize bumps into her and starts asking something I can't quite hear. She turns back to me.

"We can get into it later." She's a little drunk, which is unusual. She normally doesn't like to drink much when she's hosting, which she does with some regularity, on top of which it's barely nine o'clock. But I guess, like she said at the pool that day, it's also our last full summer at home.

"Also, just FYI," she announces in a singsongy voice, "Lucas is here."

"Wait, seriously?"

Lucas is emphatically not a partier; I don't think I've seen him at a social gathering with school people since we used to have our birthdays at the indoor laser tag park. And it's not because he isn't popular, either. It's just . . . never been his scene.

But Ivy nods. "I ran into him at the pool this morning," she explains. "So I invited him. Not for nothing, but he asked if you were going to be here." She gives another pointed glance in Calvin's direction.

I don't know what to do with that information, exactly. I look around and don't know whether I'm relieved or not that Lucas is nowhere to be found. "Okay," I say. My heart thumps in my chest. I don't know if it's nervous dread at the thought of Lucas running into Calvin or Ryan, or the odds that Happily-EverDrafter is somewhere in this house at this very moment, or the too-close feeling of all these different parts of my topsy-turvy summer colliding here in this castle of a house.

"Thanks for the heads-up, I guess."

I watch the party for another minute, wincing at the sound of something crashing in the next room. "Where's M.J.?" I ask, realizing all at once I don't see his familiar curly towhead around, either. "Did he run out to resupply?" It wouldn't be a party without Ivy's boyfriend around here somewhere.

Something unrecognizable passes over Ivy's face, but before she can answer my question somebody is asking her for extra toilet paper. She gets tugged away. The hall is a transit point between different parts of the house, and I want to stop this jostling feeling. So I make my way back to the kitchen.

There is a group of girls I only vaguely recognize from Ivy's lacrosse team standing where I left Calvin. I scan the kitchen but can't spot him anywhere. I grab a hard lemonade from an ice-filled cooler perched on the island and spot Makenna, who was in my AP government class this past school year. She tells me about her family trip down the shore, and I only catch every third word or so over the noise. Finally, she leans in. "Hang on," she says, putting one manicured hand on my arm, "Did I see you holding hands with a guy?"

"I was," I say, taking a sip of my bottle and looking around one more time. "I should probably try to find him."

It takes me a long time to do a circuit of the downstairs, with the density of the crowd and the size of the house, plus the half dozen catch-up conversations with people I haven't seen since the end of the school year. Calvin's not in the great room or out on the patio or playing pool in the game room with its antique arcade video game machines or VR headset. I pull out my phone to text him. I'm right by Ivy's mom's study, which hopefully will give me some quiet so I can hear him. I pull open the door and—

There's Ryan. The lights are dim, so it takes my eyes a moment to adjust. He's on the Chesterfield couch in front of his mom's glinting wall of golden Best Realtor plaques. He is not alone on said couch. Emily Thurnauer is with him. Well, kind of under him. And his hand is . . .

"Oh, I'm sorry . . . ," I yelp. I should just back out of here slowly, but I'm rooted, humiliation and jealousy and hurt flooding my belly. "I thought no one was in here. I'm sorry."

Ryan looks over, catches my eye, but there's nothing in his. "Jules," he says, like we're two CEOs running into each other on the golf course. He's drunk, too, his voice low and loose, eyes unfocused, smile lazy. Emily is giving me the heat-seeking missile stare of "Get out." Ryan's dimple appears for the briefest of seconds, his jawline stubbly probably for the first time, at least that I've seen. "You came to the party." There is so little of bookish, sweet, considerate Ryan in his face at the moment that my disappointment feels like a physical blow.

The feeling floods back to me, and I remember in exquisite detail all the reasons why I've spent the better part of my life hating Ryan Madigan. He expects the world to be reordered for him because, let's face it, it has been. There's *no way* he could be HappilyEverDrafter. There's no way he could ever be so outside his own big head to read something someone else wrote and react to it with sensitivity and insight.

I'm still jangling like a jar of loose change as I turn and slam the study door behind me. And, there, finally, is Calvin. He's moving in the direction of the front door. "Hey," I say. "I've been looking for you."

"Uh," he says, not quite meeting my eye. "I'm going to take off."

My first reaction is that he was my ride here, which of course isn't the point—I can get home fine, with or without him. But the fact that he was going to sneak out and leave me here without saying anything is not cool. The fact that he wasn't going to ask if I was ready to leave, like we were together, but make a decision to just bail without letting me know. What did he call me earlier? Reliable? There are worse things to be, and I don't want to be the alternative.

"Okay," I say, trying not to sound like I'm annoyed. "I'm sorry we got separated like that. I didn't mean to abandon you in a house full of strangers."

"No, it's fine," Calvin says, though his voice is considerably colder than it was back at the ice cream shop. "The whole basic, rich McMansion-girl thing just isn't my scene is all."

It feels like a bucket of cold water splashed on me. "I'm sorry, the whole *what*?"

Calvin holds his hands up. "Hey, relax," he says. "I just meant . . ."

"I'm relaxed," I say icily. "I'm just wondering who's the basic, rich McMansion girl in this scenario, exactly?" I fight the urge to tell him this house is over a hundred years old and can't, by definition, be a McMansion, but it occurs to me that won't do much for whatever impression he has of me now.

"Easy," he says, half smiling like I don't know how to take a joke. "It's not an insult."

"Isn't it?" The pitch of my voice rises even though I didn't mean for it to. "Because it sounds to me like you're either insulting me or my best friend, so—"

"Okay," Calvin says, shoving his hands back into his pockets. "Look, we had a lot of fun tonight, didn't we? Let's just . . . end the night on a good note."

I open my mouth, close it again. He sounds reasonable, the same way he did earlier at the ice cream shop when he was saying it's not my job to take care of my parents. And he's right, we did have fun. But I can't help but think that even after all everything I've told him, there's some fundamental part of me he doesn't understand.

Calvin seems to take my inability to make words come out of my mouth as agreement. Or an easy out. "I'll text you, okay?"

"Sure," I manage, though all at once I can't imagine wanting to talk to him. "Okay."

Once he's gone I head back through the house and up the stairs. Maybe Ivy's room will be quiet. It is always one of my favorite places on earth. I wish, like an ache, that I could be somewhere alone with my notebook, making sense of a world in which two of three possible HappilyEverDrafters just got knocked out of the running in one night. I get to her room and tug on the door, but it's locked. Like the smart, experienced party-thrower that she is, Ivy made her room off-limits. I head down the hall, pushing open the French doors that lead out onto the second-floor balcony. Then I stop in my tracks: there's Lucas on one of the expensive canvas lounge chairs, in jeans and a River Plate soccer shirt, his curls looking unruly, his handsome face tilted up at the sky.

"Save me," I say by way of greeting, plunking down on the edge of the chair.

Lucas's face lights up with recognition. "There you are," he says.

He looks like he was waiting just for me. Or maybe it's what I want him to look like. Seeing him feels like being desperately thirsty and realizing you've been carrying a bottle of your favorite drink at the bottom of your bag the whole time. My heart slows down, and I take a breath.

"Save you from who?" he adds.

"I don't know," I say. "Parties. Myself."

He shifts over to make room on the lounge chair, and I lay back beside him, the sides of our legs just brushing. We're quiet for a minute; the sky is velvety black, starlight doing its best to glitter through despite the air pollution of being so close to the city.

"Do you think I'm destined to be basic?" I ask after a moment.

Lucas laughs. "I don't even know what that means."

"Yes, you do," I say, turning to face him. "Boring. Predictable. The kind of person who spends too much time working and hanging out with her grandma and dreaming big dreams but not being good enough to get them, just scribbling away in her notebook but never taking it further." *The kind of person who writes about other people having adventures instead of going out and having them herself.*

"First, most of those things are perfectly good things to do," Lucas tells me. "Except the not being good enough part, which is just wrong. Did someone *say* you were basic?"

I shake my head. I don't want to tell him about Calvin. "Doesn't matter."

"Well," Lucas says, "Whoever it was doesn't know much about you. Anyway, I feel like when people are calling other people basic they're saying more about themselves than the person they're calling that. What's basic? People who are solid. Who know what they value and focus on the simple stuff. So, sure, I'd take basic over whatever the alternative is."

"Yeah," I agree softly.

He could be talking about me or about him. His body is so close, his presence warm and starlit and comforting and . . . basic. But in the best possible way. Basic to my life, to everything I know I am.

"I guess you're right," I say, no more than a whisper.

We're quiet, our breathing in sync. I am seized with a wild desire to gently twine my hand in his curls and pull him to me, imagine the quiet sound of his surprise. What it might be like the moment I know he is kissing back, happy to be kissed, eager, like he's been waiting for it. I hesitate. Should I? It could be an epic fail, after all. I float in the moment of want, of wonder. Then the French door quietly swooshes open behind us. Lucas stiffens up, sits up straighter.

"Hey, Jules? Is that you?" It's Makenna. "Can you give me a hand?"

"Sure," I say, hopping up off the lounge chair, trying

to give off a *Nothing to see here* vibe. "What's up?"

She leads me back into the hall. "Sorry," she says; then: "Wait, did I just block a thing with . . . was that Belmondo?"

"Don't ask."

Makenna nods, does the *My lips are sealed* hand gesture. Then she leads me down the hall and into Ivy's parents' primary bathroom. The giant copper tub is backlit, and it's actually got columns around it. But that's not where Ivy is. She's sprawled on the marble tile, slumped over the sleek toilet.

"Oh, Ive," I say, soft. I pull her hair back, take a ponytail holder off my wrist, tie her hair up with it. "Ivy, are you okay?"

"I'm fine," Ivy sighs, sounding miserable and not at all fine. "Just tired."

I turn to Makenna. "Where's M.J.?"

Makenna looks at me like I just said something odd. "They . . . broke up?" she says. "I thought you of all people would know."

I look back at Ivy. She's pale and a little clammy, her face tipped toward the water like she might get sick any minute. She's certainly in no shape to confirm or deny. I run through all our missed connections in the last few days, even earlier tonight when she tried to pull me into the hall and somehow we couldn't talk. I feel like the worst friend in the world.

"I didn't. Hey, Ive?" I ask. "Do you want to sit up, you think, or you gonna throw up more?"

"I'm *fine*," she says again, then heaves. I run my hand on the back of her head, wishing I could make her feel less miserable, less sad. Wishing I had known that she was hurting before she got herself so sick.

"It's okay," I whisper, like I might with a hurt puppy or a scared child. "It's okay."

It takes Makenna and me a long time to clear everyone out of Ivy's house. We shut off the music to a collective groan. When everyone's gone, it takes even longer to pick up the garbage and wipe the spills off the counters. Ryan seems to have sobered up and runs the vacuum over the area rugs. He doesn't talk, so I don't say anything, either. I feel mixed-up and embarrassed. Mostly, it's like I've misjudged every relationship in my life this summer. I didn't even say good night to Lucas, the one person who made sense to me tonight. Add that to my list of screwups and miscalculations.

When we've got the house looking somewhat

presentable, I walk Makenna to the front door and promise I'll text her in the morning about how Ivy is doing. Luckily, my plan had always been to sleep over tonight, so I text my mom good night with a minimum of fuss.

I walk Ivy to her room, then wrestle her into her pajamas. I put her on her side and tuck her into bed. I go downstairs and get her a glass of water to put on her nightstand.

Her eyes are closed, but she says, "I don't want to talk about it," even though I haven't asked her to explain.

"That's okay," I say, putting the trash can next to her bed. "We don't have to."

I dig an extra pair of pajamas out of her dresser and slip them on. They're light blue with puffy white clouds. I know they keep a drawer full of extra toothbrushes in the big bathroom Ivy and Ryan share. I open the door to the bathroom and freeze: Ryan is standing there in flannel pajama bottoms and a white T-shirt tighter than I've ever seen him wear before.

"Hey, Jules," he says, smiling at me in the mirror, "your knocking skills leave something to be desired."

"I'm sorry, I . . . ," I sputter and back up. He's just standing in front of his sink, not in any kind of a compromising position, but it feels so intrusive to walk in on him this way. For the second time in one night.

"You're fine," he says, then gestures at the vanity. "We've got two sinks."

Is he suggesting I brush my teeth in front of him? I guess, yeah, I do that in front of Lucesita or Jaime if they squeeze in, and he must do that with Ivy. This bathroom is built that way so that you don't even have to jostle each other out of position, like my siblings and I have to. It's a Jack and Jill. On the other side of the door on the right is his room.

Ryan gets his brush, electric, and coats it in toothpaste. "Is Ive okay?" he asks, putting the toothbrush in his mouth and turning it on.

I watch as he maneuvers the toothbrush. "I think so."

He stops the toothbrush, says, "Are *you*?" Then he starts it back up.

Ivy's got a toothbrush like this, too, so I know it times out after two minutes, so you don't have to sing "Happy Birthday" twice to remind yourself how long to brush. Now that he's brushing, I feel like I either need to bolt or fill the dead air.

I choose the babbling plan.

"I didn't know Ivy and M.J. had broken up, which

makes me the world's worst friend. And I missed her call, and I was . . . ," I trail off. I definitely don't want to get into any of my own romantic drama, since I'm still slightly irked at the sight of him with Emily. So I go into a long blow-by-blow recitation of how Ivy looked when I found her. I throw in the fact that I haven't eaten anything but ice cream since lunch. Just anything to avoid an awkward silence.

I reach into the spare toothbrush drawer and start the process of freeing a toothbrush from its packaging, which was apparently manufactured to withstand an assault by saber-tooth tigers. It will not budge. It makes me want to babble more.

Just how long is *two minutes, anyway?*

I stare at the toothbrush package. I'm now completely flustered. Finally, after what feels like a month later, he finishes, then rinses out his brush. He washes and dries his hands, then he holds one out to me. I hand him the toothbrush wordlessly. He opens it without looking, keeping his eyes on me.

"Listen," he says, "about earlier."

I shake my head. "You don't have to say anything."

His jaw gives a small twitch. "I want to, though. I feel like this summer we've been . . ."

Was he always standing this close? I can smell the

toothpaste still fresh in his mouth, plus that sandal-wood smell I recognize from our trips into the city. It's too subtle for cologne, I decide. It must be his shampoo. I want to suck in enough oxygen to stop the advance of heat up my neck and to my ears. But I close my eyes and picture him on that couch in his mother's study, and I get cold.

I hold my hand out for the toothbrush. "You don't have to say anything," I repeat flatly. "We're friends, right? It was a party. Anyway, I came here with some-body, too."

Ryan blinks at me, hands the toothbrush over, newly freed from its packaging. "Oh," he says, raspy. "I didn't realize." He takes a step back.

"I mean," I say, keeping my voice as even as I can, "I guess you were busy."

He studies my face, his blue-green eyes searching my face with a look I can't name and don't want to get pulled in by. His jaw gives that little twitch again. "Yeah, I guess I was," he says. He rinses his toothbrush off again and wipes his face with a towel. In that way of noticing details I don't need to notice I zero in on the perfection of his hands on the towel, nails even, fingers elegant and long, what my abuela would call "manos de pianista," hands of a pianist. Although I have no idea if he's ever even touched a piano.

He finally says, "Good night, Jules." And when he goes, I half want to follow him, hear more about what he meant to say before I stopped him. But I don't.

Ivy is already downstairs when I wake up the following morning. She's sitting in the breakfast nook just off the kitchen, a whitewashed table with a wraparound leather banquette like a restaurant booth, under a window overlooking their patio, lush with a riot of summer color. "I'm sorry," is the first thing she says.

"Are you kidding?" I shake my head. "*I'm* sorry! I feel like the worst friend. I didn't know about you and M.J., and I totally should have."

"I wanted to tell you," she says. She walks over to the fridge and pulls out a can of Starbucks espresso and cream, then gets a bag of pistachios from the cabinet. Ivy is . . . not a kitchen person. It's all foraging when she's in charge. "You were just so . . . distracted."

It hurts, but she's not wrong. I'm about to apologize again when Ryan walks into the kitchen. He's changed out of the sleeping clothes I saw him in last night. His hair is wet, and he is freshly shaved, the bridge of his nose still pink from scrubbing. He's in shorts and a dark T-shirt with a bunch of old-timey cassette tapes on it.

"The dissolute arise," he says. It's the kind of dry comment that would usually get an acid retort from Ivy.

But she laughs, looking the same kind of sweet that usually makes store clerks and pool attendants bend to her will. "Just barely. Ry, would you make those super-duper eggs of yours? I seriously need protein and grease," she says.

He looks at the bag of pistachios and twists up his face like *I can see that.*

"Sure thing," he says. Then, without making eye contact with me, he adds, "What about you, Jules? You want some, too?"

Ivy turns to me. "Ryan makes the world's most epic eggs Benedict. I suggest a yes here."

I tip my head to the side, surprised. "You do?"

Ryan nods. "I had them at a restaurant in middle school and I was obsessed with them, so I YouTubed a walk-through. For, like, fifteen minutes it made me want to be a chef. But then I figured out eggs Benedict is literally the only thing I can make."

"Okay," I agree, impressed. "I'm in. You need help?"

"Sure," he says. "I need three plates, the egg poachers. They're under there," he says, pointing, "And that big pot," he says, pointing at a pot rack. "I'll get the ingredients."

We move around the kitchen easily while Ivy checks her phone. After all, kitchens are my safe place. The vibe here is entirely different from usual between them, relaxed, like friends spending time together. Usually, at Ivy's house, it's me and Ivy doing our own thing, Ryan off somewhere else, intruding only to make a quip or a verbal jab from time to time. Or at least that's how it has been. I try to figure out what it is that's making it feel different now. It could be that Ivy is still half-asleep, with less energy for sparring.

Or . . . it could be me. Ryan and me. We've never really been friendly before, and this ease between us spills out, despite last night. It's like everyone is standing down. I like it.

Ryan poaches the eggs. He says, "A smidge of vinegar in the water," in what seems like an imitation of whatever long-ago YouTube video taught him the trick. I take the English muffins out of the toaster. He whips the Hollandaise by hand. When we're done, there are three beautiful plates with two restaurant-worthy eggs Benedict each on them. I serve Ivy's and Ryan's. He brings mine to the breakfast nook. He slides in first, closest to the window, and I slide in after him.

"So, my literary duo," says Ivy, putting the pistachios aside. "How go the word wars?"

Ryan looks at me, sheepish, and takes a bite of eggs Benedict. I don't know that I want to share after the night we all had. That image of him and Emily has flashed back to me more times than is normal for friends. But I also want to talk about whatever Ivy wants to talk about.

"Well, I've been posting on StoriedZone, as you know," I say tentatively. "And it's been . . . fun. But kind of hard, too."

"Hard why?" asks Ryan. It seems like a sincere question, not the gotcha question he might have asked before.

"I don't know, exactly. Knowing it's being seen, maybe? Knowing people are going to read a thing changes the writing, you know? I'm not sure if you feel that way, too."

"It's hard to put yourself out there, for sure, if that's what you mean. Like no matter how much you love writing, having other people *read* what you write . . . Maybe it makes it not just yours anymore? And it's so epic when it's just a possibility, and so mundane when you finally write it down. At least, that's how I feel." He takes another bite of food. "No? Don't you think?"

I nod. "Yeah, that makes a lot of sense." I lift an eyebrow. "What about you?" I ask. "How's the war between the factions?"

"Very funny," he says, "Look, I didn't know where that exercise was going."

"Nobody did. I think that was kind of the point."

"So I thought I was going in there to write this futuristic, postapocalyptic thing. Or maybe the war thing, I don't know."

"Ry is a big fan of the end of civilization," says Ivy dryly.

"So when Paige said to go the opposite way . . . I . . . Look, you *cannot* laugh," he says.

"Go on . . . ," says Ivy, making the gesture with her hand.

"Okay, so I went in the direction of thinking, like, what's the opposite of the future, but still interesting, still a time of transition and change of civilization and . . ."

Ivy's eyes get wide. "Oh my God, Ryan Madigan. You're writing Red Dead fan fiction, aren't you?"

He definitely gets red now. "I wouldn't call it *fan*

fiction . . . ," he says, trailing off. "More like an homage."

"Wait, the video game?" I ask.

"You promised you wouldn't laugh," he says, looking mortified.

"I knew that's where you were going when you said, 'change of civilization.' If I had a dollar for every time you've babbled on about how well they do the end of an era in that game . . . ," says Ivy.

"I think that's awesome," I say. "I love Red Dead. Great storytelling. And they do capture the end of the gunslinger era and the encroachment of civilization really well."

He turns his whole body in my direction. "Are you serious?"

"Yeah. So you're writing something set in 1899?"

He is still staring at me, eyes wide. "You're *serious*. You know Red Dead."

Even Ivy is staring at me a little perplexed. I doubt I've ever mentioned liking this game to her.

"Two, mostly, yeah. I haven't played the first one as much. I mean, Ryan. I live on the planet. Plus Lucesita and Jaime were obsessed for a while."

"Wow," he says, and puts the last bite of English

muffin in his mouth. It reminds me that I haven't finished mine, so I scoop up a bite of egg. Before I put it in my mouth, I say, "I'd love to read this Red Dead *homage* sometime."

And I mean it. Even if he and Emily are a thing. Even if he's not HappilyEverDrafter. I realize that even if it's possible it may not be a romantic thing between us, I have been learning to appreciate him in a way I had never expected to.

thirteen

Ivy drops me off at Las Heras for my lunch shift. The restaurant has always been a warm and welcoming place to me, a refuge, a space that means family and home. But since I overheard that conversation between my parents, it feels colder somehow. There is a dust bunny on the corner of the painting of El Aconcagua. I notice chips on wooden tables and a small tear in one of the burgundy vinyl covering the chairs, wear on the part of the rug that gets the most traffic, threadbare in one spot. I've never seen any of this before. A sinking dread settles into my stomach: a sense of things already lost, a fear of a change we can't fight off but insist on trying to anyway. I don't know who my family would be without Las Heras. I doubt either of my parents could have a traditional job, since they've been their own bosses since a little after college. My mom has always told me owning your own business is like telling the universe you have faith it will treat you well.

But what about when it doesn't?

Jaime is sitting at a table in the back, hunched over, a pile of textbooks to his left. He is about as unhappy as I've ever seen him.

"Whatcha doing here, little man?" I ask.

He sighs. "Mom said I have to do my summer reading here and she's going to look over my reports before I send them in."

Jaime's grades have been a source of tension at our house for a while now. At the start of distance learning, teachers were understanding when he struggled to keep up on Zoom, but as his attention wandered, their patience started to wane. My parents tried to come up with creative solutions. They sat with him, tried to make it fun, planned rewards. He felt bad, because although Lucesita and I both kinda hated it, too, our grades stayed fine. Over time, as teachers' nerves frayed and he got more and more disengaged, his did not.

Now he is pale and slumped, staring longingly out the window at the sunshine. I don't know where Lucesita is, but it's probably somewhere fun. My heart hurts that he's getting what amounts to a punishment for what feels like a problem. I know my parents don't mean it that way. But more time cooped up inside being forced to do stuff that's hard for him doesn't feel like the solution.

"But you're not reading."

"Don't tell Mom, but I hate this book so much." I glance over. *Lord of the Flies*. I totally get why Jaime might not like it. He's always been a gentle kid, his feelings close to the surface. There's a brutality in it that must jangle his nerves. I thought it was smart, if dated, but I get why it's not Jaime's jam. I wish, for the thousandth time, that kids could have more leeway in their reading.

I sit across from him. "Piggy?" I ask.

He looks stricken. "Yes. I don't know what happens to him yet but what I've read so far is awful." Jaime was bullied when he was younger, and he has a finely tuned antenna for anyone getting mistreated. He can't even stand to watch harsh treatment in movies. He certainly doesn't need it in his school reading.

"Oh, Jaime, I know. I'm sorry." I put my hand on

his forearm. "There's a movie," I offer, but he shakes his head.

He's got a very strong sense of right and wrong. We've all read the SparkNotes at some point. But not Jaime.

I sit with him quietly for a bit, running through all the pep talk options in my head. "It's a classic" and "do ten pages a day" and "it's a story meant to teach you a moral. This didn't actually happen to a boy." They all fail to get at the basic thing. I consider lobbying his teacher, or the head of the middle school English department, to let him pick a different title. That's not going to work, at least not in time to get him out of reading it for the summer. Our school district has been obtuse about expanding its reading requirements.

An idea occurs to me. "Hey, what if I told you there's another island survival story where things happen kinda differently? We can read these both out loud together. One chapter of this book, one chapter of the other book."

He looks at me skeptically. "So read two books instead of one?"

I laugh. "Well, if you put it that way that doesn't sound nearly as fun. But what if I tell you this: the other island survival book is about beauty queens."

"Beauty queens?"

"Yeah, they're on their way to a pageant and get stranded on a deserted island."

"No survival of the fittest?"

"Well, yeah, a little bit, but being fit involves whether you have enough mascara and stuff like that."

He laughs. "You are so random," he says.

"I am. But how about we give it a try?"

He nods. I order the audio book on my phone so we can listen to it together. Then he reads me the next chapter of *Lord of the Flies* while I get the dining room ready for dinner. Doña Faustina picks him up a little while after we finish with the promise of taking him for a late swim at the pool, and I hand her take-out bags full of stuff I've had the kitchen make to send home with them for dinner. I take an hour to walk the strip and go sit in the park to recharge before dinner.

The dinner rush is more like a trickle. By eight o'clock it's obvious that no one else is coming. It's early for a summer night where foot traffic usually means a lot of walk-ins, even if just for dessert and coffee or a bowl of ice cream drizzled with dulce de leche we make right here in our own kitchen. Most people don't know it's condensed milk boiled to death in the can, for hours.

My dad comes out from the kitchen, wiping his left hand on an apron, holding a Red Bull in his right. My mom has convinced him to keep Joaquin on part-time, "off the books," so my dad is back on the line, which requires even more caffeine than usual. My mom follows him out a few minutes later. It's obvious she's been doing some heavy lifting back there, too: her hair is messy, and she's got sweat stains on her usually impeccable restaurant-branded golf shift.

"Dale, nena," she tells me. "I saved you some churrasco. Come and sit."

The three of us sit down in the quiet dining room. My dad cuts a piece of his chicken carefully, puts it in his mouth. My mother lifts her utensils but watches me. I can't even remember what an appetite is. Something is wrong, I can tell.

"There's no easy way to say this," my father begins. "Things are tough. I know you're seeing it. Zoe quit. I think she saw how things were going. We know how you loved her. But she's gone." I put down my fork. Suddenly, I'm not hungry at all. Zoe can't leave us. She *wouldn't.* Zoe gave me my first tampon and explained how to use it. She taught me to parallel park in the parking lot. She trained me how to upsell the whole table to order dessert and coffee. I've known her since

I was a dork and she already looked like a movie star. She's been here forever.

"M'hija, tenés que comer," my mom chides.

I know I have to eat. I was ravenous a few minutes ago. I cut a piece of the steak, put it in my mouth, and let its tang make the sides of my jaw sting as I chew. I do love this food: *our* food, recipes passed down from generation to generation. Food is its own kind of magic, a wish for health and survival and strength to fight the next battle, seasoned and plated like an offering. It is a thing one generation gives to the next and says, "This is how we share our love."

For some reason, this is the thought that sets me over the edge and I start crying. Zoe has always been a survivor. If she left, it's because she thinks we're a sinking ship. If the restaurant fails, everything fails with it. All during the pandemic, when everything was so scary and uncertain, somehow it felt like they were keeping balance on the high wire: PPP loans, ramping up delivery, making it work. We can't fail *now*, at the point when everything is supposed to be getting better. Not after all the white-knuckle times of the last few years. Not after twenty years of sacrifices and long hours, and not only that, either, but all the generations of hopes and effort riding on their American adventure.

My mother gets up and cradles me in a half crouch, and my father puts his hand on my hand, then brushes hair back away from my face. I let myself ugly cry, not caring if someone is going to walk in or if my parents are shocked at my reaction. I let it all go, the months of worry about them, about the restaurant, about how to figure out how to live my life well and avoid the pitfalls they've fallen into.

It strikes me that this, their empty, failing business, and their weeping daughter are the only things that still connect them. For some reason, that's the saddest thought of all and brings on another round of tears.

Later that night, I'm in bed staring at the ceiling, too wired to sleep, too sad to do much of anything else. My phone dings. It's Abuela Bubbles. Her texts are legendary in their randomness, usually. But this one just says, *You writing?* I think, not for the first time, that she sometimes seems all-seeing. Although the explanation is probably simpler and one of my parents told her about the conversation we just had and this is her way of reminding me to focus on me and my dreams.

But whatever her motivation, it works. I get out of bed and log into StoriedZone. My head aches, my eyes still puffy from crying. I've used Ivy's trick, spoons in the freezer, and I feel a little better than I did when I first got home. But I need something. *Someone.* I need the person I am coming to consider one of my best friends.

HappilyEverDrafter's light is on green. *Hi,* I type, breathing a sigh of relief. After everything that's happened this weekend: my not-quite-fight with Calvin, that intense moment on the balcony with Lucas, whatever the heck is going on with Ryan, not to mention Ivy's breakup, and my parents dropping the bomb about Zoe—I'm feeling more confused and overwhelmed than ever. I don't know who Happily-EverDrafter is. But I do know I can't keep on groping around in the dark.

The dancing circles that signal he's replying pop up right away. A moment later: *I thought you might not sign on tonight . . .*

I almost didn't, I confess. *It's been . . . a weekend.*

I can relate, he writes back. *Want to tell me about it?*

I do, I tell him truthfully: I want to tell him about all the ways my life has felt out of control lately, so different from the stories I write where I'm the one in charge. *But I want to know who you are first.*

A pause, then: *It's not that I don't want to tell you,* he

writes back. *It's just . . . complicated. And I'm afraid the answer is going to make you mad.*

The answer could never make me mad, I write, hitting Send before I can talk myself out of it. *Because the answer will be you.*

It is the boldest thing I've ever written. I hold my breath.

The dancing circles start. Stop. Start again. Then nothing.

HappilyEverDrafter has signed off.

**10:42 p.m.: AldertonGirlAconcagua posted to
"Untitled Teen Love Story."**

Maggie knew right away what her admirer—that's how she'd taken
to thinking of him—meant in his first clue when he said "where the
seagulls gather." There were seagulls everywhere, of course, as is the
case in seaside fishing villages. But since she was a kid, there was one
creaky pier too unsteady to be used for keeping boats. The seagulls
had taken it over completely, using it as their vantage point to try to
snatch fish from incoming boats.

Maggie hadn't been on Seagull Pier since old games of hide-and-
go-seek. It had gotten creakier since the last time she was on it. She
walked it slowly, trying to imagine where the next clue might be. But
there was nothing, just quick-eyed gulls eyeing her placidly, curious
only if she'd brought snacks.

But then she saw it.

 **Posts 7** **Likes 17**

fourteen

I don't hear from HappilyEverDrafter that night. He's quiet the next day, too, and the day after that; by Thursday, when Lucas and I have our not-an-actual-date at Tierra del Fuego, I'm surprised I haven't crashed the StoriedZone server with the number of times I've refreshed my empty messages folder. I pushed too hard. I asked for too much, too fast. I couldn't just let things be and develop at their pace.

And now he's just . . . gone. Of all my missteps this summer, this one haunts me most.

A honk outside my house shakes me out of my

funk. I run down and hop in the front seat of Lucas's dad's car. Lucas is sitting behind the wheel in dark pants and a button-down, his hair combed back and gelled like he's heading into work in the city at something office-y.

"Glad to see we both went for the full-on grown-up cosplay," he cracks as I slide into the passenger seat beside him. His soccer ball wallet is in the console between us.

"Seriously." I'm wearing my most adult-looking outfit, a dress my mom picked out for me for the NHS induction ceremony, light blue with a white collar. I put my hair up in a bun to obscure most of the blue and teal, then applied what I imagine might look like grown-up makeup—not too heavy, but more lipstick than I normally wear. "Mr. and Mrs. Smith out for a Thursday night dinner."

"What, like the Angelina Jolie movie?" Lucas grins as he turns onto the main road into town. "Not sure that's the reference we want. It doesn't end well for those two."

I laugh. "No, more like the ones who come in and want to get dinner over with quickly so they don't have to pay the babysitter overtime."

"Is that a thing adults care about?" Lucas grins.

"I've definitely seen customers rushing through dinner and talking about that." I laugh. "It's what grown-ups talk about? Like . . . inflation."

"Rising food costs," he agrees.

"Pain at the pump!"

We keep riffing all the way to Tierra del Fuego, both of us acting goofy enough that I almost forget what we're about to do here. Once Lucas parks on the side street and we approach the all-black facade of the restaurant, though, my heart starts thumping. I've built up a mythical anger at this place. Every time I drive by it I send bad vibes and what I'm hoping is burgeoning hex energy. There's a part of me that understands what they're doing is nothing personal, just another group of people hoping for their slice of the dream; still, their existence in the neighborhood feels like a specific attack against my family. The fact that they're obviously doing well does not help at all.

Lucas holds the heavy door open, nodding for me to go ahead.

I take a deep breath. "Here goes nothing," I murmur, then throw my shoulders back and march inside.

"Hi there," I say, smiling my most responsible,

adult-looking smile at the hostess. "Mr. and Mrs. Smith?"

"Of course." The hostess, who can't be much older than we are, has slicked-back hair and a cream silk blouse with a bow at the collar. Her eyes linger on us a moment, like she's doing the math. Then she checks her list and smiles. "It'll be a few minutes until your table is ready, but you can wait at the bar if you'd like."

"Sure," says Lucas, doing a good job of keeping his face straight, which is more than I can say for myself. The utter ridiculousness of anyone thinking we're old enough to grab a quick glass of white while we wait for our table almost sends me into a fit of giggles.

Once she's gone he leans in close enough that I can feel his breath on the back of my ear. "I'm sorry," he says, "You *actually* booked the reservation under Mr. and Mrs. Smith?"

"I panicked when she asked for a name on the phone."

"Clearly." He leads me to the bar with his hand at the small of my back, an intimate motion that feels shockingly natural. He finds me an open stool and stands next to me, leaning on the bar as he looks around the place. "I mean, it's a little try-hard, wouldn't you say?"

he says, a disdainful look on his face.

I know he's being sweet, sticking up for the home team. But there's no way to deny that this place looks good. Everything about it is fresh and new, from the gleaming wood bar to the exposed bleached brick wall opposite it that's double height, leading to a loftlike space where there is more seating. The light fixtures are modern and sleek, the server uniforms crisp. They've leaned into the "fire" in their name, with an open brick oven in the corner and a big in-wall modern fireplace. But the place is cool for the summer, their AC clearly brand-spanking-new, and not requiring the occasional kick to the condenser on the roof the way ours does, I bet. A four-person band plays at a perfect volume, enough to make it all feel lively and fresh, low enough that conversation is still easy. The whole effect is more New York City than Alderton.

And it's working: the place is jam-packed, even on a Thursday.

"I don't know, Lucas. It's pretty good."

"The food is probably terrible," he says. "Customers always want to try the new place, but then the effect doesn't last."

The hostess comes to get us and walks us to our

table. Lucas holds out my chair. Years of being in a restaurant, I know. But still.

I pick up the menu, slick and brand-new, no melted-in coffee-cup rings or dog-eared pages. It looks like a close copy of ours: an identical selection of steaks, a fish, homemade dulce de leche on a variety of desserts. But then I suppose that's Argentinian cuisine. I try not to let it anger me. I order the arroz con pollo, because I want to give them as little money as possible. Lucas orders a steak.

"Okay," he says once the waiter is gone, leaning back in his chair; his ankle bumps my bare one under the table, there and gone again. "So. Just like, hypothetically. If I had a gallon-sized Ziploc baggie full of seven hundred crickets in my jacket right now, where do you think would be the most effective place to release them?"

I laugh so hard I almost snort my Sprite. It's nice, hanging out with Lucas. I mean, we're *around* each other all the time—at big noisy dinners with our families or at work at the restaurant or cheering on our siblings at their various tournaments and recitals—but we don't spend as much one-on-one time together as we used to. By the time the food comes, he's charmed me into not obsessing about every little detail of the place. We're here for reconnaissance, true. But that doesn't mean I don't have to let it ruin my night.

The food comes, and I take a bite of my arroz con pollo. It's got precisely the right amount of saffron in it. Damn them.

Lucas bites into his and, to his credit, doesn't try to lie and say it's bad. "Wanna bite?" he asks, holding up a forkful.

I nod, and he hesitates, makes a move to feed it to me, then gets flustered and puts it on my plate. It's good, too, and the disappointment must be written all over my face because as we're finishing up, Lucas puts his napkin on the table and clears his throat.

"Okay," he says. "I have a thought."

I inhale slowly, pull myself together. "I'm waiting with bated breath," I tease. But all at once my heart is speeding up again.

He looks serious. It occurs to me that he is going to say he likes me. I want to blurt out: Are you Happily-EverDrafter? Sitting here, this way, with this mix of care and familiarity, but also seeing him for the first time in some ways, I think I want him to be.

"What's up?"

"The band is fun. I wonder . . ." He trails off and then meets my eyes. "Maybe we should plan something fun for Las Heras. An event. Something for people to show up for."

"Oh." I am disoriented, and I try not to let my face fall. I thought for sure he was going to say something about us, about this total vibe going on between us. But maybe that's just me. After all, we're here to try to save my parents' restaurant, aren't we? Of course that's what he wants to talk about. "Yeah, okay. Like what?"

"I . . . haven't quite gotten that far yet," he says. "Everything I think of costs money. Speaking of which," he jokes as our waiter drops the check, "should we dine and dash? These shoes look fancy, but they've got rubber soles."

I laugh, although of course Lucas would never. He's too honest. He's too good. I stick out a high-heeled foot from under the table, hope for a split second it makes him look at my leg. "I'd definitely slow us down," I quip.

We pay and make our way outside. As we're turning in the direction of where we parked the car, a voice calls out behind me.

"Jules?"

I turn back from Lucas to its source.

Zoe.

"Lucas?" she adds. She is beet red, a look of fear and something else, maybe shame, all over her face. She has a hand on the door to Tierra del Fuego. All my pain and disappointment about her leaving flare up.

"Zoe, are you . . . are you *working* here?" I say, even though I know the answer before I even finish the question. She lives in town because Manhattan rents are sky-high. It makes sense she'd want a new job nearby. But here, with these people who are sinking us, it's all too much.

She's dressed for work in the stilettos I've marveled at a thousand times, plus a cap-sleeved geometric dress I've coveted.

"Jules, I'm sorry. I've been meaning to stop by and mention it to you guys."

I lean in close to her so as to not make a scene. I don't want to be outed as a scout for the competition while we're still right outside. "Why?" I ask. The side-walk feels wobbly, like in a funhouse.

"Jules," she says, almost in a whisper.

I stare at her, rooted and a little dizzy. She lets go of the door and walks over to us.

"I guess you're pretty mad at me."

"I'm not mad, Zoe. I'm sad. We treated you like family and you just left."

"I have bills, Jules. I just needed something that felt steady. It hurt so much to do it."

I thought we all had to row as hard as we could until things picked up again, us and the employees, too. Maybe that's unfair. But it never occurred to me that Zoe would just leave. That we could spend years buying each other Secret Santa gifts and that she could teach me to French braid and let me read her scripts and then one day stop working for us when we were struggling.

"I thought we were family, Zoe."

"I want you to know how much I'm rooting for you guys," she says, a tear trailing down her face.

I breathe out and nod. I wonder what I'd have done in Zoe's place. Maybe the same thing. It hurts to realize, but it does make me feel a little less sad. "Take care of yourself."

Lucas and I walk away.

The night has turned chilly. Lucas takes off his jacket and drapes it over my shoulders like something out of an old movie.

"Thanks," I say. Somehow I can't focus on the

sweetness of the gesture, because actually being inside Tierra del Fuego and then seeing Zoe makes me realize we could go on a thousand recon missions, but none of that is going to save the restaurant. The problem is so much bigger than us.

We get to the car but instead of opening my door, Lucas leans against it. "You need a hug?" he asks.

He opens his arms, and I step into them, into him. He molds perfectly around me, my face in his chest, his chin resting gently on the top of my head. It feels so good I can let go of the voice screaming that this is weird, that this is *Lucas*.

"We're going to fix it, Jules. I promise you. We can fix this."

Lucas pulls up in front of my house. It's funny and unnecessary since he lives a few doors down. The streetlamp is closer to his part of the block, not mine, so we're in deep shadow now, the blaze of the sky taking its time to fade to purple.

He puts the car in park. I glance at my house. Nothing. Maybe my parents are still at the restaurant. I squint at the garage windows, but I can't tell if the cars are in there or not.

"That was . . . fun," he says quietly. "Minus the

treachery and the heartache, of course."

"Really?" I shoot back. "Treachery and heartache are so underrated."

Lucas grins. He looks adorable in this light, serious and funny at the same time, heart the size of a mountain, a full Aconcagua of empathy and care. *Solid* . . . that's the word for him. Aren't those the things that stay? The reliable and the kind, when all the flash is gone? Although . . . I'm feeling some flash, too. I sort of hope he kisses me. I could kiss *him* . . . I study his lips. I could *definitely* kiss those.

"Maybe we could do that again. Somewhere else, I mean," he says.

"Literally anywhere else." I laugh.

"The surface of the sun, perhaps."

"The back of a burro."

"On a merchant ship."

"I'm not even sure I know what that is." I smile.

"Me neither."

"But you can have common purpose anywhere," he says.

A tingle, a different kind, makes its way through me. That is almost verbatim a quote from "Untitled." I look into his eyes to see whether there's an admission there. But they look earnest, like they're hiding nothing.

I take a deep breath. "Lucas," I start. "Are you . . . ," I trail off. If he was Happily, he'd have told me tonight for sure, right?

If he was Happily, how could he have left me hanging the last few days?

I leave the question lingering there, unfinished, wondering not for the first time how long we're going to stay suspended in this in-between: not kids anymore and not adults yet, either, not just friends but not quite more. If this were fiction, I'd force my characters toward a resolution. If I were writing, I'd know what to say. But in life I just sort of flounder and wonder and am afraid to make mistakes.

Finally Lucas clears his throat. "Listen," he says, "I've got a hell of a commute ahead of me, so . . ."

I laugh uneasily. "Thanks for dinner." And I get out of the car. He stays at the curb and watches me open my door. I wave and the car rolls away slowly.

I make my way to the kitchen and find my mom waiting there. "How was dinner?" she asks, which is all she has to say to make it abundantly clear she knows exactly whose arroz con pollo I've been eating.

I take a deep breath. My mother is the tougher of my two parents, the one to usually discipline and communicate parental disappointment. But she looks worn down, her eyes a question, no fire behind them.

"I wanted to see what was so special about them, Ma," I admit, sinking down at the island beside her. I don't know how she knows, but it doesn't matter. It's a small town, and everyone knows everyone. Better to just come clean. "I wanted to know why everyone is going there. What we could do."

"M'hijita, I understand," she says, reaching for my hand and squeezing. "But it's not your job to figure out what we can do. Your job is to go for your *own* dreams, have fun, enjoy your writing thing, hang out with friends. This is our problem to solve."

She gets up and starts cleaning the immaculate kitchen, wiping off the counters although they already sparkle. It's her nervous tic: any minute now, she's going to try to feed me something.

"Ma, can I ask you something else?"

She stops wiping. "Sure, m'hija, what?"

"Remember that story you told me once? About that boy who left you notes, right before you came to the United States for college? Do you ever wonder how your life might have gone if you'd stayed to look for him instead? If you had tried to . . . I mean, I know you love el Papi, but . . . do you wonder?"

She smiles, a faraway, enigmatic look. "Ay, m'hijita,

you have the most wonderful imagination. That was nothing. I can't believe you even remember that story."

I suppose it wouldn't be easy to tell your child you regret marrying her father, that you second-guess the life you've built with him. But I don't think of it that way, somehow. Of course I love my dad. But I've wondered a lot not whether he's good enough for her, or she for him, but whether they're right together.

I question if they're happy.

"But you never wonder?" I ask. "At least who he was? What became of him?" I think of HappilyEver-Drafter. Did my mom have suspicions about who her admirer could be, like I do mine?

She smiles, more open this time. "You'd be thoroughly disappointed in the answer. But now's not the time for that. Dale, go now, brush your teeth. No more staking out the competition. I don't know the whole answer, but I know restaurant espionage is not it."

Suddenly, footsteps bound down the stairs. Lucesita appears, hair piled on top of her head, ancient caticorn pajamas a little too snug.

"You're up past your bedtime," I say. I can sound a lot like my mom, I note.

She doesn't acknowledge my comment. She puts

her head on my mom's shoulder and does her baby voice. "Mamita linda, did you bring me that shake?"

My mom gets it for her from the fridge. Lucesita scampers back upstairs.

"You baby her," I say, brows furrowed.

"You're too hard on her. You were the baby, once."

I scrunch up my mouth. I doubt it. I can't remember ever feeling as little as Lucesita seems to feel.

She smiles. "But don't change the subject yet. Wait until Maribel finds out."

I groan. "Don't tell Lucas's mom."

"What?" she laughs, rubbing her hands together. "I've already texted her. I'm waiting for her to call me back so I can give her every single detail I know. Mr. and Mrs. Smith, huh? And wait until Abuela hears about this."

"Ugh." *Parents.*

I head upstairs and change into my pajamas, wash Mrs. Smith's makeup off my face. I'm just climbing into bed when my phone buzzes on the nightstand with a notification from StoriedZone. I hold my breath and click.

HappilyEverDrafter has posted.

Sorry to take so long with this one! he's written, breezy

like it hasn't been a bajillion years. Or, I don't know, four days. He says nothing about our last conversation, about my questions, about the awkwardness, the silence. Nothing about who he actually is. *Hope you enjoy.*

**3:12 a.m.: HappilyEverDrafter posted to
"Untitled Teen Love Story."**

Maggie:

I've read that ancient people believed that when an animal came to you in a dream, you were supposed to pay attention to what that animal's message is, and that every animal brings a different one.

Seagulls mean that there is an opportunity in everything, even in the unlikeliest of places. They mean that it may be time to take a different perspective on something you think you already know.

Or maybe that's just me hoping you'll look at me with fresh eyes.

Speaking of which, for our next clue, I'll leave a note with a friend who deserves to be looked at with fresh eyes too.

fifteen

I head over to Ivy's the following afternoon. We sit in her cavernous family room, eat waffle cones from Alderton Creamery, our favorite ice cream spot, and watch K dramas. She's upside down on the couch, because she swears letting the blood rush to her head is important for brain function.

"Anything new from the Romeos?" she asks, taking another bite of her ice cream and fixing her upside-down gaze on me. Her heartbreak has not dimmed her passion for getting the 411 on everything.

"One Romeo," I correct. "Also, that's a terrible reference, because they all die horribly in the end."

She rolls her upside-down eyes in her upside-down head. "Not *that* part. Just the part where they stand for perfect love that will do anything for each other."

"Including die."

"*Not* including die. Think balconies and stolen glances at parties. 'A rose by any other name would smell as sweet.' That part. The swoony love part, not the death part."

I raise an eyebrow. "You totally did not read it through to the end, did you?"

"I did. But I choose to focus on the positive." She digs her fingertips into the area rug. "Don't blame me, *Julieta*. Blame your parents for giving you that name." She pronounces it with the correct *H* sound at the start.

"You know that's not the Julieta I'm named after, right?"

She narrows her eyes. "Maybe? Remind me."

"I mean, you know my mom. She wouldn't very well name me after a fictional character who dies tragically and, if I may add, unnecessarily at, like, what was that? Thirteen or something? No. She named me after an Argentinian woman named Julieta Lanteri. Doctor, freethinker, activist for women's rights. My mom thought it would inspire me to be a badass, too, being named after an activist. She didn't even think about the play. Unintended consequences."

"Why didn't you ever mention this when every-one was so obnoxious about your name freshman year when we were reading it?"

"It was hard to get a word in edgewise over the kissy noises and the hoots."

She smiles an upside-down smile.

We're quiet for a moment. The TV drones in the background but we're not really watching. "Listen, Ive," I say, "about the M.J. thing."

But Ivy shakes her head. "What about it?" she asks. "It's over. And not to sound cold, but I'm kind of okay about it. It's a relief not to have to spend another min-ute of my one wild and precious life pretending to care about baseball."

She talks a good game, but I'm not sure I buy it. She really liked him. She once made me scroll, like, thirty different baseball memorabilia sites to help her land on the perfect Christmas present for him. She has made a job of being at all the games he pitches.

"Are you sure?" I ask. "Because we still haven't talked about it."

"There's nothing to talk about," she insists. "He wanted to see other people. Admittedly, it would have been nice of him to give me a heads-up before he actually started *doing* it, but it's done now."

"Ivy," I say, "come on."

"I'm fine," she insists. "Seriously, I went over to Makenna's last night and we watched like three terrible rom-coms in a row, I cried, there was Pirate's Booty and Chunky Monkey. It's done."

"You did?" I ask. I push down the feeling of being left out. It stings a little, the idea of her and Makenna hanging out without me.

Ivy scrunches up her nose. "*You* were out with Lucas," she reminds me, flipping herself over so she's right side up again. "Speaking of things we really should discuss. Sounds like that joint family vacation could be a hot time this year."

I hesitate, not sure I really should let the M.J. conversation go so easily. I can't help but feel like I missed out on a best-friend window I didn't know was closing, like I wasn't there when she needed me and now it's too late.

"It was . . . nice," I admit finally. "But I guess I wonder if he's the one leaving the messages."

"Does that even matter?" Ivy asks. "If you like him?"

"I like whoever is leaving the clues."

Ivy sighs loudly, flips upside down one more time.

"Jules . . . ," she starts, sounding kind of exasperated.

"What?"

"It just seems to me maybe you're focusing too much on figuring out who this mystery collaborator is. I just want you to be sure you're focusing all that warm, gooey love energy on someone real."

"He *is* real." I sound like I'm trying to convince myself. I was up until the early hours of the morning writing the next section of "Untitled," not wanting to give him a chance to change his mind and disappear again. I was just so relieved I hadn't lost him. So grateful for another chance to get it right.

"Fine," Ivy allows, *"maybe.* But again, has anything this person said given you any reason to think they're Lucas or Calvin or my brother?"

"What about your brother?" Ryan interrupts, padding into the family room in a pair of slim-fit shorts and a T-shirt, a water bottle dangling from one hand. He's barefoot and sleepy-looking. Which looks good on him, not gonna lie.

"I was just saying how extraordinarily strong and buff and muscular you are. And how impressive in every way," Ivy fires back immediately. She's nothing if not awesome at deflecting around her brother.

He looks at her skeptically. "If you really had such

high regard for me, you'd give me a turn at the family room. I want to play a little Red Dead before dinner."

Ivy tilts her head to the side like, *Fair enough.* "Actually, I was hoping to get in a mani-pedi before the hordes descend on Lucy's." Ivy has been going to Lucy's since her mom used to let her tag along for mother-daughter manicures. Another thing we do not share in common. I don't love having my extremities fussed over.

She turns to me. "I think I already know the answer, but any interest, Jules?"

We're cool enough that I don't have to hesitate. "Not even a little bit."

Ryan looks at me. "If there isn't any nail art in your immediate future, you could hang here and help me figure out where to get some raccoon pelts?"

"Wow," I say with a grin. "Plastic on my nails or skinning critters in the virtual world. Never before have two such enticing options been laid out before me."

"An embarrassment of riches, truly," Ivy agrees. "I'll make it as quick as I can if you just want to hang out and wait for me here."

"Okay," I say.

She gets her bag, and I walk out to her car with her.

She turns to me once he's out of earshot.

"Is that okay?" she asks quietly. "It's not weird?"

"It's not weird. Is it for you?"

She smiles. "A little, yeah. But not bad. I'll be back soon."

I go inside to find Ryan has already powered up the game. He sits on the floor in front of the TV, and I get down next to him. It occurs to me that I've never been just with him in his house before. It's always been me and Ivy, with him around sometimes but not usually. It's cozy, the big poufs and pillows on the floor, the fluffy area rug, and him right next to me.

It's been a while since I've played Red Dead. Ryan expertly weaves his character on horseback around rocks and dodges a posse of bounty hunters on his trail. When he's dispatched them all, he holds the PS5 controller out in my direction.

"Here," he says, "you want to give it a try?"

"You want me to find your raccoon pelts for you?" I ask. "I think you definitely stand a better chance of getting what you need if you do it."

Ryan narrows his eyes, like he's expecting a trap. "Was that . . . antifeminist?" he asks with mock seriousness. "You could clear out a gang hideout up in

Hanging Dog Ranch if you'd rather. It's one of my favorites."

I laugh.

"Also enticing," I say, reaching for the controller. Our fingers brush as I take it. "Here, give me."

We decide on the raccoons after all. He walks me through how to get to the spot he's read about online. It's beside a river, shaded by trees, a gorgeous place I'd love to visit in real life.

"They come out at night," he says. It's quiet, and I fire up eagle eye to find the critters.

When you spot a raccoon, a little icon on the screen gives you its rating, from one to three stars. We can only use the three-star ones for the satchel he's hoping to craft. They're surprisingly hard to find.

Then I get unceremoniously eaten by a cougar.

Ryan snorts. "That's happened to me three times on this very spot," he admits, as I pass the controller back to him. "I've also been killed by more bounty hunters than I care to admit, accidentally became wanted for a crime I did not mean to commit, and been torn limb from limb by a bear."

I laugh. He's so animated as he talks about it. "Can I ask you something?" I say, shaking my head a little.

"Why do you love this game so much?"

I mean it as a throwaway line. But his eyes get big and serious.

"You really want to know?"

"I really want to know."

"And you promise not to laugh."

"Yes."

Ryan is quiet for a moment, eyes on the screen as he sets up camp, goes to sleep in-game to hasten the fall of another night. "When the game first came out, I wasn't that into the idea of it," he tells me. "Everyone was raving about it—the graphics, the gameplay, whatever. But I kind of hadn't loved the first one, so I was in no hurry to play this one. But then the pandemic came."

On the screen, he wakes up from sleep, takes down his camp, pets his horse.

"And?"

"And, okay, this is not a thing I say a lot, but I was lonely. Zoom school sucked, and I was never Mr. Super Social, and my friends either fell into the camp of 'screw it, live it up like nothing is happening,' which I knew I didn't want to do, or they were completely locked down, and there is only so much human interaction you can get via text. So we started playing RD

Online and that was kind of how we'd hang out. Them in their house, me in mine, all of us sitting around a campfire or whatever in the Red Dead world. And then I started to play single-player on my own." Then he looks back to the screen and takes a shot. Misses.

"I do not find it shocking that in the middle of a raging pandemic when just getting within six feet of another person could potentially kill them you felt lonely. I may even be able to relate," I say.

Ryan nods. "It was that first winter when there was no vaccine and my uncle was sick and we couldn't go see him and no one knew how long it would go or how bad it would be . . . I just got, like, invested in these characters." He stops, looks at me as if to gauge whether to keep going, then does. "Their way of life is ending, you know? The gunslinger era. And something was ending here, too, and I just . . . I don't know. It helped." He blows a breath out, looks embarrassed. "It sounds stupid when I say it all out loud like that."

"It doesn't, actually." The opposite; the truth is I'm a little stunned to find all this depth of feeling in someone who was a two-dimensional character for me for so long. "I think it's cool." It's not enough to grab up all that his words make me feel, but it's what I've got.

On the screen, the sun is coming up over the

mountains, the sky turning orange and pink and gold.

"I suck at the hunting part of this game," he confesses. "I always feel bad shooting things, which, *I know*, wrong choice of game." He smiles. "Or we could switch save files and go to Armadillo. They're having a cholera outbreak."

I laugh. "Enticing."

"Or we could go play some poker at a saloon," he suggests.

I smile. "Now here is where I'm going to be a real asset."

He hands me the controller one more time, motioning me closer, and for a perfect moment, we live in the gorgeous, dying Old West—just him and me, suspended in a world you can play over and over until you get it right.

You
Improbable
Billions of years in the making.
An atom floating in a distant star
Which burned and tore apart
And floated endlessly
Made its way to an implausible planet
And
After long slumbers and adventures
Into one cell
That met another cell
Among the many millions it could have been
A day
A year
A block
Before or after
And found its way in the stumbling world
That shows itself to be
Equal parts harsh and beautiful
Stark and whimsical
Heavy and hopeful,
Averting a thousand invisible possibilities
That would have made you someone else.
And became impossibly you, now,

The glittering, endless, stardust you
Of magic and veiled, unknowable things
That make you

The you whose light I want to soak in
And know.

sixteen

In class at Fairchild a few days later, Paige is handing back assignments. It's a poem I wrote after the quiet time with Ryan playing Red Dead, about the feelings of trying to find a new world in what's left of the old. I know what I wanted to say, but I'm not sure if I found all the words to say it. I wrote it from scratch three times, and edited the heck out of the final product. I'm not sure I got it right, but I knew it was the best I had to give.

Paige's assignments aren't the only thing I've been working on: ever since HappilyEverDrafter reappeared we've been volleying "Untitled" back and forth almost every day. I've added a bunch of new chapters, my pace picking up, and HappilyEverDrafter has matched it. And readers are taking notice. The first chapter got thirteen comments. Now they're in the dozens, with one recent entry getting over a hundred. I get private messages, too, readers asking me what's next, or suggesting things they'd like to see. Happily and I chat online every night, talking about story ideas, books we've read, things trending on social media, cute videos, and anything else that comes into our minds. But I still have no idea who he is. Just when I think a clue points in one direction, a different one totally contradicts it.

Paige stops by my desk, her bracelets giving off a hidden flash in the sunlight streaming through the window. "Jules, you have a sensitive and lyrical style. But this fell a little flat. You need to raise the stakes." I look at the paper. It's covered in purple handwriting, scratched out words, question marks, comments. An explosion in my chest. My head pulses.

She stops by Wyatt's seat next to me. Paige has seemed way into his writing from the start. When she compliments his work he responds with his clipped, aristocratic tone. I feel amoeba height.

She says to the girl with the undercut, "Beautiful

character work," before she gets too far away for me to hear more.

Of course I am never going to be good enough. I've been scribbling stupid phrases down and writing to HappilyEverDrafter and wasting my time when I should have been focusing on learning math or something I can actually translate into a real job. Something bankable that won't make me dependent on a stupid restaurant that may or may not meet with catastrophe at any moment. I need to build a life with a sturdy net beneath me, and writing is definitely *not* the way to that. I don't know what I've been thinking. For like a nanosecond, this class made me think I could be a writer. What an incredibly dumb thing to think.

Tears prick at my eyes, my throat. I wish I could evaporate. I don't know what I'm doing here. I am wasting my time and Paige's, who obviously just wants Ryan's incredible world-building and Wyatt's . . . whatever Wyatt is up to.

I leave class during the midway break. I know I shouldn't. I understand that I should get thicker skin, that one bad piece of feedback isn't everything. But I just need to be out in the world, not sitting there listening to people react to the latest reading. Just this once. I head south and cut through to Central Park, walking aimless and fast in the general direction of the Port Authority.

Central Park is dappled with sunlight, filled with joggers and rapacious bikers, moms with little kids, a guy inexplicably walking around in an elephant suit, head under his arm. Someone thrusts a flyer about endangered birds in my hands, and a guy plays a harmonica. The walk doesn't clear my head, not exactly, but it expands the world a little. In this city, millions of people are trying to build their own fiefdoms, each the hero of their own story. I'm just one of them. My anonymity, my smallness, is strangely comforting.

I get out of the park at Columbus Circle, then head down Fifth and cut across Forty-Second to the Port Authority, past the painted, bigger-than-life touristy places, the Madame Tussauds and the Dave & Buster's, the blaring sign promising *New York Gifts!*, lit up bright even though it's the middle of the day. Past the kids trailing after tired-looking parents, whining in Dutch, another set in Japanese, past the couple kissing, the taller of the girls running her hand tenderly through her partner's green hair, past an old guy in dress pants and suspenders and no shirt over the bony top half of his body, past the wafting pot smells and the AMC and the white NYPD SUVs with their blue lettering.

I go inside the Port Authority, then climb the narrow stairs up to the platform, which is gray and smoggy and hot. The level of the Port Authority where the buses arrive is just a parking lot speckled with glass cages, with lanes where the buses line up to swallow up tired, cranky, sometimes ruthless, grown-ups who think nothing of muscling past you to get on the bus first. They all clearly hate that their lives involve standing on these lines every day. Maybe this is going to be me one day, trapped in these glass cages every day because I wasn't smart or creative enough to make a writing dream come true.

I walk up to the glass jail—Gate 712, the bus people would probably prefer that I call it—and there are only about ten people waiting. Bad sign. A short line means a bus just left. Already the heat in the glass waiting area is uncomfortable; an open door lets in enough bus exhaust that I toy with the idea of bringing a carbon monoxide detector with me the next time.

"Hey, Jules."

I turn around in the direction of the sound. Ryan is leaning against a concrete pillar with his trusty messenger bag slung over his shoulder. A green drink is melting in his hand. My heart leaps with happiness at the sight of him, a surprising and pleasant feeling.

"Have you been waiting for me?" I ask him. It's way past our usual bus, so it's unusual that he's here at this hour. I check my phone. My sulk through the park took almost two hours.

"What? No," Ryan says, scrunches up his eyebrows, then adds, "Not actively?"

I laugh. I have no idea what that means, and he doesn't elaborate.

A bus pulls up before I can answer. We climb into its cool interior. Ryan lets me lead the way down the aisle. I pick a row on the left and take window seat. I've learned he likes aisle, which means we each get our favorite when we sit together. The bus pulls away from the gate half-full, snakes its way through the looping roadways, and finally makes it into the Lincoln Tunnel.

"You okay?" Ryan asks, his voice close in the dimness of the tunnel. "You kind of barged out."

I think about lying, telling him everything's fine. Just a couple of weeks ago, I would have done exactly that. But I reach in my bag, where I've shoved Paige's voluminous notes on my work, and hand it over. He scans the paper, squinting in the yellow half-light and turning it sideways to make out one of the notes that is off to an angle.

"She hated it so much she had to write in multiple directions," I say miserably.

Ryan smiles at that, still looking at my poem. "I mean . . . it's not great."

My mouth drops open. "Umm . . . thanks?"

"I mean the notes!" He amends quickly. "Not the poem. The poem is . . . good, actually. I really like it."

I let out a beleaguered sigh. Him being nice about it doesn't help.

"I'm not just saying that," Ryan insists. "Look, she's tough. You should see mine." He reaches into his bag and hands me his. It's got notes in the same scrawled purple hand, almost as many as mine. "I think she just wants us to bring our A game, you know? I guess that isn't always easy."

I lean my head back against the seat. "I feel like a failure. Like I thought I could do this, but I can't."

"You can. That piece you read in class the other day. Let me see if I remember right. 'In the river, water eddies around my feet, crystal and familiar, but never the same way twice.' I loved that. I thought about it all that night. How things can feel the same but are actually always changing."

I look at his face, warmth spreading from my clavicles down my arms and chest, a feeling of safety, a glimmer of hope. Learning about him has been like seeing a sketch suddenly fill in with vibrant color, like those sped-up videos on Instagram of artists making paintings. He's so different from the snarky brother-type I thought I knew. There have been a hundred different moments, the gentle way he's let me sit when there was only one seat, the voice he'd use to read to me from a new book he'd found, the earnest hope in his eyes when he told me the idea he'd had for fixing a plot hole in his work, willing me to like it but also asking me to be as real as I can be.

When we get off the bus, he walks me all the way home.

<u>More alternate endings to **Romeo and Juliet** . . .</u>

Option 5: Romeo waited long enough to see, wow, okay, Juliet's not dead, <u>cool</u>, and they live happily ever . . . Wait, <u>did we get married in our teens</u>? They are now in their mid-twenties and Romeo is hanging out too much with the guys and Juliet resents him and . . . almost-broken-up but rediscovering each other trope.

Option 6: Aliens land in Verona. They are looking for a shady place to take a nap, and it turns out that the Capulet family tomb is exactly what they're looking for (Lichen content? Correct temperature?). Anyway, they come upon the whole mess, and Romeo convinces them to take him and Juliet up with them where they can live away from their overbearing families.

It's like outlaw cowboys, but in space.

seventeen

Lucas catches me scrubbing the bottom of a crusty saltshaker during a particularly dead afternoon shift a couple of days later.

"You are in dire need of some fun," he says.

"You just said a mouthful, sister," I retort in my best impression of some old movie whose name I've forgotten.

"I may have a cure for that."

I tip my head at him, intrigued.

"You still have that picnic blanket in your trunk?"

I nod.

"So I think it's outdoor movie time. How does that sound?"

I can't think of anything I'd rather do right now. I *love* outdoor movies, and of course Lucas knows this. When our shift is over, we head over to my car. He saw a flyer about this outdoor movie in a neighboring town, and he punches the address of the park it's in into his GPS.

If Alderton is sleepy and homey, Jonesburg fancies itself cosmopolitan, its manicured downtown lined with old-timey gas lamps and uniform-looking store-fronts with green signs and gold lettering. They have a train into the city, not just a bus like Alderton, and the downtown is built around what looks like a Victorian train station. A couple of blocks away from the main commercial district, there's a rambling old park full of ancient trees that look like they've seen everything. Every Sunday in the summer, they set up a big, outdoor screen and project a movie.

This week's movie is *Shrek*, which I happen to know is one of Lucas's favorites.

Unironically.

And—okay, fine—it's possibly one of my favorites, too.

I've brought a bag filled with sanguchitos from Las Heras, a few cans of soda, and some apples. Lucas spreads out a blue-and-white checked blanket we find in my trunk, smoothing out its red edge, and I lay out the food. He takes off his backpack and reveals a big bag of butter popcorn and enough Twizzlers to feed a small battalion.

"Not to toot my own horn or anything," he murmurs, lying back on his elbows as the movie begins, "but this was an awesome idea."

"It was," I say with a smile. "I keep meaning to come to Jonesburg more."

"I meant *Shrek*." He smiles. "Here's a question: If you could be any character in this movie, who would you be?"

I think about it for a moment, watching as a cluster of little kids plays off to the right of the screen and a mother runs after a toddler. People are watching the movie but also not, murmuring softly and laughing and passing around snacks.

"Probably Donkey," I decide finally.

Lucas nods like that tracks. "You do have big Donkey vibes, actually."

"Uh-huh." I lob a kernel of popcorn in his direction. "What about you?"

He ponders it for way longer than a cartoon character question should take. "I'm Fiona," he says. I lift an eyebrow.

"How so?"

"I mean . . ." He looks serious, suddenly, like we're not talking about a kids' movie anymore. "I don't know, forget it. I'm not trying to . . . never mind. Can I say Lord Farquaad instead?"

"I mean, you could," I reply, "But that's literally the last character that would fit you. To start with, you're kind of a giant now. Also: not a villain."

He looks down, takes a swig of his soda, then clears his throat. "I mean . . . don't think this is silly, okay? When I said Fiona I was thinking . . . I sometimes have this feeling of walking around and there's a whole different type of person inside me, but everyone is reacting to me like the person they see on the outside, you know? The person they think I am. Or want me to be."

"Did something happen?"

He tips his head back. "My parents are bugging me about committing to the accounting thing. It doesn't help that my brother is doing so well. Like, they stop a hair short of 'Why can't you be more like Jorge?' but it's always there."

I know about this. I've overheard my mom tell my dad about conversations with Lucas's mom, about what they expect from their sons. Lucas loves soccer and wants to try to get recruited to play in college, but his parents want him to focus on something more serious. It's been a conversation in his family for years. A career in sports is at least as much of a long shot as one in writing, and that's a tough sell in an immigrant family. When you've left behind all your family to take a chance at a better life, it seems to be a pattern that you want the safe stuff for your kids: law, medicine, accounting. My parents are a little better than Lucas's, but it's there with them, too.

"It's not even like I'm opposed being an accountant!" Lucas continues. "I mean, I like numbers fine. I could be good at it. I like going to the office with my dad. I know there's this whole stereotype about accounting, but my dad is cool and seems happy. It wouldn't be a bad life. I just want to take time to figure out if it's *my* life, you know? But they seem to think I've got to have it all nailed down, like, right now. I know they're trying to look out for me, but I wish they'd back off a little."

Neither one of us says anything for a moment, Shrek stomping around loudly on the screen. Lucas and I are huddled close together so we can talk but not bother anybody around us; I can smell him, the same soap and shampoo his mom has been buying since we were little kids.

I look up at the stars, doing their best to shine through. There's something profoundly comforting about being with someone who gets it all: my story, the unique feeling of "neither here nor there" you get by growing up with parents from somewhere else, the desire to reach for a goal you're not sure you can attain. The burning wish to try anyway. If there's anyone who knows where I come from—who knows exactly how it feels—it's Lucas, with his thousands of hours logged with my parents and the hundreds of dinners and side-by-side moments of restaurant crunch time.

I wriggle a little closer on the picnic blanket, the heat of his warm, familiar body bleeding straight through my clothes. "I'm really glad we did this," I murmur, so quiet he has to lean in to hear me.

He smiles at me. "Me too."

Jaime and Lucesita are still awake when I get home, the two of them sprawled barefoot on the couch in their pajamas. Lucesita is flipping idly through a graphic novel she's read at least a dozen times before, but Jaime, I note with a flicker of big-sister satisfaction, is more than three-quarters of the way through *Lord of the Flies*.

"I still totally hate it and can think of other ways to comment on how mean people can be to each other," he announces, when he catches me looking. "But I am almost done."

I grin at him, I can't help it, pride and affection and an achy nostalgia for something that isn't even over yet all tangled up in my chest. "You're a good one, Jaime Talavera," I tell him, blowing him a kiss as I head up the stairs to my bedroom. He rolls his eyes but also looks kind of pleased.

I log into StoriedZone, suck in a quiet breath: HappilyEverDrafter has posted a chapter, and there's a message from him to go with it:

I've been thinking a lot about whether our characters are meant to be, or we're just writing them that way. It's hard to know, right?

It's Lucas. It has to be Lucas, right?

I write and erase a thousand different responses. I pace around my room for a while. I spend half an hour on the internet trying to find the perfect *Shrek* quote for the occasion, but it turns out that—shockingly—Shrek isn't the most romantic movie ever written, and at least half of the lines are fart jokes. I almost write back, *Onions have layers. Ogres have layers*, just for the sake of saying something.

Finally, I send back a single heart, in a desperate attempt to communicate everything I'm thinking but can't find the words for. It's not sparkling writing, but it's true.

"Ten Movies to Know Me: A Love Story"

Zelda Diaz knew two things: ~~jelly beans sour candy ice cream flavors~~ baseball cards and movies. The former she knew because it had been a thing she'd shared with her dad before he'd ~~packed up~~ ~~croaked~~ ~~died~~ ~~disappeared~~ ~~moved on~~ left. The latter she knew because she worked at the one lone movie theater in her county and sat quietly in the back while every second-run film and old classic played. ~~Premiered?~~

<u>Wait, doesn't she have to work? Do movie theaters even have, like, bouncers anymore? (Note: Google? Maybe ask Jaime?)</u>

To figure out: how does she use this "ten movies to know me" device with a stranger? <u>Is</u> he a stranger? Are all my stories secret-admirer stories? Maybe Zelda Diaz doesn't work in a movie theater and she gets sent to boot camp by her parents who think she's out of control and it's "Ten Movies to Plot My Escape"?

"Ten Movies to Survive My Parents"
"Ten Movies to Make It Through the Summer"
"Ten Movies to Take with Me on My Space
Adventure," by Juliet in cryostasis

<u>Ugh. Am I even a writer?</u>

eighteen

Abuela invites me over a couple of afternoons later, so I grab some leftover milanesas from the restaurant and make the quick drive over to her place. It's late July now, the deepest, ripest part of summer; the air is hot and still and quiet, like there's weight to it, the scentless hot pink roses outside Abuela's apartment building buzzing with bees moving languidly in the heat.

I'm half expecting Calvin to be sitting in the living room when I arrive, watching *La Periodista* while simultaneously eating chocolate croissants and assembling an IKEA shoe rack, or, who knows, a drone or some other random and unnecessary thing. But Abuela is by herself in the kitchen, pulling a batch of bollitos out of the oven.

I can't decide if I'm disappointed. I'm obviously not disappointed in the bollitos, fist-sized balls of dough with anise and a crust of sugar on top that I could eat every day for the rest of my life. But I may be a bit disappointed that my string of not-so-chance encounters with my grandmother's handiest, best-looking neighbor seems to have come to an end. We haven't talked at all since the night of Ivy's party. Part of me thinks that's for the best, that when he looked at me all he saw was some boring Jersey stereotype who lives for the mall and the shore. But another part of me remembers how easy he was to talk to before that one weird night, how much I appreciated his let's-see-what-happens view of life, so different from mine, a counterpoint that felt crucial at the time.

It's fine, I tell myself firmly, sitting down at the kitchen table and helping myself to a bollito, still so deliciously warm. That's what fiction is for, right? I can always dream up some better version of him later on and spend as much time with that one as I want.

"How's the writing going?" Abuela asks. She pours me a glass of Sprite and sits down beside me. She looks ready for a shoot of *Better Homes & Grandmas*: every hair in place, her makeup dewy and bright. "I bet your teacher loves you."

"I . . . yeah," I say, shaky and not at all convincing. "Sort of."

I mean to leave it at that, but she fixes me with that Abuela look of hers. Before I know it I find myself unloading everything that's been happening, Paige's less-than-encouraging comments. The fact that it's pretty apparent the other students seem to show more promise than I do. How hard I've been trying for what seems like no reason.

"I just keep feeling like maybe I don't have what it takes, you know?" I ask her, popping a piece of bollito into my mouth, the top part with the sugar crust I always like to leave for last. "Like I'm wasting all this time when meanwhile the restaurant . . ."

Abuela holds a hand up. "First of all, the restaurant is your parents'," she says in a sterner voice than she ever uses. "It's their job to figure out what to do with that. Second of all, who is this Paige Bingham, anyway? Maybe I'll tell her a thing or two."

I laugh. I wouldn't put it past my abuela to hop on a bus to the city to give *New York Times* bestselling author Paige Bingham a piece of her mind on my behalf. "She's a really famous writer, Abuela. She's very good."

Abuela looks deeply unimpressed. "Pfft," she counters. "Famous. Who cares about famous? It's a popularity contest, writing? No." She waves a hand. "What about your story on the website?" she asks me. "The one you said you were working on with a friend."

"That's going well, I think," I admit. "People seem to like it. But more than that . . . I like it. I feel confident when I'm working on it. I feel like myself. Like I'm thinking and writing about things that matter to me." I feel like myself when I'm talking to Happily-EverDrafter, too, though I don't mention that part.

"There are always going to be reasons not to go for big dreams, m'hija," Abuela says. "There are always going to be . . . como se dice en inglés? Blocks road."

"Roadblocks," I add gently.

"They put the words all in the wrong order in this country. Yes, roadblocks. And people who don't understand what you're trying to say. If every writer you loved stopped when someone told them they weren't good, even this Paige como-se-llama, I bet there would be no books in libraries. They keep going, even when it's hard. That's life, no matter what you want to do, a restaurant, a book, anything. If you want to be a periodista, for example."

I roll my eyes and laugh at Abuela's unsubtle hint. I haven't watched an episode of her novela with her in a bit. I grab another bollito, and we head over to the TV to watch an episode of *La Periodista*, holding our breath as Mabel gets herself out of a tight spot with one of the gangster's goons using nothing but her wit and charm. After the episode is done, Abuela shoos me out the door. She's got a date to go hiking on the Palisades with the sweater-vest guy she met at bingo.

She gives me a long hug before I go. "Eres la más hermosa. And the smartest, and the hardest working," she tells me. "Nothing can stop you but you."

I close my eyes and breathe in her smell, sugary from the bollitos, a hint of Heno de Pravia and the discount fabric softener she loves.

We say our goodbyes, taking the stairs back down to the lobby. I'm almost to my car when there's a voice behind me: "Jules?"

I turn around. Calvin is standing on the edge of the parking lot in jeans and an old punk band T-shirt, squinting in the afternoon sunlight.

"Hey," I say after a beat.

"Hey." He crosses the distance between us and meets me at my car, tucking his hands into his pockets. "Visiting your abuela?"

"Nah, just like hanging out in this apartment building lobby. The architecture," I deadpan.

Calvin smiles at that. "It's a good one," he agrees, looking back in the lobby's direction in mock approval. Then he takes a deep breath. "I guess I owe you an apology."

My first instinct is to tell him not to worry about it. That what happened at Ivy's party was no big deal. But then I do a thing I do pretty often, which is wonder how I'd want Lucesita to stand up for herself. So I decide not to let him off the hook that easily.

"Okay," I say, since *I owe you an apology* is not, in fact, an apology. "Go ahead."

"I'm sorry," he says. "I was just, like . . . not ready for all that, I guess? Like whiplash or something. First being alone with you and feeling like I had a beat on who you seem to be. Then being in that huge house around all those people, and it was all very . . ." He squeezes one shoulder up, like he's trying to gesture the word. "Suburban? A mix of 'I don't want this' and also 'I know I'll never have this'? I guess I keep telling myself it's been fine moving here. And it *has* been, for the most part. After all, I'm like a little over an hour away from my old neighborhood if I'm desperate to go there. But it's been an adjustment in ways I didn't anticipate. The party sort of made that obvious."

He looks off in the direction of the falling sun and says, "There's nothing basic about you, Jules. The opposite. I think you're pretty incredible, to be honest." He clears his throat, taking his hands out of his pockets and straightening up a little. "So. I just wanted to say all that." He's quiet, and the silence is awkward, so he adds, "So I've said it now, so . . ." He trails off.

I stare at him, blinking. "Wow," I finally manage. "That was kinda good, as apologies go."

Calvin laughs. "My mom is very serious about taking accountability," he confesses. "No half-assed apologies around her."

"She sounds like a pretty cool woman."

"She is," Calvin agrees. "You guys would like each other."

I think of saying that I'd like to meet her someday, but for some reason I stop myself.

Both of us are quiet for a moment; it feels like a natural end to the conversation, and I'm about to say my goodbyes when he speaks again. "Can I ask you something?" he blurts, the words coming quickly, like possibly he's nervous about getting them out in time. "What are you doing right now? Not to meet my mom," he clarifies, laughing at what must have been a weird expression on my face. "I just mean to hang out for a little bit. I was actually about to take a walk, maybe get ice cream or whatever. If, you know. You wanted to tag along."

I lift an eyebrow. "Looking for a buddy, huh?"

Calvin smiles. "Always," he says in mock seriousness, and holds out his hand for mine.

If I had the power to name this
        I'd remake the world
And scatter the heart of us
        like dandelion seeds
Wished and given
        sought and offered.
I would feel at home everywhere
        if I knew how.
And never be in a house too big for me
        balled up like a seed
Wishing to fly.

nineteen

We go to Lucas's family's lake house the first week of August, just like always. It's one of the few real vacations my parents ever take. We mention them going to Maine when Jaime wants lobster rolls. Even in the best of years, business is slow in August, so they close the restaurant for seven full days, drinking wine on the deck with Lucas's parents and taking long walks through the woods while the rest of us cannonball off the dock.

The house is two hours north of the city, a big, rambling place, with blue-gray wooden siding with white trim and two levels of decks overlooking the strip of sandy beach. It's got a small, floating buoy where we launch kayaks on the left side of the lakefront, plus a big wooden dock on the right where the water deepens. It's got five bedrooms, a game room, and a pool table, which, despite years of trying, no one has ever gotten any better at. Below the lower deck, at ground level, there's a hot tub and a roomy, four-person hammock. My favorite spot is the big firepit outside, between the house and the small strip of beach, where we all sit around for hours and tell stories and roast marshmallows.

The first official act is dinner out on the big, sprawling dining table on the deck. Lucas's dad and mine man the barbecue, my dad with ubiquitous Red Bull in hand. The rest of us help with dishes and sides, like the ensalada rusa. There's not a burger or hot dog in sight ("Don't even bring up such a sacrilege!" Lucas's dad jokes). It's all Argentinian asado, mollejas on skewers, which my mom brought up from home in an ice-packed cooler, churrasco, costillas, morcillas I can't bring myself to eat but whose smell is straight-up home. It's like the restaurant has taken its show on the road. I feel the squeeze of the heart I've been experiencing every time I think about the restaurant now, our food and memories all bound up with it. I push through it as I do my part setting the table and laying a rustic cloth napkin at each place setting.

Finally, we sit. Lucas's dad is at the head of the table, my parents to his left, his wife to his right. Jaime and Lucesita come next, one on each side. There's no kids' table for us. Jorge and his girlfriend, Amelie, are next to each other, on the same side as my parents. Lucas is on the end and I'm catty-cornered to him.

I like having Amelie here, because not only is she awesome and sweet, she also takes all the parental attention away from me and Lucas. We might as well be at the kids' table, or Mars, as the raucous speculation fires up on the parental side. They want to know everything about how Jorge and Amelie met, about her family in Germany, about her studies. They ask all the cringey "So when are we getting an invitation to the wedding?" questions. I almost feel bad for Jorge, but he knows the meaning of bringing a girl home, at least to our parents, especially on something as big as a family vacation. This is no quick Sunday dinner. . . . This is commitment. Or at least it's being read that way. But when I look at Jorge, the way he gently makes sure Amelie's glass is always full and trips getting up to get her another costilla, he looks like there's nothing else he'd rather be doing than seeing her here with his family.

I lean into Lucas, "Jorge likes her a lot, huh?"

I'm expecting him to gripe about it, or at the very least make fun, but Lucas only nods.

"When you know, you know, I guess," he says. Then he reaches for the pitcher of water to refill my empty glass.

Dinner takes hours, as always. Then we move down to the fire. The grown-ups drink wine. Somehow they get into singing old songs from when they were kids, trying to remember all the lyrics. After like a half hour of that, Jaime and Lucesita go inside. A little bit later, Jorge and Amelie excuse themselves. The grown-ups are getting a little silly. Lucas leans over to me, "Let's get out of Dodge before they start getting into fútbol or inflation."

"Hey, Ma, I'm going to go inside," I say, loud, to get their attention.

She's clearly tipsy. Beyond, actually. She's not much of a drinker, and she's been on the wine pretty steadily all night. "Wait, wait, wait, before you go," she says, raising a glass. "To our two hardest workers. Keeping us afloat. Well, I don't know about *afloat*. But I wanted to thank you two for everything you're doing, despite . . ." She trails off, her eyes glistening.

My father gently touches her elbow. There's an undercurrent to her words. I've been enjoying watching her let loose, move her hips as she brought platters over from the kitchen, top up her glass. But now there's another edge to it.

She pulls her elbow away from my dad and slurs, "What, Nicolas? I'm trying to thank them. They work so hard. And it's . . . I mean, who knows where we're going to be next year? So we might as well drink to them now."

The words hang in the air, leaden and foreboding. *Who knows where we're going to be next year?* There's an awkward silence, the only sound is my mom slurping down her wine.

Maribel says, "Ay, vos, where else are we going to be next year? Right here is where. To the kids!" She raises her glass. The men follow. They all sip quietly, eyes fixed on each other, willing the moment to pass.

Lucas puts his hand on my back the way he did that night on our recon mission to Tierra del Fuego. I nod.

"Okay!" he calls out with fake cheerfulness. "We're going inside! You're in charge." It's a callback to a joke my dad always makes at the restaurant when he heads out for last-minute supplies. It doesn't feel funny, just sad.

We walk toward the hot tub, past the outdoor shower, and to the door to my room. Mine is the only one down on this level. The entrance to it requires us to walk around the tall stilts the house is on and into a small alcove that leads into a beachy mudroom, strewn with pool noodles and water shoes. The sounds of the grown-ups are muffled.

Lucas leans in close, like they still might be able to hear us, which they almost surely can't. The room is only lit up by the glow from outside. He whispers. "It'll do her good, to let everything go for a week. With a clear head, we'll think of something."

"I know," I say. I definitely *don't* know, but I appreciate his attempt at encouragement.

I look up. He is flame-lit, half in shadow, his voice a rasp, his hand still brushing against me. We are at the door to my room now. His hair is in more disarray than usual, still lake-kissed. I have a wild urge to brush a curl back away from his forehead. I tip my face up to him. His nose is shiny from the heat. He's letting off waves of heat, too, like he soaked up sun and is now emanating it. He is so close. *So close.* What would he do if I just . . .

We hang there, suspended. He takes his bottom lip gently in his teeth, lets it go. I watch, rapt.

"Okay, then. Good night," he stammers. It feels like popping a suction cup off a wet wall, a jarring removal, an abrupt end to everything that was going on a second ago.

"Good night, Lucas," I say, and slip into my room, my breath still caught.

<u>File under: rewritten endings.</u>

If the world had edges
I could find you at a corner
Measure from a seam
And have you not be somewhere else
On this rambling blue marble,

If moments were solid
and not smoke
I could mold them into
A kiss that doesn't end
And your lips on mine.

If I could crack open
And let in the world
Messy and new
I would trade our past
For our future

But the world is round
And moments are smoke
And the future
is still out of reach

twenty

The days pass, lazy but overcrowded, so that it's impossible to get any alone time with Lucas. But my disappointment about that goes away on the third day, when my aunt Chiqui arrives. She is joining us from Argentina, which I've been looking forward to since I found out about it. We usually fly down to see her, and the whole extended family there, all my aunts and uncles and cousins, in the lull after New Year's. We've skipped the trip the last few years, though. At first, it was because of the pandemic, though I'm pretty sure this year it was about cash.

"Pero mirate a vos, sos una mujer," Aunt Chiqui

says now, reaching out to tuck a strand of hair behind my ear. She's been telling me I'm a woman now since I was about twelve. She's my favorite aunt, always up for a party, one of the most hilarious storytellers I've ever met. She has the capacity to make a visit to the grocery store sound like a frolic. She's the only one of my parents' siblings who isn't married. Argentina, or at least *my* family in Argentina, is more conservative about morals than most everyone I know here, and being an unmarried woman in their circles doesn't fly. So Chiqui is a source of some worry for my grandmother (my mom's mom, not Abuela Bubbles). She's been trying to move to the US for about ten years now, and my mom has claimed her as a sibling to put her in line for a green card. But immigration wait times doubled during the pandemic, and she's been on the list for years.

"Y mi Americanito esperandome," she'll usually joke. She swears her true love is here waiting somewhere in the States, but her not being able to get a green card is keeping them apart.

She and my mom and Maribel spend most of the morning out on the deck drinking mate and catching up on gossip and family stories. There is usually a lengthy discussion of the British royal family, for reasons I can't fathom. In the lull before dinner I finally catch Chiqui alone. I follow her into her make-shift bedroom.

"How pretty you are. You don't forget us, right?" she says after giving me yet another hug.

"No, Tía Chiqui," I say.

It is a preoccupation of hers, whether we remember the ones we left back home. She fears she's like an old hope written on flimsy paper that disappears in water. She's not right. But she's not entirely wrong, either.

I ask her about my cousins and my abuela, my mother's mom. She regales me with a tale of catching my seventy-something-year-old abuela up on a ladder. But I have a specific thing I want to ask her about. Finally, at what feels like the right moment, I get to it.

"Chiqui, remember before my mom left Argentina, a boy who wanted to get to know her? A boy who left notes at the ferretería?" Because she wants to move to the US, Chiqui's been studying English for a long time, and hers is pretty good.

Her face is a panoply of expressions for a split second, then she gets it placid again. "I don't think I remember that," she says. But her bored, studied look makes it obvious she's keeping something from me. She has zero poker face.

"Tía, ever since she told me that story I've been worried that my mother chose wrong. I mean, you know I love el Papi. I would never hurt him by talking about this in front of him. But I wonder if she did the right thing. And I think you know."

"Claro que no, you shouldn't say that around your father. What a thing to think." She squares off at me, hands on hips.

"She had *love*, real passionate love, looking for her. And she left it behind and let life happen to her."

"She has love right here," she says, putting her finger on my collarbone.

I shake my head. "You know what I mean."

"What's this really about, m'hijita? This is not only about your parents."

I take a seat on the bed. "It's kind of a long story," I say.

"My favorite kind," she says, sitting down beside me.

So I tell her. About HappilyEverDrafter. About Calvin and how he makes me want to be more daring. About safe, familiar Lucas. And about Ryan and all the depth I hadn't seen.

"I mean, Mom could have had a totally different life with that guy. She could have been a totally different *person*. And I could be a different person with each of these boys. I could be spontaneous and carefree and live out of a camper with Calvin while it's cool and we're both into it, however long that might be. Or I could stay behind and run the restaurant with someone I've known all my life and be one of those little old couples who have only ever loved one person their whole life. Or Ryan and I could . . . become a literary power couple, hosting fabulous book launches and . . . getting a cabin in an Irish fishing village . . ." I trail off. There I go, getting carried away with my romantic fantasies. *My specialty.*

I add, "How do I know which of these versions of me I want to be? Which one is right?"

She takes my hand. "I have a question. I think this for myself, too. Why do you worry so much about getting things right?"

This question stops me. "I don't know."

"I think, sometimes, about what it's like to come from people who have been struggling for so long, you know? My grandparents moving to Argentina after the Spanish Civil War, looking for a better life. And then your parents coming here, and hopefully one day I'll be able to come here, too. It's like a big weight, carrying all these generations of worries with us, don't you think?"

I nod.

Tía Chiqui leans in and cups my face gently, kisses me on both cheeks. "The question isn't which boy is right for you," she tells me. "The question is which boy helps you be the best version of yourself. Or, an even bigger question, what version of yourself do you want to be, independent of them all? You don't need anyone to help you have any specific kind of life. Take it from this frustrated romantic. Just pick a life and go have it."

I take a long beat in silence. I know she means everything she says. I also know she's trying to get me off the topic of who left the notes for my mom all those years ago.

"Just tell me who he was," I add softly.

"I can't," she says, a tacit acknowledgment that she does know. "Talk to your mother."

I spend most of the afternoon doing cannonballs off the dock with Lucesita and Jaime, the sibling time I didn't know I needed. As night is falling, we come inside.

My dad says, "I have a surprise!" He's carrying a box he brought in from the car. "I figured we could broaden the repertoire this year, especially with my cuñadita querida here with us! I had some home videos digitized."

It's a thing we do every year, watch the old home movies. But there are some older ones we haven't seen because they used to be on VHS.

Lucas hooks up his laptop to the big TV in the great room. A video starts to play. It's my parents, faces so young and unlined it takes me a minute to recognize them. They're in a space that's down to the studs . . . where is that? The light streams in from windows but there doesn't seem to be electric lights overhead. My father is up on a ladder, my mother is dancing in overall shorts, a hammer slung from a loop at her hip.

The restaurant. *My God, that's when they were building the restaurant.*

I've never seen this video before. There's no sound, for some reason, but my mother, her hair piled at her crown, speaks something to the camera, laughing, then blows a kiss. I long to know what it is. What could be making her that happy?

The video cuts, My dad holds up a piece of drywall. El Maestro helps him hoist it up. I had no idea El Maestro was there even before the kitchen was. My mother must be holding the camera, and as the drywall starts to slip out of my dad's hand and pushes him and El Maestro back, the camera gets shaky, put down on the ground askew. It catches only their bottom halves as she runs toward them to help. A few seconds pass. Then my mom's legs are lifted off the floor in what must be a hug, and my dad spins her around.

My throat fills with the tension of tears. They were so happy. So filled with hope. As if Lucas can see what I'm feeling, he bumps my knee with his. It's an unspoken *it's okay*.

The video changes again. It's here at the lake house, on the deck. The lake is misty in the distance, the far shore obscured. I'm maybe eight, in a little pink sundress I remember loving, my hair still wet from being freshly washed, up in a high ponytail. Lucas's hair is even longer than it is now, a mop of curls, and he's in cargo shorts and a dinosaur T-shirt, his face pudgier than I remember it. We are dancing. Tango, we're dancing tango. Choppy, childish, laughing and stepping on each other's feet.

I'd forgotten all about this. When we were kids, our parents were unduly obsessed with making sure we took tango lessons. Which is odd, because I've literally never seen anyone in my family in Argentina dance tango. It's what Americans think Argentinians stand around doing, but that's not my experience.

"You're the cutest!" Amelie says, and claps.

Lucas looks at me sheepishly. It is disconcerting to be watching these tiny versions of ourselves here. This one does have sound, and the tinny notes of Gotan Project play in the background. We're small and clearly missing the passion of the dance, but we're pretty proficient. Those classes went on for years.

Suddenly, it flashes in my mind. I can't believe I haven't thought of it before. Ever since we saw Tierra del Fuego's band, a draw I knew we couldn't afford, I've been trying to figure out what we might do to give customers an excuse to come back.

"Oh my God! I know what we can do! Tango Night! Out on the deck behind the restaurant. One cover buys you all you can eat asado, then we do a tango demonstration and give a free lesson! Something to give patrons a new reason to come and check out the food. Maybe get the local paper to cover it."

My dad looks delighted. My mom does, too, but mixed with something else. "Tango instructors are expensive, m'hija. We're not in a place where we . . ." She trails off.

"*We'll* do it," Lucas volunteers. "Jules and I will." He offers me a smile that's just this side of bashful. "I mean, you remember most of it, right? YouTube can help with the rest, I'm sure. Just, like, the first few times, until we raise enough money for actual instructors." He raises his eyebrows hopefully, like he really wants me to like the idea. "What do you think?"

I feel the first excitement for the restaurant I've felt in a long time. Not because I think we're going to revolutionize the world of tango, or restaurants, for that matter. But because it's something to try, a step toward trying to change things.

"Let's do it," I say. Lucas stands up and mock-dramatically tangoes me across the room to the deck while the whole family cheers.

twenty-one

Lucas and I are out on the dock early in the morning. The sky is barely cracked with light. The dock is the farthest you can get from the throng of people here, but it's still within view of the great room. There's at least a fifty percent chance our moms are behind the glass doors, shoulder to shoulder, gripping coffee cups and commenting on how cute we are. Knowing moms are all up in the mix is part of being from families like ours. It's annoying but unavoidable.

"You ready?"

"I mean, I guess," I say, connecting my phone to

his Bluetooth speaker and setting them both down on the dock.

After the idea last night, I was filled with a burst of energy: I looked up the old songs and created a playlist. I got online to look for a proper costume I could afford with tip money, which this summer isn't a lot. I spent hours looking at photos of tango dancers, then researching ways to make a dance demonstration fun. The key is audience participation, the internet informs me.

"Though, fair warning: I'm pretty sure I'm about to completely embarrass myself."

But Lucas shakes his head. "Not possible," he says softly, holding his hand out as the familiar bandoneón tones begin. "It's just me."

I take a breath. Lucas stands in front of me, holds out his arms. I step into them. He pulls me in but not too close, tentative, trying to feel out the space between us. I pull in closer.

For me, Argentina is all about wishing for something that once was, or could have been, and I think that's why tango reaches in so deep. Argentina, and tango, are inherited memories, wistfulness for things I never lived, memories borrowed from my parents, bigger and more grand than anything in my own life. As soon as the music starts, I'm somewhere else. Lucas steps in, begins the pattern; he's doing the boxy, basic step, but it's a start. We're doing it. He hasn't stepped on me. We haven't fallen into the water. Although I'm wondering if the dock was the best idea.

The next song comes on. He pulls me in a little closer, which makes his lead better. I surrender to the flow of it. There's an exhilaration that comes from letting myself be in tune this way, letting my body feel what the next step is instead of having my mind dictate it. It was one of the things I liked about dance, I remember, that moment when I was able to leave my mind behind and let my body intuit. On the next turn, I loop my leg around his, a flashy move that we'll need to master for a demonstration. He raises his eyebrows in surprise, pulls off a tighter spin in response. I smile. I close my eyes and picture us on the night of the demonstration: me in slicked-back hair and a slit dress, him in all-dark clothes, a faceless group around us cheering us under the patio lights and the stars.

We may be able to pull this off.

We dance half a dozen more songs until my heart rate is up and his lip is sweaty and the sun pierces the trees. Everyone will be up soon, and we're on breakfast duty this morning.

"I have a good feeling about this," he says.

"Me too," I say.

"It feels different here this year, doesn't it?"

I nod. "It feels different . . . lately."

I want to say something more. Something about messages? Something so that if he is HappilyEver-Drafter he knows it's okay to tell me.

"You've been a part of my story for so long," I say. "I like this new chapter."

I glance up to look in his eyes. He holds my gaze.

I try to communicate telepathically. *Please, say it. Please tell me if it's you.*

"I like this new chapter, too," he says. "And most of all I want to see what happens next."

He keeps looking in my eyes as if considering my unspoken request. I lean my shoulder on his upper arm, his eyes a tractor beam pulling me in. He moves in my direction, so small it's almost imperceptible, but also closing nearly all the distance between us in a way that catches my breath and makes the sun sparkle more on the lake. My eyes begin to close, all on their own, as I tilt my face up to meet him.

A burst of giggles breaks out alarmingly close. I whip around.

"¿Viste? ¡Que hermosos!" Our moms are literally at the start of the dock, where it meets land, holding mugs and looking at us.

"Ma!" Lucas bellows.

"What? We're just having our coffee," says Maribel. "Although I did want to say that your corrida is looking good. Your adornos . . . not so much yet, sweetheart. But you'll get there. Practice makes perfect."

Jaime and Lucesita are inside the French doors, giggling.

Lucas stands up. The moment is so totally blown. He helps me up, and we stomp off to the house to the sound of our moms laughing.

Top 5 Reasons Why Friends to Lovers Is the Best Type of Love Story

- Don't they say you should always be friends first?
- Friends have almost definitely seen the haven't-combed-my-hair side of you and have moved past it.
- You already know who is going to fill the sugar containers and who doesn't like to do the ketchups.
- He knows your taste in memes and cat videos.
- Shorthand.

twenty-two

"That's it?" Ivy bellows as I recount my Lucas almost-kiss to her, nearly flinging herself off her bed in frustration. She almost knocks over the framed photo on her nightstand, the same one I have of us as kids inside the big plane at the Alderton carnival. Alderton's claim to fame is our tiny aeronautics museum, and every year three ancient planes and a hovercraft that doesn't hover get rolled out onto the green for our end-of-summer carnival. Ivy and I take a photo there every summer. This was one of the first ones. "One measly almost-kiss and nothing else the entire rest of the trip? How can that possibly be?"

"I mean, we were there with both of our entire, extremely-nosy families," I remind her, then take a swig of my kombucha. It's the following week, and I'm back at home in Alderton; technically I came over to work with Ryan on an assignment for Fairchild, but he's stuck in traffic on the way back from some undisclosed location. I'm glad for the chance to catch up with Ivy instead. "It wasn't exactly a romantic getaway for two with a heart-shaped hot tub and rose petals on the bed every night."

"But still," Ivy grumbles.

"You're telling me." I take another swig. "I just feel like I missed my chance, you know? Not just to have the full friends-to-lovers experience, but also to find out if he's HappilyEverDrafter. Like if he didn't tell me there, maybe he's not going to get the nerve at all."

She hops down onto the area rug with me. "Respectfully," she says, fixing me with her stare, "Who cares if he is or he's not? You wanted him to kiss you regardless, right?"

"I mean, yeah, but . . ."

"Well, there you have it." Ivy springs upright. "Don't let the thrill of the hunt for some perfect mystery guy distract you from a really good thing that's right in front of your face." She gives me a wicked smile. "And, you know, *other* body parts."

I burst out laughing. "That's very good advice."

Ivy has way more romantic experience than I do. She's basically been a serial monogamist since she was six. So probably I should listen. But the things HappilyEverDrafter has shared—on the page, in our chats—have meant so much to me. I'm not sure how you could get someone so unfiltered without that safety of anonymity, of distance. So although it's been frustrating, I'm also grateful that we've been able to get to know each other this way.

"What about you?" I ask, changing the subject. "Did you spend the whole week lying around thinking about how much you missed me?"

"Obviously," Ivy replies. "I spent a lot of time at the pool with Makenna. We're thinking about maybe starting a podcast."

"Oh," I say, picking at a thread at the edge of my cutoffs. "That's cool."

Both of us are friends with Makenna, on top of which we're seventeen, not seven, so there's no actual reason for me to feel jealous about Ivy hanging out with someone who isn't me. Still, it feels like something is shifting between us this summer. The ground is slightly uneven under my feet. *I'm still your best friend,*

I want to remind her. *I'm just . . . busy. And stressed. And maybe my family is losing our business. And I want to get everything absolutely perfect. But I still need you.*

But I don't say any of those things.

She's about to say more, maybe about the podcast, when the house vibrates with the sound of the garage door opening. Ryan is in the house a moment later, yelling a casual "Yo!" up the stairs. In a few beats, he knocks on Ivy's door.

"Yeah," she says.

He eases the door open slowly: "Everybody decent?" he asks.

"Do you imagine we just sit around in here naked?" Ivy asks.

"I mean . . . now I'm going to need therapy to erase that image, thank you," Ryan says, a mock pained look on his face. "Jules." He nods at me. "Sorry I'm late."

"No worries," I say. I feel a burning need to know if he was out with, I don't know, maybe Emily Thurnauer. Although I was literally just talking to his sister about wishing another guy had kissed me, so I am hardly entitled to that information. "You ready to get to work?" This is obviously the summer of me making no sense whatsoever.

"Yeah, for sure," he says. "Just come find me whenever you two are done with . . . whatever it is you do in here."

"Plotting the overthrow of patriarchy, mostly," Ivy deadpans.

Ryan nods seriously. "That I'd help with, so keep me posted."

"I can work now, if you're ready," I tell him. I hold out a hand so he can help me up off the floor. It's just an instinct that comes from the familiarity we've built over this summer of commuting, talking, and, yes, just enjoying each other's company way more than I think either of us expected. But when he takes my hand and helps me up gently, I catch Ivy's eyebrow raise and I let go in a hurry. "I'll be back," I tell her. "I want to hear more about this podcast."

I follow Ryan downstairs to the formal dining room, which is outfitted with a carved oak table that must sit like sixteen people. It's ringed with plush velvet chairs with ornate carvings on them. The rigid backs make sitting up super straight inevitable.

"Okay," he says, opening up his laptop to the outline we put together on the bus back to Alderton yesterday. Paige's assignment was to find a partner and try experimenting with a genre neither of us had ever written before; it made practical sense for Ryan and me to work together on account of our shared commute, though I don't know that that's the *entire* reason we chose each other so fast. "Where did we even leave off, do you remember?"

"The clones are on the run," I say.

We're doing a near-future dystopia about teenagers who don't know they're clones being raised as new host bodies to replace the old and failing ones of their wealthy "originals."

I add, "I'm just saying, if the whole first act hinges on her being a normal kid who doesn't know she's a pawn in this creepy conspiracy, she can't just turn ninja all of a sudden at what she thinks is a doctor's office and pull off that amazing escape. Like if you found that out about yourself now, would you put it together that fast? Her realization needs to develop in stages."

Ryan nods. "But the end of act one is when she meets Reg, right? And he's been watching the clinic and knows he's a clone, so he explains stuff to her."

I smile. "I'm pretty sure she just goes with Reg because he's smoking hot. Also because goons are chasing her."

He rolls his eyes. "May my formal complaint to the

objectification of this character be noted."

"Noted," I quip, and pretend to write in an imaginary notebook.

"Anyway, okay, that's good. We just need to tone down the scene in the clinic, then, before she gets outside." He pulls my laptop across the table, types in his choppy, mad-fast staccato. "And then?"

"The chase through the subway."

His eyes light up. He's better at action sequences than I am, and I'm better at making Reg smoking hot and impossible to resist, so we complement each other.

We work for the better part of the afternoon. We stop once to gorge on clementines and pistachios while he shows me some truly hilarious Red Dead fail videos. While he's searching for one he saw the other day and wants to play for me, I watch his long, nimble fingers, the cast of his lashes on his two-tone eyes. I am struck by how much I like being this way with Ryan. Our easy back-and-forth feels exhilarating, like it makes me better somehow. I love how willing we are to listen to each other's even most outlandish ideas, using the improv rules we agreed to earlier, the "yes, and" of brainstorming that builds and doesn't detract. I like the way he seems to be able to know what I'm thinking before I can even get the words out.

It almost reminds me of working with . . .

I mean, obviously, he is the most logical candidate for . . .

I think I'd really like it if he was HappilyEver-Drafter.

"What?" Ryan asks, cocking his head in confusion at me.

"What?" I echo, a little too loud, pulled out of my HED revelry.

"Why are you staring at me like I've just sprouted face tattoos?"

"I'm not," I stammer.

"You're definitely looking at me funny."

"I was just thinking . . ." I break off. *Ask the question, Jules. Ask him.* I stumble around in my brain for the words. *Have you been secretly working on my project with me all summer? Are you this good at collaborating with me because we've been doing it all this time? Are you my soulmate, even though I've kinda mostly hated you our entire lives and you've seemed to hate me back?*

"Are you dating Emily Thurnauer?" is what falls out of my mouth instead.

Ryan regards me steadily. I notice for what seems like the first time that his eyes are really a bunch of colors, golden yellow by the iris, then a kind of green, and a dark blue by the whites. They're distracting, eyes to fall into.

He says, "There's a question I wasn't expecting," instead of answering.

"I'm just curious," I mutter, deeply regretting the question.

"About my dating life?" He is still fixing me with a tractor-beam stare, his voice even.

"Okay, I think the Reg thing just distracted me." I shake my head. "Forget I asked." I point at the screen. "Back to the subway escape. Can we plausibly get them to City Hall Station even though that's been closed since like the 1940s?"

"No, wait," Ryan says, holding a hand up. "You can't just drop that question like that and then be all *whatever.*"

I sigh. "Ryan—"

"*Jules.*"

I blink. It's a little disconcerting how much I love my name in his mouth. I say, softly, "What, Ry?"

Ryan gazes at me across the table. I look at a point on his forehead to not get lost in his endless, fascinating, complicated eyes. But then I can't, and I lock on. For what feels like several lifetimes we sit there, staring, the crackle of lightning between us, the room receding back to static, disappearing. My throat tightens up in anticipation. He seems like he's going to say something important, like he's weighing just how to do it. My breath is slow, deep, expectant.

But then he just shakes his head. "To answer your question, Emily and me at the party was a one-time thing," he says quietly.

It's not at all rational, or proportional, how many butterflies that sends dancing through my whole body.

Then he adds, "Is there anything else you want to know?"

There are a thousand things I want to know, about him, about us, about HappilyEverDrafter, about me most of all. Like a reflex, my fingers inch just a millimeter closer to his, too small and subtle for him to notice. I just want to touch him.

I shake my head.

He studies me some more. "While we're being all disclose-y, I wanted to tell you I voted for you for class president sophomore year."

I blink at this, willing this information to compute. "What?" I ask, to give myself more time to process it. "The year you ran against me?"

"Yes. My dad thought it would look good on college applications. He made those flyers and took out that ad in the school paper. I didn't really even want to run. I thought you would have done a better job than I did. But I wasn't brave enough to just not run, which is what I should have done. So I voted for you."

None of this makes sense. "But you were such a . . . you weren't exactly a gracious winner," I said.

He nods. "When you came up to me to congratulate me, and I just kind of walked off?"

"Yes."

He looks out the window. "I can see how you might have seen that as not gracious. I was honestly just pissed that I'd won. It was more work I didn't want to do. They'd just announced it, and I'm bad at hiding how I feel about things, so I didn't want you to see me upset at winning. So I just left. I'm sorry if I was rude. I wish it would have been you. I approached you about helping me run stuff after that, remember?"

I think back. Funny, I'd forgotten that part of the story. It was maybe a week later. He stammered something out to me in the hall outside the art room the school paper used for meetings. It hadn't felt like a request for help. But maybe it had been and I just hadn't understood what he was trying to say. He said something about "better man" and "copresidents" and a request to the faculty to provide better Wi-Fi for studying outside, and I was so hurt and embarrassed at having lost I told him I'd think about it and never talked to him about it again. Avoided him for months, actually.

"I'm sorry," I say quietly. "I didn't understand."

We're both quiet for a while. Finally he smiles, "But the real question is how we're going to get the clone crew to break into the company database to find out where her clone sister lives now."

I laugh and turn back to the computer. "I have thoughts on that."

And the moment is gone.

Her secret admirer's next clue had stumped Maggie for one full day and the better part of the next. She was surprised to discover how nervous this made her, what an outsized impact it had on her. It was the part about leaving a note with a friend that she just couldn't crack. She even obliquely wondered aloud to a few friends if they had a note for her. But every confused look made her realize she had it wrong. If he'd been suggesting they shared a friend—which they must—he wouldn't leave a note with another person. That would put an end to the scavenger hunt too soon in case the friend cracked and revealed his identity.

No, it had to be some kind of riddle. But it was one she just couldn't crack.

On the second day, nervous that her slowness to crack his code would make him lose interest in the game, she'd briefly checked in at the sail shop to make sure he hadn't left anything else, tossed her bag behind the counter, and went back out to walk. She had no destination in mind. She just knew that when the salt air kissed her skin, she felt more alert, more alive.

She headed down the lane where her family store was and to what could ostensibly be called her town's main street. It wouldn't hold up in any main-street competition. It was only a few blocks long, with some seasonal T-shirt shops that were shuttered for a few more months yet, a restaurant that catered to locals, and an art gallery that held work by area artists whose preferred media were shells and dried starfish. Everything she had ever done had happened on this sun-bleached street, the games of tag, the skinned knees, that hurried, awkward kiss with James Whitmore in the seventh grade. It was soaked into her, never to leave her, but she also thrummed eagerly with the thought of leaving it behind.

The end of the road was punctuated by a large round green, around which the road took you in a circle just to make you head in the opposite direction. Beyond that, breakers and sea. In the center of the green stood an old metal sculpture taller than she was by orders of magnitude. Everyone called it Old Harry when using it to give directions to the infrequent summer tourists. "If you've reached Old Harry, you've gone too far."

She crossed over to Old Harry now. He was portly, wearing a fisherman's sweater made of metal like the rest of him, his fuzzy beard and mustache jutting from his jaw but not obscuring a kindly grin. Around him, several metal harbor seals frolicked. She tried to remember what Old Harry had done to earn him a statue, but it had been here since before her parents had been born, so if it was once news, it had long been forgotten. She walked over to the plaque. It read: "Harold Stinton, a sea captain who made his home on what is now known as Stinton Lane, known far and wide as a friend to all manner of creatures of the sea, contributed greatly to the knowledge of . . ."

Maggie trailed off. A friend to all manner of creatures. She'd heard this in school, she now remembered. They'd had to color in a picture of Old Harry in some early grade. It was an old illustration of this statue, labeled, "Old Harry, Friend to Seals."

This had to be it. Maggie searched all over the statue. Finally, she found it in the mouth of one of the seals, a note carefully tucked into a plastic sandwich baggie to protect it from the moisture of the nearby sea.

She took it out, unfolded it—her heart glad, her smile wide.

⏻ Posts 14   ♡ Likes 47

twenty-three

I don't think either Lucas or I realized, back when we came up with the idea for Tango Night, just how much work we were signing ourselves up for. The next couple of weeks are a total blur of prep and planning: menu and decor and music and publicity, my to-do list a mile long. We put a notice in the local parenting magazines billing it as a date night. We reach out to the Calling Alderton Twitter account, which tweets out news of upcoming local events, then troubleshoot the ancient reservations system so we can accurately track how many diners to let in.

And that's all before we've even rehearsed.

"Let's take a break," Lucas says now, breaking into a shrink-wrapped tray of Sprite and handing me a room-temperature can. We've been practicing in the basement of the restaurant the last couple of days, pushing aside fifty-pound bags of flour and boxes of extra flatware to work on our forward cross and back cross.

"Good idea," I say, setting the soda down on a nearby shelf and bracing one hand on Lucas's shoulder as I bend down to unbuckle my dance shoes. We've been working so hard I've got blisters, and my whole body is a catalog of twinges and aches. "This is going to be worth it, right?" I ask him, sitting down on a box of take-out containers. "All of this?"

Lucas nods. "It's going to be worth it," he says with more confidence than I can possibly feel.

We've been saying it to each other all week like a mantra whenever we're tired or accidentally step on each other's feet. We've been reciting it like a prayer. It's going to be worth it. It *has* to be worth it, because if it's not . . .

"It's going to be worth it," I repeat, downing my Sprite, then getting to my feet and reaching for his hand. "Let's try that again, tighter."

He nods. He never says no. He's never the first one

to stop. He goes again as many times as I ask him to. It's one of the many reasons to love him.

Finally, aching feet winning out, I tell Lucas I'm ready to stop. "Okay, great, because I've actually got some stuff to take care of at home. I'll walk you to your car?"

I cock my head at him in curiosity. What could he have to take care of at this hour? I can't help but wonder if it's the next chapter of "Untitled." But I'm too tired to wonder for long.

"No, it's okay, I may wait for my mom." I may not, but I don't want him to feel so responsible for me. He leaves. I sit downstairs for a while, then say my good-byes upstairs and head to the street.

I listen for the click of the locked door behind me and head out into the night. It takes a minute for my eyes to adjust and realize Calvin is leaning against the lamppost by the street. He's in jeans and a sweatshirt.

I stop in my tracks, stare at him for a moment. "This is an odd spot to take in the sights," I say with a smile.

"Oh, I don't know," he says. "I like the sights here." We've hung out a couple of times since that day outside my abuela's, checking out a swing band playing in the library courtyard and browsing a new indie bookstore he thought I'd like. But something about him showing up here like this feels different. For a moment, I'm worried somebody's going to see him. Not that I'm doing anything wrong. I think of Lucas, who's working so hard to save a restaurant like it's his own. Then Ryan, who brought me a cup of Earl Grey with lemon to the bus stop this morning, just the way I like it, melting me in a way I had to fight not to show.

"So what's going on?" I ask.

"They're doing fireworks over the river at ten," he reports. For a guy who's new to town, he's full of local intel like this. He told me he reads that little freebie town paper everyone else lets molder in their driveway. It's just like him: quirky and out of step with everyone else I know. "Thought I'd see if you wanted to check 'em out."

I consider making a crack about why he can't text like everybody else. But I already know the answer to that. He isn't like everybody else.

I hesitate. I'm bone-tired. I have an unfinished assignment due tomorrow. I owe Ivy a call. There are flyers I need to print for Tango Night, and our ancient printer is going to need some coaxing and possibly an infusion of fake ink. There are ten thousand responsibilities I could—*should*—disappear into. But I like the thrill of trying on being this person instead, the one who takes spontaneous invitations. I take a deep breath and nod.

"Sure," I say. "That sounds like fun."

We walk to my car, and Calvin slides into the passenger's seat. As we do, he delivers a hilariously detailed update on the misadventures of Mabel and Reinaldo as I head for the river.

"She's risen through the ranks and is now famous in her own right, obviously," he tells me, rolling the window down so the night wind ruffles his hair. "She's the top reporter in Reinaldo's family's newspaper empire, but of course that's not good enough for Reinaldo's scheming mother—who, I don't mind telling you, is kind of a nightmare. So she's concocted this sham engagement for Reinaldo to this absolute harpy who hates Mabel and is rich and spoiled and totally terrible."

"Riveting," I laugh. "I cannot believe you are still watching that telenovela with my grandmother. Are you secretly seventy-five?"

"Ageist," Calvin teases, "Your grandmother is pretty awesome. Plus I think I've landed on the perfect language immersion technique. It comes with the yummiest food ever."

"All good points."

We arrive at the water just as the fireworks are starting. We get out and sit on the hood of my car. I'm about five years old when it comes to fireworks, which is another reason I agreed to come to this even though I'm dead on my feet. I love the flash, the colors, the promise, the sheer celebratory power of fireworks.

"Anyway," Calvin says. "The whole thing is fun, you know? But it does make everything so complicated. I don't think life has to be like that." It takes me a minute to realize he's still talking about the novela.

"How does it have to be?" I ask, glancing over at him, the lights of the bridge twinkling to our left.

He leans back on his elbows and tips his head back to watch the dance of lights above us. "Sometimes it's just simple."

Actually, Top 5 Reasons Why Boy Next Door Is the Best Kind of Love Story

- I mean . . . he's next door.
- I guess Heathcliff kind of qualifies as "next door." "Whatever our souls are made of, his and mine are the same," is still the best line in a love story. Even if, yeah, problematic.
- You can call him when your sink explodes.
- He's brilliant, thinks deeply, and he has a Hidden Talent. Like carpentry.
- Sometimes it's just simple.

twenty-four

Tango Night has finally arrived. I am in a red dress with a slit, hair slicked to the nape of my neck, standing in the restaurant kitchen. There's a tiny, high window near the grill where, if I stand up on tippy toe, I can peek out to the deck. It is jam-packed, the tables cleared away to the edges to make more room for seating. The main dining room is packed too, people who saw the ad who wanted to come for the food special and not even watch the dance or take the dance lesson. We've been spreading the word like mad, and it's worked. My parents have had to bring in all their extra servers to keep up with demand.

Lucesita and Jaime are going around to each diner to sign them up for our new frequent-diner program, inputting their info right into an app on their smartphones at each table. I helped set it up, along with a program to send an invitation for free dessert for everyone two weeks before their birthday. In all my reading up on how to revive a restaurant, this is one of the things I learned. That's been part of the prep for this night, too, sitting with my parents to figure out things we can do. We've agreed that with some of the extra money from tonight, we're going to start a program to mail postcards to all new move-ins to the area, among other things. My parents have always been set on relying only on word of mouth. But maybe these times call for something more.

My heart thuds. Lucas and I have practiced a lot, usually after closing. I think we're okay. We're not like some of those dizzyingly good dancers I've watched on YouTube, footwork blazing fast, tension and heat emanating from them, lithe dancers' bodies making their moves crisp and perfect. But we've got the steps down. *I hope.* I know how we dance isn't going to be what makes people decide whether to come back, but I can't help but feel the pressure. I trace my high-heeled dance shoe toe on the kitchen tile to steady myself.

Lucas comes to find me. He's in a black button-down with one button undone, and slim black slacks. He's gotten a haircut, and his hair looks almost tame, combed back. He's let a little bit of stubble—as much as he can manage—grow on his jawline to dampen the effect of his baby face.

He looks . . . there's no other way to say it: he looks hot.

I take a few deep breaths to try to get my galloping heart under control. The kitchen is in full swing all around us, El Maestro barking out orders, Joaquin's face slick with heat and exertion. We're in a tiny oasis near the window, all the kitchen workers doing their own graceful dance around us to make sure everyone has the best meal they've ever had. They look harried but happy. Most everyone here has been with us for a long time. Their hopes are riding on us too.

Lucas says, "Hey. You ready?"

I look up at him, "I'm nervous, Lucas."

He takes my hand. "We've *so* got this, Jules. Don't worry. We're going to crush it."

His certainty stills me a little bit. "Okay," I say. "Let's do it."

He taps on the window as the signal to start the song. As we walk into the corridor leading out back I hear the first notes of "Por una Cabeza." We chose it because it's probably the song most American people recognize as tango, played in movies like *Schindler's List* and *Scent of a Woman* and *True Lies*, dramatic and sweeping. I chose the tinny, old Carlos Gardel version because it's the one I grew up hearing, and because it's one of the few versions that's not instrumental only, and I love the words. It's about gambling, about how love is like a gamble on a horse race won by what Americans would probably call "a hair." In Spanish, it's "por una cabeza," "by a head." Something about how old the song sounds feels important, too. Recorded in 1935, it's almost ninety years old. Its scratchy rendition says something about the power to endure. It's a song that my mother, and my mother's mother, and maybe even my mother's mother's mother have danced to. This exact one, across kilometers and time. I feel them all with me, all the people who did their best so that I could be here, in this moment.

Lucas leads me out to the patio by the hand. My parents are standing close to one another near the stairs, the hope in their eyes so raw and real that it makes my heart thud harder. I don't let myself look at individual faces, because if I know anyone watching I'll just be in my head too much. I'll just look at Lucas.

He walks us out to the middle of the clearing onto the makeshift dance floor.

He pulls me in and everything stops but the music. He begins. My back is rigid, and the steps feel stilted. For a moment, the panic sweeps up my body. *This is going to be a disaster.* All eyes are on us, and I am a broken robot. Lucas pulls me in a hair's breadth tighter at the waist as if willing me to pay attention only to him. I look into his eyes. He nods so subtly I must be the only one who can see it. I let my body relax. He takes me into the first spin. I surrender to it. Carlos Gardel sings "Borra la tristeza, calma la amargura."

The rest of the song melts away, too. I just let myself react to him, and we are perfectly in sync. He puts more into it than at any rehearsal, more drama, more flair. He hits his steps sharper, spins me faster. I didn't know he had this performance gene in him. It's like he's coming alive with the audience reaction, a small smile playing on his face where we nail particularly challenging footwork, standing up to his full height with pride. This is his music, too, his heritage he's sharing, and even though it's not his restaurant, it's part of his story, his life. My heart swells with gratitude for him. He is giving it his all.

When the song finishes, everyone stands up and

claps. I'm out of breath, from the intensity of the dance but also from the nerves. My parents make their way to us.

"You did great!" says my dad, his eyes tired but his smile real.

My mom has a faraway, wistful look on her face, but she hugs me tight. I let myself look at the crowd. And I recognize faces, everywhere: neighbors, old clients we haven't seen in a while, Mrs. Richards and all her friends from the book club, plus her husband at her side, looking drained but smiling wide. My abuela sitting nearby, with Sweater Vest next to her. And Ivy. It's all encouragement, everywhere. The drop in adrenaline and the relief at it being over is like warm syrup.

We lead the couples who want to in a demonstration of the basic step. Some, a handful of already experienced ones, dance to the tango fusion music we put on next. Others don't even attempt the moves but hold each other as they sway happily. One woman gleefully does the YMCA arm motions to "Santa Maria (Del Buen Ayre)," not even trying to do anything resembling tango. And it's perfect.

After so many months of worrying and being

afraid for Las Heras, finally, a triumph. I know one night won't change everything. But it's a step. One foot in front of the other. I squeeze Lucas's hand and he squeezes back, and I am all happiness.

"... a star danced, and under that was I born."

—Shakespeare

twenty-five

Ryan and I get the collab assignment back. It's got some purple on it, but Paige has also written, "Excellent work!" at the top. Ryan has long ago moved his seat to be the one in front of mine. He turns around and flashes me a big smile.

When class is over, Paige calls my name. I nod at Ryan, and he says, "I'll wait by the front door."

I wait for people to file out and go up to Paige's desk.

"How have you liked the class?" she asks me.

It's a little sad to think we're closer to the end than to the beginning. It feels like we just started.

"It's . . . surprised me."

"I liked that flash fiction piece you did on the time-stopper's loneliness. But you strike me as the kind of kid who has always been able to ace school. And because you haven't had to work as hard as some others, you've kept it at arm's length."

The comment makes me feel exposed. But she's not wrong. School has always been an exercise in figuring out what teachers want, then giving it to them. That's why what Paige has asked for has been harder. She hasn't wanted hoops jumped through but truth. It's been tougher to find.

"That's true. But it's helped me learn why this is important. It's more satisfying, you know? Even though it's scarier."

"Authenticity is the scariest thing. But you know what? You're good at it. You should lean into it more. Stop looking for the right answers and just give yours. They're pretty special."

I smile, aglow, and we say our goodbyes.

The day is gray, but I still have to fight the urge to skip all the way to the Port Authority. I'm so happy I drag Ryan into a little hole-in-the-wall Italian place I've been meaning to check out all summer, right in the shadow of the Port Authority, across the street from where the Dean & DeLuca used to be. It's so small there are only a few stools to sit on, but we order gorgeous sandwiches full of prosciutto, a salad to share, and we sit on the stools facing the windows out to Fortieth Street, watching people go by. My mom has always told me she knew she was home when she saw New York because no one ever looked at you, no matter what you were wearing or how you were acting, and she liked the freedom to exist without being examined. I love New York for the opposite reason. It's the place where I think you can feel the most seen.

The short time we spend in the restaurant means that the line for the bus is way longer than usual by the time we do get to it. Normally, it would make me cranky, but nothing can stop my mood. Ryan is vibing on it, too, acting goofy and telling me stories I've never heard before, like about one misguided time he thought he could steer his bike with his feet, culminating in a scar he shows me on his shin.

By the time we get to the front of the line for the bus, all the seats are taken. Ryan says we can wait for the next one, but in this mood I could stand all the way to Alderton and maybe even the moon, should this coughing old behemoth suddenly find itself able to fly there. So I pull him on. The bus pushes off with a lurch. I fall into Ryan, and he puts his arm around my waist to steady me.

We move into the yellow gloom of the tunnel, the traffic at a crawl. People are cranky. For all their faults, New Jersey Transit buses generally have decent AC, but this one, packed with bodies, is struggling to fight off the swampy, smoggy tunnel air. Finally, we make it out of the tunnel to find that the weather has taken a turn. It's been dreary all day, but now it's like a low, marbled, drab ceiling is pushing down from the sky. As we make the loop where we get our last glimpse of Manhattan, a single bolt of lightning cracks the gray near the Empire State Building.

The bus speeds on the highway, the way clear on the Jersey side of the tunnel, mercifully. The huffy sound is like the bus used to be a smoker in its youth and its bad decisions are finally catching up with it. The route takes it off the highway a few miles away from our stop, wending its way through several small downtowns, Jonesburg first.

Past the old-timey, Regency-style movie theater on the far end of Jonesburg, there's a neighborhood full of dignified old colonials. Some are white with black shutters, others are blue with white. There are neat lawns and a preference for rosebushes. The bus makes its first stop, then coughs again, jerks forward, coughs, makes a movie gunshot sound . . . and creaks to a stop.

The harried bus driver stands up. "Okay, folks, listen up. I'm gonna need to go see what . . ." He trails off, like it's not even worth explaining, and steps off the bus.

A cop car comes, then another. The air-conditioning has stopped altogether now, the soup of humanity getting restless. The bus driver comes back on. "Okay, folks, listen up," he repeats, like it was in a handbook of how to deal with ornery riders. "We're gonna need a tow, here. Dispatch has sent another bus, but the tunnel is jammed, like you saw, so it may be a while. Maybe the bus behind us will have some room for a few of you, but not all of you. You gotta hang tight until we can get you all resituated."

A collective groan goes up. The woman sitting in the seat by which I'm standing gets up abruptly, slings her huge leather tote, weaponized with her laptop inside, straight into my belly, then pushes past everyone standing and grumbles an "excuse me" in her wake.

Ryan looks at me. "Alderton's like a twenty-minute walk, tops," he says.

"You wanna?" I say.

He looks out the window. "Better than standing around who knows how long."

We get off the bus and start our walk away from the cranky passengers. Some of them seem to hope the right complaint, the proper request for details as to the cause of the trouble, will unlock a magical bus-fixing device. Others are on cell phones, loudly, making their displeasure apparent to everyone around them, conversations about door codes and missed appointments. "I *know*, honey, but what can Daddy do? I'm going to call Young now to see if she can drive you to practice, okay?" "Look, I don't know where in godforsaken New Jersey I am. Let me get off the phone so I can share my location with you. Hurry, okay?"

We leave them behind and start the straight line connecting this neighborhood with Alderton's main drag.

"I can't believe we've only got a couple more weeks of class left," I say. I'm going to miss our trips into the city, though I don't say that. I wonder if things will go back to how they were once we're done at Fairchild, the two of us in our own separate orbits, making occasional contact long enough to lob vague insults in each other's direction before floating away again. If he's going to go back to being Ivy's inconvenient, prickly brother. I hope not.

Ryan doesn't seem to have those worries. "I know," he says. "I can't believe how fast it went." He shakes his head. "Can I tell you something?"

I nod.

He goes on. "I'm kind of nervous about what Paige is going to say about my final portfolio."

"Why?"

"I can't get a beat on her, honestly. I can never figure out if she thinks I'm wasting my time with writing or not. I kind of need something that can make me stand out on my college applications, you know? My grades were . . . not stellar this past year."

"Really?" This surprises me. Ryan has always made school seem effortless, like he sprung forth with all the textbooks already in his database.

"Yeah," he admits. "Chem kicked my ass, and I didn't make honor roll third marking period. My parents are still recovering."

"I . . . can imagine." The Madigans may not be around much, but that doesn't stop them from expecting excellence. It's kind of a nonnegotiable to them.

"They're iffy on the whole creative-writing thing

as it is," Ryan continues, "and if I don't pull out something splashy in this program, I'm not sure how that's going to go. I've already had to promise my dad I'll at least minor in prelaw. Since my dad is a lawyer, he's impossible to argue with. And you know my mom."

"I . . . have met her, yeah." I look at the sidewalk, with its tiny flakes of reflective material, which as a kid I used to tell myself were ground-up diamonds. "It sounds stressful. I'm sorry."

"It sucks," he smiles sadly. "I'm over it."

"But don't be nervous about Paige," I say. "She basically told me that stubbornly holding on to the dream is what gets you there. And if stubbornness is the key, then you've got this in the bag."

He laughs. "But you, though. You've got some natural inner thing. Watching how you go all in has made me want to be better, too."

I glance at him. His ears look red. Maybe he thinks he's said too much.

"You always have," he adds, almost a mumble. I smile, more inwardly than anything. That is quite an admission from the great Ryan Madigan.

We're only a few blocks away from my house now. I feel so calm, so at ease with him. I don't want this walk to end. I consider suggesting we always get off earlier and walk the last part of the way home. I wish I could go back to the start of the summer to know this feeling, to suggest the extra time back then so we could have had a whole summer of this. Getting to know him has been infinitely slow, like moving inch by inch toward a fidgety creature, a buck, maybe. Only now am I feeling like he's let me stand near enough to see him really.

The sky is ominously dark now. A raindrop splotches on my nose. I turn to him as he's whipping around to me. Another hits my forearm.

"Damn," he says. "How the hell does this keep happening to us?"

"Summer in New Jersey?" I remind him. And in an instant, buckets of water start falling.

Ryan laughs. "Run!"

I put my messenger bag over my head. But it's one of those entirely unreasonable summer storms that won't be stopped. In less than a minute my bag is soaked and I sling it back over my shoulder, letting the warm rain run over me. The ground was so unprepared for the onslaught that the drains on the corners can't swallow the rain fast enough and it sits in eddying pools. Ryan stomps into one, and I do the same. We're wet already, and it's warm. The ground sends up the vibrant scent of grass and fertile earth, the flowers brighter with rain. There's no sense in trying to stop it, so I lean into it, aiming for puddles, which are warm like bathtub water, throwing my head back and my arms wide to meet the drops as they fall. Ryan runs under an awning where a misplaced downspout is making a vertical river, the rain flattening his hair comically while he sputters and smiles the most unrestrained smile I've ever seen on him. I take a turn after he does. The onslaught of water makes me feel as free as I've ever felt, letting it happen, this thing we usually try to duck from, drinking in all of life without reservation.

We make our way through the puddle-pocked streets. When we finally get to my porch, we're as soaked as if we'd jumped in a pool. To underscore the randomness of life, the rain slows to a drizzle when we step under the overhang.

Even though it's been a couple of blocks since we ran, I'm still catching my breath, every skin cell awake and searching, alive to the moment, my senses alert. Our porch is small, and he's huddled close. He's breathing hard, too. I look up at his face. He's not laughing now, he's intent, looking in my face as if for an answer. A go-ahead. It crackles between us, the moment, all the moments leading up to this one, the things we want, as if they'd been said out loud. For once, I don't have to wonder. It's written it on him, and I can tell that he sees it on me.

His face is covered in rain. I wipe some of it from his cheek, then his brow as it's about to run down his face. It's only once it's done that I realize the boldness in it, the wild step it is to touch him that way. I can't believe I did that. But he doesn't flinch.

Instead, he leans his body closer to mine. My heart thuds, and it's not from the running. But at the same time, a warm ease spreads over me, a melting of a shield I hadn't realized I was holding. My lips part like I want to breathe in more of the moment. I want to tilt my torso into his, ease him back with my body, up against the railing of the porch. I want to know what his lips feel like. He's angling his face toward mine and our foreheads are inches apart now, his dark T-shirt wet against every angle of his lean shoulders. I raise my hands to place them on there, but catch myself and lower them back down.

"I'm . . . ," he begins. It's a sentence without a plan. Finally he gets something out, "There's no one I'd rather be caught in the rain with than you," he says.

It is wildly personal, a step I didn't imagine he had in him but which thrills me. I want to kiss him so much not doing it feels like a physical exertion.

"There's no one I'd rather get caught in the rain with than with you, too. Either?" I smile.

He smiles one-sided, like joking isn't going to break this moment. He runs a thumb on my wrist, down the top of my hand, and sensation explodes in the spot. It is like he has the power to move atoms.

Here, Ryan's touch still alive on my skin, I am not sure of anything except the fact that I want to kiss him more than I've ever wanted anything.

The front screen slams open. Lucesita says, "Eeeww! You two are soaked!"

Ryan jumps back almost a foot, so comically fast Lucesita must notice she's interrupted something. Or maybe not. She walks between us and sticks her hand out to test the rain. She's not going away.

Doña Faustina materializes in the doorframe. "¡Mi hija!" she says in a tone one usually might reserve for telling someone they're on fire. "¡Y tu sin sombrilla!" Her Cuban accent gets more pronounced when she's upset.

"I don't think an umbrella would have helped, Fau. It was pouring and the bus broke down."

She opens the screen door to shoo me inside. Few things make Doña Faustina go into Code Red like someone who has come into contact with precipitation. "¡Te va a dar una gripe!"

"I'm not going to get a cold, it'll be okay." Talk about ruining a mood. I glance at Ryan.

He smiles, takes a step down, and says, "I should go."

I'm suddenly colder with his body moving away from mine.

"You want to come in and dry off?" I ask. Doña Faustina is giving him the stink eye, like he's personally responsible for the rain and *definitely* responsible for me being in it.

He shakes his head slowly, his eyes locked on mine. I want to believe he's thinking that he wants this rain, that moment between us, to stay on him as long as possible.

Because it's what I want too.

7:51 p.m.: HappilyEverDrafter posted to
"Untitled Teen Love Story."

Maggie:

I have such memories of how much they told us Old Harry's story in school when we were kids, always emphasizing his friendliness. Do you remember? Or was this clue vague? That old tattered children's book they have at the town library and which they read to us every year during the lighthouse celebration was always one of my favorites. I thought you might remember it, too.

I am enjoying this game, but I wonder if you are. I wonder if you want to keep going or if I might just bore you, make you think my identity isn't worth discovering. Plus I know your days are counting down here, and I'd love to meet. Re-meet, I guess, meet under the circumstances of you knowing that I have feelings for you.

If you are, leave a lantern outside the shop door. That's good, old-fashioned seaside-town imagery, don't you think? If you don't leave it, I'll understand and won't have hard feelings. I'll bother you no further. Whatever happens, I wish you so much luck and love and happiness.

twenty-six

Ivy wants me to meet her at the pool on Friday, but I need to work on my final portfolio for Fairchild. That's mostly the reason I don't meet her. We're supposed to revise three of our assignments and turn in a draft of something brand-new. But the truth is I'm also a little nervous about running into Ryan. We've barely talked since our almost-kiss in the rain the other day. He skipped one day of class with a curt text of *I'm not going today*, then our schedules have been different because Paige has been scheduling one-on-ones. I can't take much more of this. I need to know the truth.

My phone buzzes with a notification from Storied-Zone. It's a message from HappilyEverDrafter.

I read it. I . . . can't believe it. I stare at it. I read it again. Then a third time.

Then I call Ivy.

"Still not too late to avail yourself of the awesomeness that is the Alderton Town Pool?" she answers. The pool noises are loud in the background, little kids screeching, laughs from what sound like middle schoolers running, a lifeguard telling them to walk. But my heart thudding wildly in my ears is louder than all of it.

"He's ready to meet," I blurt out.

"You're . . . going to have to be more specific."

"HappilyEverDrafter! He just wrote to me." I put the phone on speaker so I can read the message out loud. "'It's time for me to come clean. I'm not the one you're expecting, but you've had the clues to find me all along. Read carefully.' It's a scavenger hunt, right? Like the one in our story," I ask her.

"Sure sounds like it."

"It's got to be Ryan or Lucas," I guess. "Calvin doesn't know about the ones you and I used to do all the time."

"I mean . . . ," Ivy starts.

I'm racking my brain trying to figure out where the first clue might be.

"He must mean his chapters in 'Untitled,' right?" I tell her. "That's where his clues have been the whole time? He's never given anything away while we've been chatting. No mention of family life, school, nothing like that. So that can't be it."

"Jules."

I open up "Untitled" on my laptop, skim Happily-EverDrafter's first entry. "You know, a thing I never paid attention to before, his character gives directions, he mentions a Little Free Library on a street called Marchmeadow. I remember that sticking out for me because we've got a Marchmeadow in town and it's not exactly a common name. I thought of it as one of the clues that he did know me and our town and he wasn't a rando with a murder problem, like you always thought."

"Yeah, that street is a couple of blocks away from your house. It's got a Little Free Library, too," she adds quietly.

"Does it? I've never seen it."

"Yeah, if you're walking down to the creek. On

the right side there? Tucked in behind that big oak. After that house with that giant metal sculpture of the seagulls."

"Will you come with me?" I ask.

Ivy hesitates. "Jules," she says, "listen. Before you do this, I really want to—"

"I know." I cut her off. "I *know* you think this is a wild-goose chase and that I should pick instead of being so caught up in it and that I'm just going to be disappointed. But for me? Will you come? I want to do this, and I don't want to do it without you. Please? You're my best friend, Ivy. And I don't think I'd want to do a scavenger hunt without you. There's no way I'm going to be able to solve this without you." I shut my laptop. "Besides, if your ongoing suspicions that he's a *Dateline* episode waiting to happen, your tae kwon do skills will come in handy."

"I haven't done tae kwon do since the fifth grade."

Behind her, the sound of a colossal cannonball splash is followed closely by a sharp lifeguard whistle.

"Please?"

Ivy sighs. "I'll be right over."

The house with the Little Free Library is three blocks away from the bus stop. I am obsessed with Little Free

Libraries . . . I can't believe I've never seen this one before. It's shaped like a tiny schoolhouse, painted red, complete with a ringable bell in the tower and miniature American flag outside. I pull out the books one by one.

"Whoever is stocking this Little Free Library definitely has a thing for Tom Perrotta," I say. "I can't believe I missed this clue. Not only did he write it into his chapter, but *Election* is actually in here. And *The Leftovers* and *Little Children*," I say.

She responds, "I accidentally saw the movie for *Little Children*. I can say this much: not appropriate for little children."

"How do you accidentally watch *Little Children*?"

"Okay, it wasn't entirely an accident. I was in my Patrick Wilson phase post-*Phantom*."

There, behind a romance with pink, yellow, and blue lettering I spot it: a note, folded four ways. I unfold it. It's typed.

It read, "Check me out where we're calling Alderton."

I hand it to Ivy. "I'm usually a pretty good escape-room, scavenger-hunt girl, but I think this guy may think I'm better at clues than I am."

"I doubt that." She smiles.

"Check me where we're . . . he can't be at a *place*, right? Because he doesn't know when I'm going to do this thing. So he's not going to be sitting there waiting for me, wherever this is."

"Calling Alderton," she says, slowly, trying to puzzle it out.

"Oh, like that Twitter account," I say. It clicks, I think. "Hey, don't they have a place in town hall where you can leave them notes if you don't want to tweet at them? After the senior citizens in town complained that there was no place to write them a note?"

"Entirely missing the point of social media," she says.

"And electronic communication of all kinds, yes. But the grammar school made them a big mailbox, remember? Someone came to the restaurant asking us to fill out a card shaped like a heart because the whole top of the box is notes from every merchant in town in a whole rainbow of colors. They charged us each ten dollars as a fundraiser for the account, to host a website and stuff."

"So . . . town hall?"

I nod and put all the books back carefully, slipping *Little Children* into my messenger bag. "Remind me to bring them something to replace this one," I say.

"I will," she says softly.

We get to town hall, an old, colonial-style building that was once a sprawling house in the center of town, back near its founding, but now holds town services like the building department and the DPW. The Calling Alderton message box is inside to the left of the front door.

The hearts covering the top look a little worse for wear, some bent, some torn outright. This has been here a few months, at least. There are dozens of them. I begin reading them all. There's ours. It would make sense for Lucas to choose this as one of the places to put a clue. He was there when the Calling Alderton reps came into Las Heras to ask us to support the project.

Finally, I spot it. It's newer than the others. It says, "Psst, AldertonGirlAconcagua!" on a fuchsia heart shaped a little differently than the others. I pluck it off and flip it around.

It reads: "Creamy goodness, my treat! There's only one place in town."

I hand it to Ivy. "If you were going to think the only creamery in this town, like the *main* ice cream place, what would you think?"

"I mean . . . Alderton Creamery."

It's a few minutes to Alderton Creamery. The owner is behind the counter. It's lively but not as packed as it'll get after the sun goes down. Maybe my family should have gone into the ice cream shop business. But then I remember how it's closed October through April, and that I always wonder how they possibly survive that way. All through the pandemic I was afraid they weren't coming back the first spring, then the second. But, somehow, they did, adapting by offering outside service and, later delivery. I'm happy about that. Very few things say summer in Alderton to me like this place.

Ivy waves the pink heart at the owner. "My friend got a note that she may have a free cone."

The owner looks at Ivy quizzically. Ivy hands over the pink heart.

"Uh . . . yeah, sure, let me see," she says, looking down at it. "Yes, look here," she says, like she's delivering the lines from a play badly. "There's a coupon code." I lean over to see. There's a series of letters.

"Hold on, I've got something for you," she adds.

She goes in the back and comes back with a tiny airplane. It looks a little like the old-timey ones they trot out for the carnival in town. It's got a small, typewritten note on it: "As you write the next chapter, remember."

The lady behind the counter adds, "I'm supposed to give you whatever ice cream you want. It's prepaid."

"You have to tell me who he is," I say to her. "You *have* to. Please. He set this up. He was here. You know who he is."

The woman looks from me to Ivy, then back at me again. She smiles sheepishly. "I . . . just scoop the ice cream."

Ugh, *so frustrating*. Like being riiiight there, but not quite. But at least there's ice cream in it. I turn to Ivy. "We can share. What are you in the mood for?"

She studies the menu. "Hmmm, you choose."

"Blueberry?"

"Perfect."

The owner gives us a bowl that looks a little fancier than usual, and Ivy and I take it to one of the tables outside. She takes a spoonful and asks, "So what does this clue mean?"

I stab my spoon into the ice cream to make it stay. "I forgot to check for another clue!" I study the little airplane. It's very pretty, detailed and exquisite. There's another note folded up in its little cockpit. I can't believe I didn't see that right away.

It reads: "You've probably cracked these clues by now, but just in case: meet me by the planes on

Saturday night at 9:00 for a do-over."

This one is signed: "HappilyEverDrafter."

I hug the plane gingerly to my chest and close my eyes. He wrote this, came here, set this all up. He is ready for what's next, too.

"So?" Ivy asks, her face serious. "Did you figure it out?"

I shake my head. "It doesn't say. It says to meet at the carnival on Saturday."

"There's . . . nothing that gives it away? The carnival's huge."

"By the planes."

"Our planes?" she asks.

I nod absently, squinting down at the note. It's typed, so there are no clues in the handwriting, but maybe the font is supposed to tell me something?

"What do you think he means by a do-over?" I ask. Maybe some reference by either Lucas or Ryan about our near misses, the way we should have gotten it right earlier but haven't.

"I don't *know*, Jules." Ivy's voice is impatient. I look up at her. She looks more like Ryan than usual, the old, imperious Ryan, the one I was sure disdained the world. But, then I realize what her mood is about. *Ugh.* Of course she has limited bandwidth for endless romantic drama, being kind of fresh off a breakup I'm pretty sure she hasn't processed. And there's the ick factor of this possibly involving her brother.

I'm not playing with Ryan's feelings. I want her to know that, but I can't quite say it. I haven't told her about the day in the rain. It feels like a lie by omission, because I've told her everything forever. But I just can't. Not yet. I don't want to be an idiot and make it weird with her and with him without knowing about him and me for sure.

I squeeze her hand, then push the rest of the ice cream in her direction so she can finish it. "I'm grateful you came to do this with me," I say.

"That's what friends are for," she says. Then she shoves a spoonful of blueberry ice cream into her mouth.

"There is only one plot: things are not as they seem."

—Jim Thompson

twenty-seven

Most of Saturday I am on the verge of pure immolation. I change my outfit what feels like a hundred times—a dress, shorts, a dress, pants, a dress. Finally, I decide on my lucky frayed-edge denim Converse and my favorite white blouse with little yellow daisies on it, plus jean shorts. Casual. Not the typo of outfits. But a poem, not a chapter. I focus on my clothes to put aside the gnawing questions about tonight. *Will he show up? Will I know what to say? Will I get it wrong? Will he be glad? Does this mean to him as much as it does to me?*

I was hoping to get Ivy to come with me—after all, we've been going to the carnival together every year since history began. But she begged off. So after dinner, I drive over to the green by myself. It's absolutely packed. Sugar-fueled little kids are running amuck. Middle schoolers are trying desperately to look cool. Old couples are strolling arm in arm. Everywhere there are familiar faces, people I've been seeing here since I was little. Neighbors, young, old . . . it looks like all of Alderton is here, happy for the fullness of summer and for being together. The weather is ideal, warm and clear, the ground not the soggy mess it sometimes can be this time of year in this low-lying ground near the water. It's not even that buggy, a minor miracle.

I take my phone out of my bag and look at the time as I walk by the ticket booth—8:58. I pick up the pace on my way to the planes. I spot it from a distance, the old biplane with the double wings with enough distance from the bottom and the top one for a grown-up to stand upright, although the old-timers who take care of the planes spend the whole carnival chasing off anyone who tries. And a smaller one behind it, painted bright red, with two propellers. Alderton's pride and joy.

I stand in front of the bigger one. Its baby-blue wings are cordoned off, holding back the crowd. I look in the direction of the entrance.

The minutes tick by. I scan the crowd—my senses humming, and my nerves open and raw, my eyes peeled for Calvin's distinctive hair or Lucas's beat-up sandals or Ryan's neat haircut. No one turns up. I start to feel dumb. What if he's not going to show up at all? What if I ran down here, obsessed about my outfit, and this really is all something I made up out of nothing? What if I did get it tragically, pathetically wrong?

A tap on my shoulder.

My heart lurches. I whirl around to see who it is.

I furrow my eyebrows, confused. "You changed your mind?" I ask.

"Surprise," Ivy says, doing a mock curtsy. She's wearing a pale blue sundress and perfect little white sandals, the effortlessly chill ensemble of a person who I know from experience has never changed her clothes fourteen times before a social event. As usual, her hair is perfect, her nails a demure pink.

"This is . . . interesting timing?" I say.

She must realize she's waltzing right into the middle of my big, romantic climax? I mean, it's distinctly possible I am going to do just fine stammering through ruining my own sweeping rom-com moment, but my best friend suddenly showing up isn't going to help.

"I'm meeting HappilyEverDrafter."

"I know," she says, raises her eyebrows, and gives the small nod you give a little kid as you wait for him to get how math works.

"Okay, so—" I jerk my head in a way that hopefully communicates *I love you but bounce.*

Ivy laughs. "Jules, for the smartest girl I know, you can be sort of dense at times," she says. "It's me."

I blink. *I know it's you,* I want to say, but I'm not sure how I'm going to keep the irritation out of my voice. I stare at her blankly, then glance around to see if any of the boys are going to decide to show.

She adds, "I'm HappilyEverDrafter."

I focus back on her. She's saying words, but they don't fit together in any way that makes sense.

"I don't understand what you're saying." All of a sudden, I feel like sitting down. I lean against one of the things roping off the plane.

"It's me. *I'm* the one who's been writing 'Untitled' with you. Which reminds me, I actually have some ideas for what we should call it."

I play back all our endless chats, all the things we've shared. I try to remember if I said anything gross or cringeworthy. But that's not how it was with Happily. It was easy. *Like I was talking to my best friend.*

I feel queasy.

"But . . . ," I sputter. "But you don't even like to *read*."

"I mean, you're not wrong," Ivy admits. "But *you* do. And more than that, you like to write. So at first I just went to see what you were writing. But when I noticed that you could collaborate with someone on StoriedZone, I just—I don't know, I thought it would be a fun way for us to spend time together. You seemed so busy, but you always had time for that. I never really meant for it to be a secret. But when you went right away to thinking it was some grand, romantic thing, I didn't know how to tell you."

"All summer," I say. The shock is melting into anger. "All summer, you let me think it was a guy writing to me. And not just any guy."

"It wasn't supposed to happen like that!" Ivy interrupts, holding her hands up. "I wasn't like, trying to trick you or make you feel bad or anything. I thought you'd know it was me right away. Marchmeadow? The seagulls? Like remember how we used to love to feed the seagulls when my parents used to take us down the shore? And we'd make up names for them and stuff? And all the times we've seen a statue of a rando somewhere and wondered what makes it so that people get statues? But then you just assumed it was Calvin or

Lucas or my brother. And I tried to tell you. I did."

"Not super hard, Ivy." I say, my voice rising. "When, exactly, did you try to tell me?" I feel so dumb. Just completely duped. And let down. There's no great Romeo with sweeping romantic gestures. There's just my friend taking me for a fool.

"It's been hard to get a single word in with you all summer, Jules!" She sounds angry now, too. "And I tried everything I could think of to convince you that not only was it *not* one of the guys, but that it didn't actually matter that it wasn't one of the guys. That you could decide, not wait to be chosen. But you wouldn't listen. When I got the idea for the scavenger hunt, I thought for sure you'd get it then."

"How would I possibly have gotten it from that?"

"Because *I*, in the entire history of your life on this planet, am the only person who has ever made up scavenger hunts for you!" She shakes her head. She looks hurt, actually. "*Our* scavenger hunt! Our favorite ice cream shop! Our plane!" She gestures wildly at the plane where we've taken so many pictures. "Like, at the very least I thought you'd figure it out when I said that thing about the do-over. I thought we'd come here and take our corny photo again and have a big laugh about the whole thing. But you had such tunnel vision about it being one of the 'Romeos' that you looked right past me. Same as you've been looking past me for a while now."

I take a step back. "What does *that* mean?"

"You know what it means."

"I don't."

Ivy sighs loudly. "Okay, let me ask you something," she says. "Where am I thinking about applying to college?"

I have no idea what that has to do with anything. I think back. "Rutgers?" I guess. "Vassar, maybe?" I dimly remember something about that being where her mom went.

"Wrong," she says. "I toured Rutgers and hated it with a capital *H*. What's the first episode of the podcast with Makenna going to be about?"

"I—" I break off. I never got around to asking her about it.

I don't know. She hasn't said. But I haven't asked, either. I'm an unreliable narrator, I realize with a small, unpleasant jolt to the breastbone, narrating my own story but leaving out wide swaths of what I haven't paid attention to. Worse than that, I'm pretty sure I'm a bad best friend.

But I can't even think about that right now. Ivy

lied. She saw me making a fool of myself and let it keep going. I cycle back through the moments with the guys. Did I misread all those, too? Did I see more than was there because I believed one of them was HappilyEverDrafter?

I was so sure that after tonight the decision would be made for me, that I'd be sure I could choose and get it right.

"I can't believe it's not any of them," I murmur.

"Oh my God," Ivy interrupts, throwing her hands up. She gets a look on her face I've never seen before. "You know what, Jules? Let's *not* anymore."

She turns around and stalks away, leaving me alone in the noisy, teeming crowd of the carnival. I stand in front of the old plane, numb and stunned. This night could not have gone any worse. I didn't just not get the guy. I think I lost my best friend, too.

twenty-eight

The restaurant is slow the following night, surprising after the big high of Tango Night. But it's the end of August, and one Tango Night isn't going to change everything all at once. Still, the place feels desolate, which matches my mood after the debacle at the carnival. I haven't heard from Ivy since our argument, and I can't bear to face any of the Romeos. I just read everything so incredibly wrong.

I wander into the kitchen to find my mother leaning against the stainless steel prep table. She looks small, her tiny shoulders jutting through a black polo shirt she doesn't fill out.

"Come into the dining room with me," she says. "We'll lock the door."

I glance up at the clock in the kitchen. It's nine forty-five.

I follow her to the dining room. I sit in the booth furthest from the door while she locks the door, then sits across from me.

"You're sad," she says. "You've been sad since the carnival."

"Yes," I say.

"Abuela says to drink more mate."

Despite my mood, it forces a smile. That's my abuela's cure for everything.

"Why don't you tell me about it?" she asks.

"I don't know. I mean, I told you the basics."

"I know. But what are you thinking about it? I feel like I haven't been around enough for you."

I put my hand over hers. They're cold. "You have. You know, just love stuff. And not love stuff."

She smiles sadly. "But how are you feeling?"

"I don't know, Ma. I guess I've spent so much time trying not to fail. To get it perfect. And it made me ignore what was right in front of me. I wanted it to be perfect and fated. Not like—" I stop myself. I don't want her to feel bad.

"What? Keep going. You were going to say . . . like me and el Papi, maybe?" She has this uncanny mind-reading capacity with me. I guess when you know someone from the minute they're born, they're pretty easy to read.

"I don't know, Ma."

"What? You can say whatever you're thinking. You're not going to hurt my feelings."

I scrunch my legs up under myself on the old chair. "Well, yeah, I'm not trying to be mean. But you and el Papi don't really look like you're in love that much, you know? No offense."

"None taken. No, it doesn't look the same way twenty-plus years in that it did in the first few months. But that doesn't make it any less. In most ways, it makes it a lot more."

I search her face. Is this classic Mom-talk, trying to pep me up by papering over the cracks?

"Ma, but did you ever really love him?"

She raises her eyebrows in surprise. "What? Your father? Of course I did! And I still do. I used to walk to my dorm the long way from classes so I could see if his light was on. I joined the Young Entrepreneur's Club just to be near him."

"But the other guy."

"What guy?"

"The notes. In Argentina. At Abuelo's hardware store."

She laughs. "Ay, dios mío, that again. You've blown that up into something so much bigger than the throwaway comment it was when I told you."

"But you haven't wondered all this time? Who the great love of your life was? Or could have been?"

"Your father is the great love of my life. Always has been. I mean, sure, I wondered about the notes. Who wouldn't? But then I came here and met el Papi and it was just a strange thing that had happened. And then, a few years later, around the time you were born, in fact, I found out who it was."

Now I sit up bolt straight, put my feet back on the floor. "You know who it was?"

"Yes, I do. It was la Chiqui."

I stare her, confused. "Tía Chiqui? Your sister?"

She nods.

"But I don't get it. Why would she do that?"

"She was, what, maybe twelve or thirteen when it was time for me to go away for college? She was the youngest, and I was the oldest, and she had that worshipful thing little sisters have with big sisters.

A little like how Lucesita is always trying to impress you."

I've never noticed that, but I'll leave that point for another time.

"Anyway, so she came up with this silly plan. She thought if I was interested enough in the thought that there was a boy madly in love with me there I might cancel my plans to study abroad. To come here. She conspired with a friend to write them so I wouldn't recognize the handwriting."

I run all my bits of information through this new filter. My mother's apparent disinterest in who the mystery guy was, which I mistook as feigned. Her easy dismissal of my questions about it. How much Chiqui loves her, and the fracture you feel when a piece of you goes away. What it's like to live with your family in another country.

She goes on. "I guess that's why it breaks my heart so much to see how long it's taking us to get her here. While I was at college, I think she held out hope it was just temporary, that I was moving back home. For a few years after that, too. Then she tried to build a life over there, tried to find a guy. But it never quite worked out for her. I think all she's ever wanted was to have her big sister back, you know? And when I started to try to fix things, to get her papers to come over here, and I couldn't, it felt like I was failing my little sister all over again. But now maybe it's for the best."

"What do you mean?"

"We've been trying to figure out the way to tell you this. I wanted el Papi here. But I don't want to wait anymore."

"What?"

She puts her hands over mine now.

"Las Heras. We have to let it go."

It's only now I notice that her bloodshot eyes, the dark circles under them.

"But Tango Night . . ." Even as it's out of my mouth, it sounds silly, not enough.

She rubs her forehead, spent, talked out, but trying to keep it together. "It doesn't work that way. One night doesn't make up for the hole we've been digging for the last two-plus years. And, anyway, our landlord won't renew the lease."

I scan the dining room. The painting of the Aconcagua is slightly off-balance. To its left, there's a picture I've seen so many times I've stopped noticing it. My mother and father, impossibly young, faces slim, narrower at the jaw, hopeful. They have their arms around each other, she's holding a bunch of his shirt, squeezing him toward her. Behind them, boxes, a ladder, evidence of construction. It's like the video we watched at the lake. It is the first picture they took in this space before it was even what it turned out to be: where we spent all our birthdays and holidays, where we fought and made up and lived their American dream, which became ours by default, even before we existed. The thing they built to carry the weight of all the people who came before them. I don't even know who we are without this place.

My mother traces my line of sight, looks at the picture. "Look at those two fools," she says. "They thought they knew everything."

"You did," I say. I need to believe that. They must have. How else do grown-ups get to be in charge?

She shakes her head. "We didn't."

The tears come harder. "What are we going to do? For money? To pay the mortgage, all that?" I ask. She's told me a thousand times how there's no other way for them to get by in the world except for this business, the mother of all baskets where we've put every single, fragile egg in our lives.

She tips her chin up, trying to look brave, but her voice is small. "I don't know," she says. "But we're going to figure it out. I promise. And you focus on following your own dreams. You got that?"

"But how can I, now? After this?"

She squeezes my hands. "Especially after this. I followed my dream, and I've never been sorry. Not even today."

I'm confused. "What dream?"

She waves a hand around. "This. A little dream, maybe. But a good one."

"Las Heras?" I ask. It's been a lot of things. A comfort. A place like home. A fourth child in the family, the crankiest and most demanding one. But a dream? "I thought the restaurant was el Papi's thing."

"Oh, he majored in business because he wanted to be sensible. But you know him. He would have been happy living on the beach painting portraits for tourists. It was my idea to start it, after we visited friends in this town. I figured it could be our little thing. He'd charm the customers, make Abuela's costillas; I'd do the books. That's how I realized how much I really loved him. When he heard my dream and worked so hard to help make it real. We got married. I quit my computer job. And six months later we started this."

I put my face in my hands. Hearing my mom talk about Las Heras like a dream, nostalgic here at its end, feels terrible. But there's something else, some kernel in all this sadness. Something about dreams, and the people who believe in yours.

Ryan. I flash back to a dozen conversations on the bus. When he listened about how I doubted myself. When he told me what he liked about the latest thing I'd written. When I was down about Paige's feedback and he told me to keep going.

Trying to figure it out all this summer, finding the clues, when the clues were right there the whole time.

"But what do you do when a dream fails?"

She thinks it's a question about the restaurant. "This dream hasn't failed. We don't fail because Las Heras closes. It's given me so many of the happiest moments of my life. We'll have those, forever. And we'll find ways to make new ones."

twenty-nine

I spend the next day in a fog in my room. By the afternoon, I can't take the terrible feeling anymore. I go outside and walk and walk and walk with no direction. It's hours later before I find myself on my abuela's block. She must know about the restaurant, too, and suddenly I want her warm presence, a big-bellied hug.

I knock softly on her door. She opens, hair in curlers, and gives me a hug. "Viniste justo a tiempo," she tells me. "Come on, we can watch the last episode of my novela. Mabel and Reinaldo."

It has been way too hot in here all summer, with her "allergy" to AC, but the temperature turned to a

338

glimpse of autumn a few days ago, a cool breeze bringing with it whispers of leaves about to give way. She spreads out sanguchitos, mate, and a new recipe she's learned since she met her new guy at bingo: Polish latkes. I glimpse under the rollers to see her hair color is brighter. She's got on blue eyeshadow. She looks so peppy and full of life.

The last episode starts. I can't quite follow it all, because I've missed a bunch of it, but Reinaldo is pretending to be a window washer. Mabel, now a rich and famous journalist, glances at him disinterestedly as he sways out there on his platform, then goes back to her work. She gets a text on her phone, and she checks it just as Reinaldo reaches her floor.

Reinaldo unrolls a sign, presses it up against the wall. It reads *Marry Me*. But Mabel isn't paying attention. She's striding out of the room to leave, to go chase the story. Reinaldo bangs on the window. Mabel has slipped on some earbuds, and she can't hear him as she puts on her elegant jacket. He bangs again, the rickety window cleaner's platform swinging dangerously.

She stops. Maybe she's heard something. She takes an earbud out, turns around, looks at the window.

He unrolls the sign again, which he'd let fall as he banged. It takes her a moment to put together what's going on. Here is Reinaldo, rich, beautiful, usually impeccably dressed Reinaldo, all scruffy and in perilous circumstances, just for her. To show her he can get down and dirty, that he's not just a spoiled rich boy.

She runs up to the window, tries to say something to him, to apologize, to explain. He can't hear her. The scene cuts to him, the wind whizzing by him. He's saying things she can't hear, either.

I consider making a crack about how it is that he did not think through this flaw in his plan, but my abuela is scarfing down latkes and grinning with such enthusiasm that I don't have the heart to do it.

Mabel runs to a terrace just out of the camera's view. It's beautiful, modern, all concrete, metal, and glass. She calls to Reinaldo. He makes his way to that side of the platform. There's a hair-raising moment when he climbs over the side of the balcony and the window washer's platform lurches sickeningly.

"That's definitely against regulations," I quip at Abuela.

She mock-slaps my knee. "Shh."

And they're on the balcony, hugging tight, saying sorry, explaining, kissing, promising forever. She's saying he should never pull a stunt like that again, which

I can't disagree with. It's not that Reinaldo has lost all his money and has had to take up window cleaning. It's that he wants to show he'll do anything for her.

Out of nowhere, a volcano I didn't know was in me erupts, and I start sobbing. It's so bad I cover my face with my hands, lean forward, try to catch my breath.

My abuela puts her hand on my back. "Ya, mi niña," she coos over and over again.

I sit up. Abuela Bubbles's wise old eyes size me up.

"This is about a lot more than Mabel and Reinaldo," she says.

I nod.

"I'm sorry about Las Heras. Is it that?" she asks.

I nod again, find a few more tears at the bottom of the well.

"And the boy?"

"Well," I admit. "A boy, anyway."

That gets her attention. "Tell me," she prompts.

So I tell her about HappilyEverDrafter. "All summer it's felt like I've had these three different love stories laid out in front of me, you know?" I ask her. "Lucas, this safe, dependable one who has been in my life forever, who totally understands me and my family and where I come from. Calvin, the boy next door who makes me feel like anything is possible, who sees life as an adventure and makes me see it that way, too. And who obviously had the abuela seal of approval, too. And Ryan, who's, like, a completely different person than the obnoxious, privileged rich boy I thought he was—this smart, sensitive, brilliant writer, who challenges me and keeps me sharp and has some adventure in him, too, who will run through the rain." I stop, wipe my face, wondering how much of this is making sense to her. "It feels like I'm choosing more than just a romance, Abuela. It feels like I'm choosing the kind of person I want to be. The kind of life I want to have. And I thought if I just knew which one of them was HappilyEverDrafter, then the choice would be clear. But now . . ."

She hands me the mate, tells me to sip. I do.

"Did I ever tell you how your grandfather asked me to marry him?" she says.

I shake my head. She hasn't talked about him much since he died. She smiles, "Mi Pedrito. Nobody would have made a novela about him. He took me to a shoe store in Luján. He told me to pick any pair of shoes that I wanted. None of them were off-limits, he said. He delivered fruit for money, then, had had to drop out

342

of high school to help support his family, so this was a big sacrifice. We didn't have much, but his family was even poorer than mine. I knew his own shoes were falling apart, not because he didn't care for them, but because he worked so hard in them.

"I said no, I couldn't accept a pair of shoes. He insisted. I picked this quiet little pair, dark blue, with this tiny cream pattern embroidered around the edges, a low, modest heel. I was fifteen, and these were my first pair of heels. So beautiful. He bought them for me. I still have them, in a box. I always tried to wear them lightly and take care of them, because I knew the sacrifice they represented. Then he told me, 'I know I may not seem like much now. But if you marry me, you'll never be without shoes.' This was the biggest sign of safety he could imagine then, the most impressive thing he could dream of offering. Not one for sweeping romantic gestures, mi Pedro. But you know what? I never was. Never without anything I needed, not while he had a breath in him to get it for me. He was a good man, a solid man. Dependable."

"Do you miss him?"

She closes her eyes, lets out a big breath. "Every day. You have his eyebrows. And the color of his hair when he was young. Not the blue, of course." She smiles. It's a sad smile. "I try not to think about him at the end, you know? About him in that room alone, a nurse holding up a phone right before they put the tubes in him and me telling him he better hurry up and get better because I needed that back door fixed. A lifetime together and all I could think of was to joke, to nag, when I wasn't allowed to be with him.

"I didn't tell him he'd constantly surprised me, how much I loved that his rough fingers were so gentle with kittens and chicks and baby birds that fell out of nests. I didn't tell him how much it meant to me that he was the only person left here who remembered me as a girl and that sometimes, when he looked at me, his eyes seemed like that version of me was still the one he was seeing. I was embarrassed there was a stranger in the room with us, holding up a phone for us to talk to each other. So I told him about the back door."

"Oh, Abuela, you did the best you could. He knew how you loved him."

She wipes away a tear. "Ay, m'hijita, I know, I know. You say dumb things when your whole heart is breaking. After he was gone, I didn't get out of bed for three days. I had no idea how I ever would again. I had to sell that house because it squeaked and banged and thudded his name, every piece of wood and siding, every day. The table he built. The curtains he hung for me, moving them three times until I was happy with them, then carefully patching up the extra holes without complaint. His tools, all shiny. The way that man took care of tools, better than most women with their jewels. He was so careful with everything. So grateful for every little thing he got to have.

"But then I did get up. And I did move on. And I came here, and you all made me so happy and reminded me of the best of him, and why we keep going. For what comes next. And I found new friends, and new places to go. And my Mabel and my Reinaldo."

I smile. She's kidding about this last part, of course.

"You think I'm kidding," she says, like I said my thought out loud. "But no. You know why I like my novelas?"

"¿Sos chismosa?" I joke.

She laughs. "Un poquitín, si. But besides liking gossip and knowing people's business, I like these stories because of what they teach me."

I raise my eyebrows skeptically.

"It's true!" she says. "You know I've always said so. One day they're poor. The next day they're rich. We all want to have a life that's steady, predictable. Safe.

Where we never have to worry where the next pair of shoes comes from. In this world maybe we've been taught to expect it, like unexpected things should be unusual. But that's not how it is. The unexpected is really to be expected, life up and down all the time. We can't wish for a life without bumps. If there's anything these last few years have taught us, it's that. The best we can wish for is the strength to face the bumps, to learn from them, to overcome them. You know what I mean? Life is like that. You never know what's going to happen. We keep going not because we know we're going to succeed, but because it's the only way to live all out."

"But that scares me," I say softly.

"It scares me too. But being open to life surprising you can open you to the biggest heartbreaks, yes, but also to the most amazing moments. There's no avoiding the ups and downs. There's only knowing that no matter what comes, you can face it. You especially, mi niña. You are so strong. You get that from Abuelo Pedro, too.

"Let me ask you something," she says, sitting back and looking at me shrewdly. "Putting the boys aside for a moment. When you were imagining all those different lives for yourself—telling yourself all those different stories about your future—when did you feel the most like yourself?"

I sit up a little bit straighter, eyes narrowing. "That . . . is a really good question," I admit, and it's not until right now that I realize I haven't thought to ask it. It sounds ridiculous to admit, but the truth is I've been so focused on figuring out the correct answer—so focused on getting it right—that I don't know that I ever stopped to consider which version of the story I liked most. Life isn't some whodunit novel, where the key to the mystery is revealed by a tuxedoed detective. It's a choose-your-own adventure.

And I'm the author.

All at once I get to my feet, wanting to ride this fuel in this moment. "I've gotta go, Abuela," I say, flinging my arms around her neck and squeezing. "I've . . . got some revising to do."

When I leave, the sky is turning purple, with hot pink clouds blazing in the sky. I'm walking past the apartment complex parking lot when I see Calvin. I say his name, and he stops and turns my way.

"Jules," he says.

I smile. It's been a while since we've talked. We haven't texted, either. I guess it felt like a natural stopping point. And right now I'm filled with a certainty that doesn't include him.

It's like he can see it on my face. "You look like a girl on a mission," he says.

"I don't know if I am. But I want to be."

"I haven't heard from you."

I weigh what to say. There isn't much to tell at the moment. There's only possibility. And choosing.

"I've been trying to figure myself out a little. And I think I have?" I take a breath and continue. "I hope that even if you and me aren't going to hang out in that way anymore, we can still be in touch."

He smiles. "I'd like that. So that way it's not awkward if we run into each other at your abuela's house. The next telenovela is starting next week, and my Spanish is seriously improving."

Now it's my turn to laugh. "No, it won't be. It's nice to think she's got a neighbor like you."

The sky is on fire, and for an instant I remember why I thought he might be HappilyEverDrafter. I projected a lot of my own wants and imaginings onto him, but the real person under them is pretty awesome, too. Even if he's not "the one," his different worldview made me see things in new ways. I'm grateful he was a part of my topsy-turvy summer. I lean in and give him a hug.

Maggie couldn't believe she was finally going to meet this admirer who had turned her last few days upside down. These notes had made her feel like anything was possible, like maybe she'd be the kind of impulsive girl who would realize she had real love in her life and postpone going off to the desert dream just to let fate guide her. Not that she wouldn't pursue her education, of course, but what if love was knocking at her door and it was the passion of a lifetime? She could enroll in the local state school, commute, stay home. Plenty of kids in her town were doing it. And maybe now she wanted to do it a little, too.

Here's the thing about grand, romantic moments, though. They hardly ever live up to the hype. As she approached the agreed-to spot on a sandy stretch of shore away from the hustle and bustle of the piers, she recognized him at once. It was Charlie, a boy she'd played jacks with and chased gulls with when they were small. His father owned a dependable old fishing trawler, and although Charlie was whip-smart at math and won an unfair number of spelling bees, she had the sense he was one of those lifers who stick near the sea and do what their parents and grandparents did without a lot of fuss.

She'd thought him handsome, in his way, back when she'd first discovered boys. But she hadn't thought of him in that way in a long time. When she'd started to wonder who might be leaving the notes, who

might have that sense of romance and adventure in him, she'd considered a lot of suspects, but never once Charlie. He was quiet, with hands
marred by tangles with ropes and fishing hooks, with dark, serious eyes
and wind-tossed hair. He was not who Maggie had expected at all.

Even before she approached him to sit down on the old, worn
beach boulder, she knew that their small flare of mutual interest would
not change her plans. Maggie was leaving, and unexpected Charlie
was not enough to stop her.

Posts 52   Likes 89

thirty

I find Ivy lying in her usual lounge chair at the town pool, her bikini a pale turquoise that shows off her hard-earned tan, her sunglasses taking up the entire top half of her face.

"You're in my sunlight." She looks at me over the top, then pushes them up imperiously.

"I'm sorry, Ivy," I sink onto the chair beside her. "I messed up."

She peers at me over the tops of the sunglasses again. "Go on."

"I'm sorry," I say again, more emphatically this time. "For not realizing that you were HappilyEverDrafter to begin with. You're right. I should have seen the clues. I'm sorry for being so distracted all summer, so in my own head. I'm sorry I was such a jerk at the carnival the other night."

"You were disappointed," Ivy says softly. "I get it. I really never wanted it to go that far."

"I wasn't, though," I tell her. "Or maybe I was in the moment, because I didn't see the big picture. But I'm definitely not now. Collaborating on 'Untitled' made me feel so seen. So understood. Like, of *course* it felt like I had this amazing, once-in-a-lifetime connection with HappilyEverDrafter. It's because I *do*. I just had to see it for what it really was and not wish for it to be something else."

Ivy smiles. But then her expression wobbles. "I felt like such a little kid this summer," she confesses quietly. "Like I was the only one who cared that we're going to be going our separate ways next year. Like you didn't have time for me because everything else was more important, the restaurant, the Romeos, the big, creative, exciting life you've already started because you're, like, the only person our age I know who knows exactly what she wants to do all her life. I felt so left behind."

"But you were hanging out with Makenna all the

time." I guess Ivy isn't the only one with little-kid worries.

"You think I wanted to process my entire breakup with Makenna?" Ivy looks off at the pool. "Like, look, she's fine, I'm not going to trash-talk her. She's proven to be a good friend this summer. But if I have to look at one more clean-eating account on Instagram, I'm going to make a vow to subsist on cheeseburgers for the rest of my life."

I laugh. "It's probably a little childish that I'm relieved."

"Maybe. But maybe it's okay."

I hold out my hand. She squeezes mine, her perfect acrylics uncharacteristically neon orange. I hold up her hand for a mock inspection. "And what's this?"

"Don't ask. Makenna says eighties neon is definitely coming back. She insisted."

I laugh, let go of her hand. "If you've got any processing left to do, about your breakup or anything else, I would love to be the person you did it with."

Ivy considers that for a moment. "Maybe later," she says. Then she nods at the tote bag on the chair beside me. "You've got your notebook in there, don't you?" she asks, pushing her sunglasses up again. "Because what I really want to do is finish this damn story."

2:17 p.m.: AldertonGirlAconcagua and HappilyEverDrafter posted to "From the Desert to the Sea."

Maggie did leave her sleepy seaside town for school in the high desert. Charlie did get over his initial disappointment at Maggie's reaction to his romantic gesture. He took to the sea like his father, after all, becoming one of the youngest fleet captains in all of downstate. He had an uncanny knack for finding the most fertile fishing spots and a nose for avoiding storms.

But a strange thing happened in the time Maggie and Charlie were apart. Charlie forgot. Maggie remembered. She thought often of the heady days of feeling wanted by a mysterious stranger. She cried bitterly at how thoughtless her words had been that day on the shore, how her eyes had been so set on the horizon she had not looked right in front of her.

The first note she wrote him was on a postcard she picked up as an afterthought in the crystal shop where she worked weekends to help pay for school. It was a picture of Arches National Park. On the reverse she wrote, "Your very own copy of the arches. I hope it's okay to write you sometimes."

It took him so long to respond, she had given up imagining he might. But he'd been out on a long fishing trip out past the banks, he said, and hadn't seen her postcard as it sat waiting for his return. His letter was in his neat hand and spoke nothing of love but plenty of the sea. Writing to him became a pastime, and later felt more like a lifeline. Maggie loved school, and the stark beauty of the desert, but the unthinkable had happened: she missed the sea. Even more shocking, she missed the Charlie she got to know in their many long and lovely letters. She longed to feel close to him.

When they saw each other next after Maggie's first year of school was over, Charlie was less shy, Maggie more so. She spent the summer on the deck of his boat, when he wasn't out fishing. He walked her home in the gloaming and kept a respectful distance. It went on this way maddeningly long, until the week before Maggie was set to go back to school. It was always impending distance that seemed to nudge them into action. Except this time, it was Maggie who made the move. She leaned into Charlie as he stood at the end of her walk and gave him a kiss. His lips were salty with sea water, hers sweet from her cherry ChapStick, each a delight and surprise to the other.

🎵 Posts 217   🤍 Likes 399

thirty-one

I go to Lucas's house and slip into his yard. It looks like it is frozen in time. It's mostly grass, with an ancient old oak in the center, and the tree house his dad built when we were six. Lucas's dad is an accountant, not particularly handy, but that summer he got it in his head that he was going to build a tree house, and he downloaded all these plans from the internet. My dad teased him in that way that Argentinian men can have with one another, but ended up helping. And it was like a slice of heaven just growing on their tree. We spent hours in here, Lucas and his brother, me and, later, sometimes Jaime and Lucesita.

I climb up the rope ladder to the tree house. My hips nearly get stuck in the doorway. It is so much tinier than I remember it.

From inside, I have a direct line into Lucas's room. His light is on and the play of color on the walls means he's either watching TV or playing a video game. I call him. It rings for so long I'm almost sure he's going to let it go to voice mail. But he picks up, finally.

"Hey, can you come out?" I ask. "I'm in Groot. I can see your light on."

He materializes in his window. I flash the lit-up screen of my phone at him so he can see it, then I put the phone to my ear again.

"I'll be right down," he says.

A few minutes later, he comes out his back door and walks barefoot across the grass. His hair is tousled, as usual. The tree house winces as he comes up the rope ladder. He fills the entrance entirely.

"This place used to be bigger," he says.

"We used to be smaller, I think," I reply.

The air is moist. A faraway jasmine scent wafts in it. Gone are the pillows and blankets we used to keep in here and the small, perfect flower curtains, probably long ago repurposed or thrown away. The deliberately crooked cutout window is a frame for the full moon and plays a shadow on Lucas's face.

I finally say, "It's been a summer."

He looks toward the window. "It has been."

"I have to admit something: I thought you might have been the one writing back on my StoriedZone account."

He fixes me with a quizzical look. "Did you? Is that why it's been different with us this summer?"

"Kind of, yes."

"Well, it wasn't me."

"No, I know that now. I thought whoever it was was some version of 'the one,' you know? And what I needed to realize was that it doesn't work like that."

"And you've decided I'm not 'the one'?"

I glance over at him. I can't tell if he sounds disappointed. Or hurt. I can't stand the thought of hurting Lucas.

"I don't even know what that means, to be honest. I know you're my oldest friend. I know I hope you're still in my life when we're both a hundred. I know that no one will ever understand my family and my history like you can. So I've always kind of wondered about us. . . . But now I don't think we're supposed to be together in that way. Did you?"

He draws in a long breath, lets it out slowly. "It would have been nice, I think. It would have all fit so easily. God knows the parentals would have loved it."

I can't help but laugh. "They so would have."

Finally he looks at me. "I guess I feel a little stupid, you know?"

My heart pinches. "Lucas, every single thing that happened was real. And not for nothing, but you were a total smoke show at Tango Night."

He smiles. "I did look pretty good, didn't I?"

"You sure did," I say.

"That stubble was a total bitch, though. I had a rash on my face all weekend after shaving it off."

I laugh. Then I get serious again. "Hey, for real, though, don't just do that Lucas thing where you make a joke and then it's all supposed to be fine. I never want to lose you as a friend."

"We're okay. I promise."

We're quiet for a long time.

Then he says, "I'm sorry about the restaurant."

"I know. Me too." And if there's someone I know who gets it, the big, vast meaning of all that, it's Lucas. And I'm grateful for that. And for knowing I have someone as solid and real as Lucas in my life.

* * *

Formal classes at Fairchild are over now; all that's left this last week is what Paige is calling "exit interviews," individual meetings where she returns our final portfolios and shares feedback on work in the class. The meetings aren't in our usual classroom but across the quad, at the school library.

It dawns on me that I haven't been in here all summer. I recognize it immediately from "fantasy library" Instagram posts I've drooled over. I didn't know this iconic building whose picture I've seen a thousand times was the library. Inside, there's a circular open space in the middle, leading up to what, indoors, feels like the clouds but is a giant, round skylight, making the whole space ethereal and bright. This main floor is double height, held up by carved, light-wood columns.

Story idea: a girl runs away from home and lives in a massive library. Like Where the Heart Is *but not pregnant and so much better than Walmart. But, the rub: there's a secret society that meets there and is plotting to remove her? And she has to uncover their dastardly deeds? Or join them?*

I follow the directions for the meeting room. It's right behind the massive wall behind the desk. I make my way around the bend and am met with an almost churchlike painted ceiling, and two levels of dark wood bookshelves, connected by one of those slide ladders. Paige is sitting on a low leather couch.

She points to a seat in front of what looks like a castle fireplace. I wonder if it's just decorative. I plop down.

"It's something, right? I love bringing students here because it helps me relive what it felt like for me to see it for the first time. I always believed like I could study better when I was here. There's a great reading room on the seventh floor you should check out, too. It's magical. And if you're into libraries you should check out the Morgan and, of course, the Rose Main Reading Room at NYPL, if you haven't already."

"It's amazing. I . . ." The space makes me want to say something about my dreams, what I want, but I stop myself. I'm not sure why. Maybe because speaking the wish will finally make it seem too big, especially in front of someone who knows what it takes to achieve it. Or because I'm afraid she's about to let me down easy, suggest maybe I should follow a more sensible career path because I don't have what it takes to be a writer.

But she must read the hope on me, too, because she says, "So you're going into your senior year, right?

What are your plans after that?"

Here goes. I pull up straighter, for courage. "Well, I mean, I think I'd love to major in creative writing. At the very least I'd like to figure out how to make writing my career. But I don't know if . . ."

She leans in, smiles. "Are you going to ask the talent question? Like do you have what it takes?"

"Well, yeah. I mean . . . a lot of people imagine they want to be writers. Not everyone's got the talent."

"Listen, I'm a hack, so you might hear differently from the snoots, but my personal position is that talent is crap."

I stare at her. Does she mean I don't have any and so I shouldn't feel bad? Or . . . what does she mean?

"Like . . . are some writers more naturally able to turn a phrase? Maybe? It's a moot point, like wondering if some person, in their perfectly natural condition, is an inherently faster runner than some other person. I mean, maybe, but the one who trains hardest generally goes the fastest, right? It's even more pronounced in a field like writing.

"When I was in college, I knew a lot of students who were way more talented than I was. Who got the school prizes, who made classmates cry at their readings. I spent those four years wishing I could be as good as they were. Today, I have the best career of all of us. And that's not to toot my own horn. I was not the most talented one. I was the one who never gave up."

"But my . . ." I point at her folder. "What I've written. Is it good enough?"

She smiles. I get the sense we're having two different conversations. "I don't know if it's all humans or writers in particular who want that gold sticker. You want me to tell you you're good enough. So I will. You have a way with words. You listen to direction and feedback, course correct when it's needed. You obviously have the enthusiasm. But what I'm telling you is this: I don't *get* to say if you're good enough. Publishing, not even readers, they don't get to say, either. You decide you're not going away, you're not going to stop writing. It's a business full of rejection; I'm not going to lie. Full of heartbreak and setbacks. It's glacially slow. Feedback is maddening and contradictory. And don't get me started on contracts and book deals.

"You've read the big, splashy stories about how I first published as an undergrad. What you haven't read about is how it took me five years to get the next deal after that, and how many books I wrote that no one read until *Lakeside* made it big and everyone went back to 'discover' me. About how many lattes I slung for a living when the advance money ran out after the first one. About how much my dad pushed me to get a nice, safe desk job.

"So I can tell you you're good enough. You are. But my question to you is: Are you willing to never give up? Because that's really the only thing that matters."

I nod. "Yes," I say.

"Then it's all entirely in your hands. Now, let's talk about what you did here in this piece about time travel."

thirty-two

The shuttered restaurant is probably the last place I want to be, but also one I can't not go to. My mother needs to clean out the office and take down the pictures and sentimental things before the restaurant close-out company comes to give her an estimate for what they'll pay for our equipment. I'm not sure why it feels so imperative that I be here, too. It's like trying to catch the last grains of sand as they slip through our fingers, grab one to put in a little jar.

We've got most things boxed up. The pictures. The first $20 they ever made, in its frame. Keepsakes and thank-you cards and one each of every ad, every Valpak, every coupon in the paper, all in a photo album with a crackly spine. For some reason, they chose to measure our heights here instead of home. Maybe because we spent so much more time here than there. They start down near my knees, me, Jaime, Lucesita, in pencil and pen, scribbled year after year, on both sides of the doorframe to the kitchen, our initials beside the date and the line so we can tell them apart. She makes me stand next to it as she takes a picture to get a record of it before it's gone for good.

In all, it takes a surprisingly short amount of time to gather up a lifetime of meaning. The rest of it, the laughs soaked into walls and the many games of tic-tac-toe and twenty questions and the hours of homework and the exact spot where a customer finally helped me understand algebra . . . those we can't carve out and put in boxes. I run my hand on the grain of one of the tables. Soon they'll all be gone.

In the window is an artist's rendering of what they're going to put here. They plan to knock down this building, and the one next to it, which our soon-to-be-former landlord also owns, and build what looks like an impossibly tall, gleaming tower in the place of the two-story structure the restaurant is in. It promises luxury retail and office space, and reads, in Starship

Enterprise letters, *Revitalizing downtown Alderton*. So it's not that the space where our restaurant used to be will be something else. It's that it won't be at all, smashed into nothing and built entirely differently, with new materials. I don't know if that's worse or better, actually. At least I won't have to drive by and see another family building a different dream here. But, on the other hand, when I'm old, if I ever want to show where I spent most of my childhood and teen years, it won't exist at all, except in these few things we've got in boxes.

My mother sits at the same table where she told me we were losing Las Heras. She doesn't look as spent as she did that day, which feels counterintuitive. For more than two years, we stood on a crumbly precipice, and then it gave way beneath us, and we fell. And I thought if we could do everything right, we could stop it, but we couldn't. In some ways, we're still falling. But there's some peace in having the worse happen. There's no more to dread. There's just the solid truth of it: This happened. There is nothing left to fight.

I sit across from her.

"I wish I had known what else to do," I say to her.

She cocks her head at me. "What do you mean?"

"Maybe if I'd worked harder."

She grabs my hands, and hers are surprisingly strong and hot with life. "No. Don't even think that. How can you think that? There's no way of know-ing what could have made it different. Or if anything could. And it wasn't your job. You did so much more than you should have been expected to."

"But not enough."

"Look, this is my fault, I know. I was so heads-down trying to figure out what to do, I didn't do a great job of protecting you from all the problems. Of telling you to go home, to go be a kid. Of being the mother. I'm the one who's sorry. Please forgive me."

I shake my head. On top of all this, I don't want her to feel bad. But I also want to soak in her words, which feel soothing, like cream on a burn. "It's okay," I say.

I squeeze her hands back, but she uses them to pull me up and around the table, to get me in a big hug. We stay like that for a long time. Then she says, "Dale, vamos, let's get this stuff in the car."

We each carry a box at a time, and we're done in faster than I want us to be. We come back to stand in the doorway one last time, backs to the sun that is starting to make its way over the buildings across the street, into the gloom of the unlit restaurant.

I look out onto the far wall, bare now, dusty shapes

left where we've taken down photos and artwork. It is all too much, the leaving of all of this. It is a thick knot in my throat.

"So much love in this place," she says, and takes my hand.

"Yes," I say. And so much sweat, and fear and joy and boredom and . . . life. I don't say all that. I want to curl up into a ball in a corner, maybe chain myself to a beam so they can't do anything to stop this place from existing. But then, it already doesn't exist. I squeeze her hand, and we stand there until the sun is warm on our backs and makes the Las Heras stenciling on the door begin its sun-dial trip across the floor for the last time.

Dear Las Heras:

You were never just a place. You were always an idea, a gutsy move, a wing and a prayer. It's been a few weeks since we said goodbye to you. Most leaves are still green, but others are fully brown. Today, I walked past where you used to be. I'd been avoiding it, to be honest. But finally I decided it was important, this witnessing.

The sidewalk in front of where you used to be bears our initials in the corner, near the street. There they were today, all five of them. We carved them on the day they'd repoured the old, cracked sidewalk, like, five years ago. But that was the only recognizable thing there.

There's a larger version of the artist's rendering that was in your window on that last day. It is . . . beautiful, somehow. Is it disloyal to you to think so? It's the kind of building that, if I saw it in a city I was visiting, would make me think, It must be nice to live here. There's no hint of you. Strangely, there's something okay about that.

Seeing the empty space where you used to be feels freeing in a way that's entirely surprising. It is confirmation of what Abuela said to me once: we don't give our whole heart because we are guaranteed that our efforts won't all one day be knocked into dust. We give it all because it is the only way to trust ourselves to handle anything.

People like us, the newcomers, the small ones, we're the ones who <u>make</u> this world with our hopes and our small wins.

Somehow, seeing the empty space where all our dreams lived for so long makes me realize our dreams are not so easily knocked down.

I love you always,
J

thirty-three

The last of summer seeps away, the nights taking on that telltale coolness, the first leaves turning brown at the edges. I spend a few last afternoons at the pool with Ivy. I take Lucesita shopping for back-to-school clothes and help her pick out her first lip gloss. I resign myself to the fact that the story of my summer romance that could have been might have to go unfinished. When Abuela made me see I had to write my own ending, the resolution was suddenly obvious.

But somehow I can't find the words.

I could slip a love letter into his mailbox. An oldie but goodie.

I could skywrite *I like you* over his house.

I could invite him to play Red Dead Online and tell him in there. I have fought off the urge more than once.

I could dress up like an Orc, or a character he loves, and sing at him until he opens his window.

I could find him in the middle of the street, grab him by the shirt, and lay one on him. But I haven't. There are the big, sweeping things I dream, and the person I actually am. And the person I am does not stalk and kiss.

In the end, he finds me.

I'm sitting on my porch with a book. He drives by, slows down, then parks in front of my house. I've been reading out here a lot. With no restaurant to go to, Paige's class over, the pace of the end of summer slow and full of time to think, I've let myself get lost in book after book. He gets out of his car with the confidence of someone who knows he's expected, although he's so unexpected my heart breaks into a gallop that threatens to bust it out of my chest.

He makes his way up my walkway. I put down the book, open to save my page. I tug at my messy old cut-offs, stick a finger in the hole by the pocket. He is in a more relaxed outfit than I've ever seen him out in, an old band T-shirt that looks so well-worn it might just be his dad's, or from a vintage shop, and roughed-up cargo shorts in a charcoal gray with wear at the seams. But he's still got his corner-office-in-training vibe. He's still Ryan, after all.

"I didn't win the Best Work Prize," Ryan says when he finally reaches my top step.

The afternoon is cloudy but doesn't threaten rain, for once in our history. It's a couple of days before senior year starts.

"Me neither," I admit.

The house is quiet and empty. Lucesita is at town camp. Jaime is at a friend's. My parents are both at work. Once they announced the restaurant was closing, several of the old regulars reached out to find out what my mom was going to do next. Mrs. Richards, of the book club, offered her a job managing her art school. My mom oversees the running of dozens of classes each week in a gorgeous old industrial space, hosting parties, and inviting famous artists to give talks. It turns out Mrs. Richards' husband has been sick for a while, and she needed someone trustworthy to step in and was excited to offer the position to my mom. It takes all of my mom's skills without giving her any of the worries. When she got her first paycheck, and, a few days later, an actual health insurance card, she did a little dance in the kitchen and snapped a picture of them both on her phone. My dad is working at a friend's food truck, and painting more. Unexpectedly, he looks happier too. Sometimes, what looks like the worst is actually the start of the next great thing.

"We should have known Wyatt was going to pull it out in the end," I add.

"Wyatt is a poser." Ryan laughs, taking off his sunglasses and tucking them into the collar of his shirt. The blue in his eyes is overpowering the other colors in this light. "I mean, he's what happens when we teach children that Hemingway is canon and no one disabuses them of that notion, right?"

I laugh at the callback to the conversation that feels like it happened years ago.

He takes another step closer to me. "Honestly, what does that guy have that we don't have? Has he ever even found a single solitary perfect raccoon pelt?"

"I bet he is not equipped for that, no. Plus I'm sure he has no idea how to get clones out of the predicament of being caught by the evil company who created them."

"Hack."

"Wannabe."

"So . . ." Ryan leans back against the porch railing. "I was driving by. You were out here. I figured I'd be spontaneous and stop and tell you . . ."

I wait, look at his face, earnest, struggling. A little muscle of uncertainty moves in his cheek, revealing a dimple for an instant.

"Yes?"

His teeth play with his bottom lip. He smiles, says, "I had fun with you this summer. I . . . kinda miss it, actually."

I take a step closer. "I did, too. And I miss it, too." He stands up straight, off the railing, makes an infinitesimal move in my direction. I take another step, tilting my face up to his. We're close enough that I can feel the heat of him now, powerful and riveting. This summer has been about him all along, and having him here, so close to me, makes me feel what I've known all this time but didn't let myself see through my haze of aiming for perfection and writing the ideal romance with HappilyEverDrafter. But even more than that, this summer has been about me, too, about finding the words and the courage, about letting go and going all in, whether I succeed or fail.

He smiles, his face serious. "You're all the way over there, Jules," he says softly, and holds out his hands.

I slip mine into his, and he gives me the gentlest pull. I step in closer still, let go of his hands and lift my arms up around his shoulders. He puts his around my waist. It's so good, so unexpected, so overdue, that I just let myself linger here, feeling his body against mine, my eyes closed. But then I open them, and his face is inches from mine, pulling me in, his lips suddenly right by my mouth, his breath warm.

I tilt my face up more, and he leans down, and I don't know if I kiss him or if he kisses me, but we're suddenly grazing each other's lips softly, tenderly, the world all gone now, just him and me and the cool air. It's slow at the start, then builds to a cascade of sensation. He feels inevitable and entirely unknown, his body pressed on me, his arms tight around me, his hands on my shoulder blades, his lips searching mine, hungry and unafraid as I put my hands on the back of his head to bring him in as close as I can get him and kiss him some more. I have dreamed of this moment. I have written this moment more than once. But the actual thing is 3D and rich, saturated technicolor, a vibrant symphony of a moment.

He pulls his lips off mine and lays a line of kisses on my cheek, all the way to my ear. "I've been waiting for you to do that all summer," he whispers. "Longer, if I'm being honest. A long time."

"Seriously?" I pull back and look at him.

He smirks. "Jules," he says, like it should have been obvious. "Why the hell do you think I spent all summer taking the *bus*? I assure you it was not for the mood lighting."

I laugh at that, at him and at myself and at the ways even the most familiar stories can surprise us. At how a summer can hold the pain of the end of the restaurant but also the wonder of him and me, of finding out what I wanted and not just what I was supposed to do.

"You want to come in for a while?" I ask him. He nods, his gaze riveted on me, looking at me in a way that is new and exciting and . . . everything I've been hoping for all this time. I lace our fingers together and tug him in the door, then close it behind him. It's the first time he's been in my house, I realize, but it feels completely natural. Once we're inside, I kiss him again.

"I'm so happy you're here," I whisper.

"Me too," he says, raspy, in my ear. "One of us had to finally overcome our desperate inertia, right? I figured society says it should be me."

I smile, lead him over to the couch. We sit and I put my legs on his lap. "What do you want to do?" I ask.

He laughs, wiggles his eyebrows suggestively. "I mean . . . now that I get to do *that* . . ."

I laugh, too. "I'm serious," I say.

"Well, let's see, let me focus." He mock cools himself off. "Okay, what have you been writing?" he asks.

I reach for my notebook, which is on the scuffed-up old coffee table next to Jaime's latest graphic novel and Lucesita's violin bow. "Let me read it to you." I smile.

Real and True

The dust on my boots says we've traveled long
And I've lost my way from time to time
But found you all the same.

I've been too long afraid
Trading the true for the safe
But still you waited patiently.

Waylaid at a false balcony scene
Confused by a passing dance
Still there you were where X marked the spot.

I found you once, real and true
Through alteration and rhyme
By picking up words like gems and following the
dotted line.

Through every misstep and wrong turn
And thanks to everyone
who cheered me toward the finish line
Or the starting line
Depending on how you look at it.

acknowledgments

Books are time capsules. I worked on this book during the pandemic. You'll see that in its pages, from the loss of Abuelo told in shreds of memory to references to how the restaurant struggled, as so many businesses did, including those of the people closest to me. Living in a world of crushes and mystery admirers made the scary days better for me. But the tough moments still seeped into the story. I wanted to write a joyful book about a girl finding out who she wants to be in the world, but I also wanted to acknowledge what we've all experienced. And all the people who made this book a reality.

As always, to my agent, Sara Crowe, your emails

make me smile. To the Alloy team, Sara and Viana and Josh, and everyone else that makes that lovely machine hum, for your smarts and for roaming around the empty building with me. To the Harper team, my editor, Alessandra Balzer, first and foremost. To a non-comprehensive list of Harper magic makers: Caitlin Johnson, Jon Howard, and Mary Magrisso, plus the fantastic team that makes things look beautiful: Jenna Stempel-Lobell, Chris Kwon, and Julia Tyler for the design, and Ana Hard for the beautiful illustrations. To the indefatigable sales team who gave the book a voice: Andrea Pappenheimer, Kerry Moynagh, Kathy Faber. To the awesome marketing people: Audrey Diestelkamp, Lisa Calcasola, and Patty Rosati. And to Taylan Salvati in publicity. Finally, to Elisa Melendez for narrating the audio book and Almeda Beynon for producing it. Omission from this list is by no means a diminishment of the importance of your role. Thank you and the whole team for the great gift of getting this book in the hands of readers. I still pinch myself on the regular when I remember I get to work with you.

To my email subscribers and social media followers, to readers, teachers, librarians, administrators, book reviewers, award-committee members, and everyone who makes the whole world of books go 'round: you are awesome and inspiring. You make me remember that getting to do what I do is total magic.

To my beta readers and critique buddies and my dear H*****s, thank you for making me laugh and being so darn smart.

To Tracy Adams. During the writing of this book, you reminded me of the meaning of that Richard Evans quote, "It is often in the darkest skies that we see the brightest stars."

To Yvonne Ventresca, you teach me what friendship is every day, and your work ethic and dedication to the craft of writing inspire me to up my game.

To my family, Pablo and Daniela, Mami, Zach, and Andreanna. Thank you for reminding me that there are always more reasons to smile than not. Thank you for the quarantine Zooms and the outdoor Thanksgivings and for indulging my absolute mad love for Red Dead Redemption 2. (Arthur Morgan, although the fever has broken, you'll always be the outlaw with whom I rode out quarantine).

It's been a weird time, y'all. I'm lucky to have had you to help me through. Jules would definitely give you a free alfajor after dinner for all your awesomeness.